Sweet.Alice

Also by Coral Lansbury

Ringarra
Felicity
The Grotto

Sweet Alice

CORAL LANSBURY

E. P. DUTTON NEW YORK

For Angela

First published in the United States in 1989 by E. P. Dutton, a division of Penguin Books USA Inc., 2 Park Avenue, New York, N.Y. 10016.

Originally published in Great Britain.

Library of Congress Catalog Card Number: 89-51271

ISBN: 0-525-24825-0

10 9 8 7 6 5 4 3 2 1

First American Edition

Chapter One

If Homer had been a woman she would have struck her lyre, stamped her feet to the cadence of the verse and sung of the deathless exploits of Alice Morell. The literal-minded would have yawned and said that Alice Morell was simply a forty-three-year-old blonde born at Morell Manor just in time to accelerate the decline of the gentry into the gutter of exhausted credit. In fact this was correct, but who wanted to gnaw the crusts of literal truth when there was a modern Homer recounting the wonders of Alice Morell of Morell Manor?

The Homer in question was Lupin Tanner of the Salon de Coiffure and Beauty at the corner of Mount Street and Alfred Crescent in Barnsley. Some old people remembered when it had been a barber's shop with a striped pole outside run by Lupin's father; now there were three shiny wigs in the window and a long swathe of purple velvet surmounted by a silver-gilt crown. It was unquestionably the most fashionable hairdressing establishment in the Cotswolds, not because Miss Tanner had any special talent with perms, tints and streaking – the latter generally produced a badger effect on her clients and her permanent waves were renowned for their frizz – but because only in her salon could you hear of Alice Morell, beautiful beyond belief, raised to expectations of splendour and doomed by the family curse to poverty and disgrace.

When Miss Tanner raised her comb and looked heavenwards at the word 'disgrace', heads fell from dryers and a palpitating *frisson* ran through the lacquer-laden air. Everyone felt a sudden thrilling pain and crossed her legs quickly. The long-handled comb would slowly descend into a clump of pin-curls as Lupin's voice thrilled to the passion and heart-wrenching tragedy of a woman blessed with beauty, riches and noble birth, yet condemned by malevolent fate to a misery of poverty and shame.

The most eagerly sought appointments were on Thursdays at ten o'clock, when Alice Morell herself came in for a shampoo and set. Before she touched those pale gold tresses, Lupin would look slowly around the salon at a hushed group of faces framed in rainbow rollers, all of them breathing rapidly with lips parted, eyes wide with the pity and terror of it all.

'I remember your dear aunt saying that just after you were born, the young Duke of Bedford came to your cradle and said he was going to marry you one day.' Lupin's voice was silvery and hushed as she trimmed Alice's feathery bangs.

'I really don't remember,' Alice said.

'And a Moroccan prince offered to buy you on the spot.'

Alice was thinking of the rust which kept clogging the kitchen sink and did not answer. Most of her waking thoughts were concerned with dry rot, drains and gusts of wind that blew through every room and which she could no longer call draughts.

'Princes and peers, all of them coming to Morell Manor, seeking your hand, and then . . .' In deference to her client's presence, Lupin would pause at that moment and sigh deeply while a tide of emotion swept her audience. They knew of the curse that had befallen the house of Morell, bringing in its wake disasters which made the House of Atreus look like a model family.

Alice always reached vaguely for her purse when Lupin had circled her head with a diadem of Twinkle Sheen Dianet Spray, and Lupin would then fall back against the basin with a choking whisper.

'Mrs Morell, please – it's an honour and a privilege, and I would be so happy if you would try this new lipstick and tell me and my ladies if you find it emollient or streaky?'

As Alice pocketed the small offering and left, Lupin swung round to face her listeners with arms outflung, henna-red page bob vibrating with emotion.

'We should all be grateful! To have had so much . . . of everything . . . and now to be starving. Starving up there

6

at Morell Manor with a worthless son, after having danced with princes and been fêted at foreign courts and wined and dined by American millionaires. Alice Morell, whose aunt was the mistress of Edward the Eighth!'

Only once was Lupin interrupted, and the whole embarrassing occasion was held to be the result of Bertha Craddock's being menopausal and finding out her husband was having an affair with a traffic warden renowned for her hairy thighs and availability behind the bus shed.

'Rubbish!' Mrs Craddock said when Alice had just left with two cakes of lavender toilet soap.

Lupin was so stunned that she stood like an angular motif from a Sumerian funeral relief.

'Rubbish! Alice Morell was wearing hand-me-downs and borrowed boots when my two girls were taking ballet in Oxford.'

'Mrs Craddock, the only hand-me-downs that ever touched Alice Morell's skin were heirloom laces belonging to her aunt and priceless silks which had been in the Morell family for generations!'

'Miss Tanner, I happen to have known Alice Morell since she was a child – all she ever had was a name and we know how she lost that, don't we?'

'I hope you're not referring to the Morell curse, Mrs Craddock. Speaking for myself – and, I have no doubt, for all the ladies present – blaming Alice Morell for what happened is like reproaching someone for having cancer or a heart attack.'

'She's a Morell, which means she's mad, but some mad people pay their bills. You're the only living person who's made money out of Alice Morell. You certainly haven't made it out of your hairdressing!'

As she said afterwards, that cut Lupin Tanner to the heart, and everyone sympathized with her. How could you walk into an epic poem or a romantic saga with such bumblefooted, cloddish insistence on motives and facts? It was as if Swift's Houhynyms tried to thread needles and do fine embroidery, or an elephant attempted to dance on a pin.

7

Nobody wants the dull monochrome of life when the fire-works of fiction are offered in your own backyard. Lupin Tanner had created a stirring romantic saga in which every woman in Barnsley played a part. They had all sat in the same chair as this ruined glory and passed the time of day with a radiance now dimmed to ashes. And it made them feel terrific!

In a Greek tragedy, the chorus always has the best time, and the more they complain the more you know they're enjoying themselves. It makes people feel better when they can see someone like Oedipus sitting blind and wretched outside Colonus. Disgruntled workers in the city were given a half-day to go and look at the old king; invalids said they felt more improved after seeing Oedipus than after taking all of Hippocrates' smelly potions.

Lupin Tanner had always known that there is nothing so heartwarmingly comforting and cheerful as contemplating the ruin of the rich and powerful. Old and faded beauties make pimpled adolescent girls feel gorgeous, and the spec-tacle of erstwhile millionaires in soup kitchens produces orgasms of delight in bank clerks. Bertha Craddock was driven from the salon with derisive hoots and cat-calls and was forced to patronize Labelle's Beauty Shoppe in Byford, which improved her appearance but left her social standing in shreds.

'We should all be grateful,' Lupin continued to say 'that no matter what befalls us in life, we have never been raised so high nor dropped so low as Alice Morell!'

There is no question that Alice Morell was as much affected by this Calypso of the comb as everyone else in Barnsley. If some of Lupin's stories were exaggerated – well, they could quite easily have happened to Penelope Morell, that blazing flapper of the twenties who had jumped naked out of so many pies that people said she could breathe under crust. Alice treasured her memories of Aunt Penelope – and all of her clothes, which she still wore.

Lupin Tanner's fictions were so appealing and so much more plausible than the brute facts of her existence, and

8

over the years Alice's memory had begun to move in accord with Lupin's romance. Film stars have believed their own publicity before now, and Lupin Tanner had gifts which made the best press agent in Hollywood sound like the safety instructions on a plane. After all, the ultimate *tour de force* of the creative artist is to impose her vision of life upon society, which is exactly what Lupin Tanner had done with Alice Morell and the whole of Barnsley. And let it be said on Alice's behalf that it was not all Homeric simile; there were some hard, jolting and very disturbing facts in her life.

Alaric Morell was always painfully conscious of them and of his mother's ability to avoid the lot after a refreshing visit to the hairdresser. Before he left for London that morning, his last words to his mother had been explicit and voiced in a tone of passion rare in such a normally quiet and restrained young man:

'Mother . . . if you sign a cheque, if you try to obtain credit or attempt to borrow so much as a penny from anyone, we will both be sent to prison.'

Alice had remonstrated gently with her son, protesting that it all seemed rather melodramatic and that the last time she had heard about anyone being sent to prison for debt was in one of Dickens's novels; she couldn't quite remember which because there were so many characters, and they all had such dreadful things happening to them all the time, and besides they were such peculiar people. A Morell might read Dickens, but would be most unlikely to meet him. But Alaric had gone to the station and caught the seven forty-five to London and she was left to bicycle into Barnsley to buy groceries. For some reason that no one had satisfactorily explained to her, the tradespeople were no longer delivering to Morell Manor.

At a rough guess, Alice Morell's mind was sixty years behind the times. This was not because of mental retardation or through any fault of her own, but simply the result of being brought up by aged relatives who browsed like dinosaurs over the Cotswold hills. And when she did reach an age of partial understanding, she found herself in the web of that seductive Circe, Lupin Tanner. Once the Morells had been a comfortable clan of gentry, despising the aristocracy as upstarts mostly sprung from royal bastards, and patronizing the local farmers with a cordial condescension which was gratefully acknowledged with dropped curtseys from the women and pulled forelocks from the men. Unfortunately, although the Morells could trace their line back before the Conquest, they had never achieved fame or fortune. Indeed, over the last hundred years they had been so busy trying to save money that they had never had time to make any. One piece of land after another had been sold off, the family portraits had gone under the hammer at Christie's, and now all that was left of any value was Alice Morell and her son Alaric. There were some unkind people like Bertha Craddock who said that the two of them were not simply worthless, they were a menace to society. Certainly, if they all accepted the legend of Alice Morell as depicted in Lupin Tanner's romance, they acted on the reality of Alice Morell and would not give her credit for a loaf of bread. Bertha Craddock said that Alice Morell had been caught shoplifting more than once, but that was just spite.

To all of this Alice was oblivious as she wheeled her bike up Elmwood Hill, pausing for a moment to watch a flight of swallows circle down to Barnsley Church. It was there one Sunday morning long ago that Aunt Penelope had quietly watched the Communion service and then, just as the vicar raised the chalice, had called out, 'Bring on the champagne!' From this point she could see Morell Manor, drowsing in the early morning sun like a red fox in the grass. At this distance the boarded windows were not visible, nor the decided tilt to the roof with one tall chimney trying to emulate the Tower of Pisa. She vaguely recalled the croquet parties on the lawn – or were those in Aunt Penelope's time? She did remember vividly the day when she first met her cousin, Henry Morell. But that memory

10

was always bullied out of her head by her grandfather's explosion of rage.

'You, a Morell! A whore! A slut! A bitch on heat would have shown more discretion and decency, by God!'

Everyone crying and grandfather shouting, 'Your Aunt Penelope never married. She made some money out of it!'

Aunt Matilda kept saying that she had lost a woman's most priceless possession, apart from the inheritance Aunt Penelope had left her. It had all left Alice feeling depressed and confused, but even as she acknowledged her fault, something in Alice told her that it had all been quite wonderful. Nobody had told her much about sex, and what she had seen on the neighbouring farms had hardly filled her with any joyful anticipation. Aunt Matilda told her that a decent woman closed her eyes and spelled chrysanthemum slowly while it was going on, and if it was still continuing then you spelled out herbaceous and bougainvillea in that order. No man, Aunt Matilda had said with considerable satisfaction, had ever been able to outlast a bougainvillea.

Alice had not even tried to think of flowers. Whenever she remembered Henry Morell she still found herself with a strange stirring in what she had been taught to call 'the private parts' and a distinct blurring of vision. It was because she was thinking of Henry that she did not see the furniture van pulling into the lane by the manor house and then backing into the shadow of the willows by the pond. The unfairness of it all – or so it seemed to her – was that she had not run off with Henry, she had not got 'into the pudding club' as the Barnsley locals would say, but instead she had insisted on a wedding with four bridesmaids and a dance and a honeymoon in Provence. But of course, when Henry was revealed as a rotter and a cad, her grandfather, her uncle and her aunt all stood up as one to sing their reproaches and engage in individual solos consisting of a catalogue of retroactive warnings. Only Aunt Penelope had sat nodding and smiling at some memory of her own, but then Penelope had found her own enchanted country a

11

long time ago. There were times when Alice had an uncomfortable feeling that she took after Penelope, if only because of her cheerful disposition. Everyone had expected her to be miserable, because she deserved to be miserable, but there was a glowing spark in Alice that only needed to watch the wind through the rushes, or hear a lark, to suddenly burst into joy.

After Alaric's birth there had been a family conclave with Alice sitting on a low chair holding the baby, her uncle and aunt on either side and grandfather at the table with his hand on the Bible. Whenever grandfather had something particularly unpleasant to say – like calling in a tenant to tell him he was going to be turned off, or accusing the cook of stealing the butter – he always used the Bible as a support. On this occasion, after assuring Alice that she was damned and unclean in the eyes of the Lord, he agreed to have Alaric educated like a gentleman, to send him to Eton and Oxford like all the male Morells, and to provide him with a modest allowance, provided that his mother acknowledged her disgrace by never going into society and never mentioning the name of Henry Morell. Naturally, Alice had agreed and proceeded to devote her life to Alaric . . .

'Mrs Morell, I can't! I swear it's more than my life's worth to give you any more credit!'

Susan Padgett had once worked for the Morells before she married Joe Padgett and set up a grocery shop with him. Padgett had told her before he left for the races that she was to run Mrs Morell out of the shop unless she paid the £78 she owed him.

Alice smiled gently. For years tradespeople had been getting more and more difficult; she remembered when a simple, 'Charge it!' from her Aunt Matilda would have had as much effect in a local shop as a warning salvo from a British gunboat off the African coast in the days of Queen Victoria.

'My dear Susan, I don't want credit, simply our normal business arrangement. I could pay cash . . .' Alice pulled out a £20 note from her purse, 'but I promised Alaric that I

12

wouldn't break this, and it does seem quite ridiculous when all I need is bread, milk and a pound of Cumberland sausages. You know how fond Alaric is of your sausages, Susan.'

Susan stared at the £20 note which Alice was putting firmly back into her purse and she thought of Alaric – Alaric and sausages – Alaric's golden head in her lap one day when Joe had gone to the races.

'Mrs Morell, it's not £20 Joe wants,' she said plaintively. 'It's the balance, and that's — '

Before she could finish Alice had interrupted her with a laugh.

'Oh, Alaric will attend to the balance. I only want a few odds and ends.' She leaned forward confidentially. 'You know, he's gone down to London to straighten out all our financial affairs. Alaric is quite brilliant when it comes to business matters. When he comes back he'll attend to balances and debits and all those wretched things that men find so important. Now we're women, Susan, and therefore we're much more practical, so I'll take the milk and a two-pound loaf and three pounds of sausages and leave balances and all that sort of thing to Alaric and Joe.'

As though hypnotized, Susan was wrapping the sausages and handing over the bread.

'No, dear, not that whitey-looking one, the nice crusty brown one. That's right. If I had the time, I'd bake my own, but this is such a season for greenfly amongst the roses . . . and the mildew – it's this humid weather.'

As Alice floated out and placed the bread firmly in the basket on her bicycle, Susan began to chew her thumb with frustration. How could you argue with Alice Morell, how could anyone cope with any of them? Even when she had been instructing Alaric, he had seemed to be with her and enjoying himself enormously, yet somehow absent. And why, in the middle of it, had he called her Philomel? The Morells were odd . . . and now the balance was £81.56 pence. Almost abstractedly Alice had reached over the counter and taken a packet of freshly sliced ham.

Like everyone else in Barnsley, Susan Padgett knew that the Morells were not simply insolvent and bankrupt – the old grandfather had sailed into the bankruptcy court and cruised out making everyone feel in debt to him, and Alice's uncle had drunk himself to death on Napoleon brandy he had never paid for – but now Morell Manor was about to be demolished, and yet Alice Morell was bicycling down the High Street humming under her breath, shaking her head occasionally because a blonde curl kept straying across her eyes.

In a strong, unfriendly light Alice Morell could indeed have been taken for the forty-three years she was, but something had happened to her when Grandfather Morell had shut her off from the World and Society. She had certainly grown older, but it was as though the visible aspects of age had ceased at that time. There had been admirers (not princes and peers) who had all been driven off by her grandfather and uncle. She made an occasional trip to London, although Ascot and Mediterranean cruises were banned even if there had been enough money to afford them. Aunt Matilda told her with mournful relish that she was being deprived of such delights because of her 'one great slip'. She read assiduously, but nothing published after the fifties when the world had gone Commie or soft as Grandfather used to say at regular intervals. What sustained her were those weekly visits to Lupin Tanner's salon, her breathless confidences and little gifts, and the piles of bright new magazines. Thanks to the latter, Alice knew precisely who had been presented at Court and when, and why chiffon was out for evening and lamé was in, and about the distinct possibility of stripes making a hit next summer. There was a cadence to her voice that came from another era and seemed to echo Lupin's refrain, a cast to her mind that would have become a dowager duchess or her Aunt Penelope.

At one time Aunt Penelope had been a lady-in-waiting to Queen Mary, before she began to ramble in a very exotic countryside. She had indeed been one of Edward VIII's particular favourites, and when she was not pleasing the prince she was delighting a great many other discriminating gentlemen. Everyone said that Penelope had taste and stamina and if she had never married this was because of her sense of devotion to the Queen – or so Alice was told. Aunt Penelope's jewels – a quite extraordinary number of diamond bracelets and gold lockets – had been the legacy which Alice had squandered when she met Henry Morell.

For years, Penelope had drifted from her bedroom to the dining-room and out to the swing under the apricot tree in sunny weather. She was always elaborately dressed, with white hair in ascending puffs that she arranged herself and a faint smile that greeted everyone and no one. She was a perfect dinner guest, nodding pleasantly at whatever was said and never requiring any more attention than to have a plate passed to her. But there were *moments*, and now as Alice recalled one she almost collided with a Ford at the traffic lights. It was after the first hunt of the season; everyone was at dinner – the vicar, the local magistrate – and the conversation was lumping its way from one chewed platitude to the next when suddenly, in clear, ringing tones, Penelope looked up and trilled, 'The Rajah threw rubies and pearls at my feet!'

The entire table paused, jaws agape, food dropping from forks, but Penelope had bent over her plate and was delicately separating a morsel of gristle from her mutton. Then everyone went on eating and complaining about fox covers.

Alice knew what Penelope's world was like. Once, while swinging, she had looked up through the branches of the apricot tree and said, 'Your hand is burning my thigh. It's cooler further up.'

Occasionally she would tell Alice about balls where notes were passed from a lady's nosegay into her bosom, and weekends when you would wait for a certain knock at the door – and how frantically exciting it had all been when two other men had discovered the secret knock. For the most part she was silent and only that private smile

15

revealed what she was enjoying at the expense of the world and time and reality. Alice could never really believe that her aunt was as mad as people maintained.

She had died in a fall from the swing. Late one afternoon she had asked Alice to push her. The movement was gentle, then suddenly Penelope's hands had tightened on the ropes, she threw her head back and began laughing as she sent the swing flying higher and higher, while Alice begged her to stop, to come down. Triumphantly, she had cried, 'Oh, I'm coming! I'm coming! Oh God, what joy!'

She fell from the swing and her neck was broken. At the funeral the vicar was deeply moved when he recalled Aunt Penelope's last words as she greeted her saviour. It was, he said, a blessed end and one that all should devoutly pray for. Whenever Alice thought of Henry, her memories seemed to blend with Aunt Penelope swinging up into the branches of the apricot tree and laughing. Was she already entering that magic world which her aunt had discovered, and would people one day whisper that she was mad? And would there be an Alice to sit and listen to *her* stories of secret meetings and champagne drunk from something more intimate than a slipper? Briskly she shook the clouds from her mind and hoped that Bessy, the last remaining Morell servant, would have tea ready when she got home. And she did hope that Alaric had attended to all the business matters of the estate in London.

*

Cautiously Alaric approached the roulette table at the Ritz. He had caught a bus to Piccadilly and walked down past Fortnum and Mason's to the colonnade of the hotel where he proposed to recoup the Morell fortunes. Alaric Morell was not a gambler by nature; in fact, it was difficult to describe his character since it was so unformed. At Eton he had played games with zest and discovered a passion for Latin and Greek which sent his form master into ecstasies. It is the remarkable quality of a good English public school that it preserves the juvenile mind so that it does not reach

16

maturity until senescence, and that it can make a boy more familiar with Themistocles than Thatcher, and a better authority on the rise and fall of the Athenian drachmae than the fluctuations of the petrodollars. If Alaric had been closely examined, he would have revealed a mind which saw Athenians playing cricket and Spartans having a brisk work-out on the squash courts before the battle of Marathon. Like his mother he was a distinct anachronism in the modern world, but he had done splendidly at Oxford and Merton had rejoiced when he took a First in Greek and a Blue in cricket. All of which had made him unemployable. There had been talk of his joining the Foreign Office, but these days a strange interest had sprung up there in barbarous tongues like Russian and Arabic; even Chinese was being spoken of with favour.

Grimthorpe, the family solicitor, had long ago given up trying to make Alice Morell accept that she was so far below the poverty level that no known statistic could reach her. Instead he tried to reason with Alaric who, after some effort, had accepted that the Morells were ruined beyond all hope of repair. Sourly, Grimthorpe had told Alaric that he would have to work for his living, and that had really stung the boy. He had spent most of his life in libraries tracing the variations of an obscure Boetian noun, or toiling at the nets to perfect his cover drive, and to be told that he had to work when all his life had been toil, and accepting the responsibility that he must care for his mother, who was getting on in years and as irresponsible as old Aunt Penelope who had jumped out of a swing in a religious frenzy . . . It was galling. He had tried employment agencies where clerks looked at him and then at his credentials in disbelief.

Alaric's problems were complicated because he shared to the full the Morells' fabled good looks. He was blond and tall, with the face of an angel who has never fallen from grace. Women found him irresistible and Alaric had never learned any of the ordinary arts of courtship because he was always being seduced. He did prefer women to men, but

17

Alaric's main problem in life had been to protect himself from over-use. Fortunately, he was so often abstracted and lost in contemplation of a Greek hexameter that he missed some pretty blatant attacks on his anatomy. Now, he thought with satisfaction, at last he had the means to make thousands . . . millions if there were no awkward limits placed on the tables. He pulled out his file cards and felt his top pocket to make sure his tuning fork was in place.

The doorman nodded and touched his cap as Alaric passed him, looking pale and abstracted. He immediately recognized the college tie and the shabby elegance of Alaric's tweeds which had been cut down to size from one of his uncle's suits. The gaming salon with its chandeliers and muted lights stunned Alaric for a moment with its subdued opulence. There were Arabs and ornate Europeans at the tables and the sound of voices barely rose above that of the humming of bees in a summer garden. Alaric found himself wondering if this was the quality about the Corinthians which had led the Athenians to speak of them as depraved. Then, as he made his way to the roulette table he felt a sudden twinge of guilt. A group of elderly women were bent over the wheel, opposite them was an Arab with a blue-black beard, and on either side of him two more Arabs of lesser rank. The bearded Arab was obviously myopic, if not legally blind. At every turn of the wheel he threw himself across the table, then chuckled with glee as he raked in another pile of chips from the croupier: impassive, moving only to call the terms of play and the numbers. How could he, Alaric felt – armed with the knowledge he had – deliberately walk up to the table and rob these people? They had no chance against him and his system. He swallowed hard as he remembered his games master saying slowly, 'It is the game that counts, not the winning of it. Better by far to lose honourably than to win by cheating. Play to win, but win with a straight bat, not with a crooked mind.' Alaric had been rather fond of that master, a feeling which was more than reciprocated at dusk in the cricket pavilion. However, there was his mother and

18

a number of other painful facts which made juvenile morality seem a little absurd.

Alaric decided that the only decent thing to do was to take the croupier into his confidence – at least let him know that he was there at the table to appropriate the money of the house and of anyone else reckless enough to wager against him. He thought of his mother – helpless, ineffectual and dependent – and the duty which had been entrusted to him. 'Care for your mother, my boy. No one else will. Remember that you are the visible witness to her shame.' Alaric flinched. That blot on his past at times had the power of assuming the proportions of a vast ocean of guilt closing in upon him on all sides.

He had £80 to his name, which was the full extent of the Morell fortune. Then he looked at two old women at the other side of the table, barely able to lift their hands under the weight of diamond rings. Could he bring himself to rob two old ladies who were beginning to remind him of Aunt Penelope whose last words to him had been, 'Not tonight, my dearest, there is a royal prerogative.' When he mentioned that to the vicar, that man had clasped his hands and said, 'Such a good soul, no doubt planning to spend the night in prayer with our Lord.' But there was his mother, and Morell Manor about to be demolished, and he had tried so hard to find a job but nobody would take him seriously. Suddenly he recalled Perseus who had not hesitated to rob the ancient Graeae of their single eye, and his mind was made up. Abruptly the two old ladies left the table, muttering remarks which would have made Lawrence of Arabia spin in his grave.

Alaric decided to take the croupier into his confidence. The bearded sheikh was raking in his chips and arranging them in piles in front of him like multicoloured minarets. Alaric knew that every minaret represented thousands of pounds, and in that same moment he saw the jewelled scimitar at the sheikh's side and a watch that glittered as it counted the golden hours. Obviously the man was rich, disgustingly rich, but Alaric felt he must make sure – and just as you did not play squash with a weighted ball, so you did not play any game without informing the referee that you had a foolproof system of winning.

The croupier had cast the merest flick of a glance at Alaric and immediately placed him. The Merton tie, the tweeds, the blond tousled hair – obviously county, aristocratic and quite possibly a younger son bent on squandering the last of the family estate at the gaming table. Croupiers at the Ritz have inherited generations of social insight that is more reliable than *Debrett* or the latest edition of *Burke's Peerage*.

'There is a chair available, if you would care to play against Sheikh Mohammed ben Isfadil, sir.'

Alaric smiled faintly and wavered; the Arab was looking at him and positively gloating. However, he remembered Eric Twining, his games master at Eton.

'I should like to explain something before I play, if I may?'

'But of course, sir,' and the croupier nodded without smiling, expecting the usual request for credit which would entail a discreet inquiry from the manager.

'I must tell you that I simply can't lose!'

'Ah, yes, sir.' This was accompanied by the faintest elevation of an eyebrow as the croupier called to mind all the eccentrics he had ever known, and how the great majority had come from Merton and Oxford. There had been Lord Cresforth, who refused to gamble without a tame squirrel which sat in a pocket of his suit specially designed for it, and made sudden forays across the table in pursuit of the marbles which it obviously thought were nuts; and the Honourable Michael Wilston-Haughey, who insisted on squeezing orange juice on the dice before they were thrown; and the Marquis of Spenlow who – poor Spenlow, that had required the police and a straitjacket – and now this young, fair boy had a system.

'You see, I have a system.'

'Most gentlemen do, sir.'

'But mine *works*. I must know if I can use a tuning fork

before you spin the wheel.'

'A tuning fork poses no problems, sir. Provided it does not disturb the other players.'

'It's not at all noisy, but I have to gauge the tonic vibration before I select the winning number.'

'The winning number. Yes, of course, sir.'

'I derived the system from a fragment of Artychus that I found in the Ashmolean.'

The croupier nodded, wondering if the walls of the Ashmolean were padded and whether the readers were given weekend passes to the outside world.

'It was an absolute revelation to me because it was attributed to Parmenides, but I knew stylistically that it had to be much earlier. I could prove conclusively that Diels and Kranz were absolutely off the mark.'

'There is a chair available for you now, sir. I think his highness is anxious to begin play.'

Alaric did not really appreciate being interrupted in the middle of an explanation, but then some people had said that if the house were burning down Alaric would give a lecture on thermodynamics instead of reaching for a hose. The sheikh was grinning at him, pausing occasionally to whisper to the attendants at his side.

As he sat down and pulled out his tuning fork, Alaric continued, determined that at least they would know why they had lost their money.

'Everyone knows that Artychus investigated cubes and modulated numbers, but the ratio of tonic variations to numbers introduced an entirely new concept.' As he spoke, Alaric tapped his tuning fork on the edge of the table, listened intently and then said with quiet confidence, 'Thirty-two will win.'

*

The sun was dazzling as Alice pedalled back to Morell Manor and she almost regretted that they no longer had a car. Two men had come and driven it away the day after

21

Uncle Theodoric had breathed his last, and there had never been another. What she did miss was a dog. Once, the kennels had been full of hounds and every time you opened the front door of the manor house you were almost bowled over by an assorted pack of terriers, spaniels and an aged pekingese that had belonged to Aunt Penelope. But they were all gone now, even her beloved Sailor who used to run beside her bike, making occasional lunging rushes off into the hedges to pursue rabbits. All of them dead now, every one of them buried somewhere in the garden: Sailor the labrador in the middle of the rose-bed, terriers amongst the hollyhocks and Pekingese under the apricot tree. She did not notice the van parked by the pond as she wheeled her bike up the drive. There was just time to pick some roses before the sun spread the petals and stole the perfume, she thought. Yes, and she had a pair of scissors in her bag.

The roses were all hybrid teas and their perfume made her think of Henry again and the inn in Provence where the jasmine climbed in at the window. She really must make herself concentrate on greenfly – she could see where they were attacking the buds – and she reached for a spray of yellow gold blossoms just above her head which would fill the Wedgwood bowl on the dining-room table.

At that moment the sky fell on her, or so it seemed. One moment the light was pink and gold and bees were murmuring around her; the next there were shouts and a huge wooden contraption on top of her.

'My Gawd, lady! Watch it!'

She felt brawny arms lifting her up and carrying her on to the grass. Then she saw that the 'wooden sky' which had collapsed on top of her was in fact Aunt Matilda's grand piano, and behind it another burly carrier was dragging Aunt Penelope's favourite chair through the roses, while two other men were lugging her grandfather's Georgian clock down to a furniture van. The front door of the manor house was wide open and furniture, all her furniture, was pouring out of it like a flooded stream.

'We didn't expect you back so soon Mrs Morell. We knew it would upset you. But we had our orders.'

Alice looked up at the grimy whiskered face bending over her.

'Mr Mulligan! You were here last week for the furniture! I told you then you had come to the wrong place.'

Mulligan shuffled and rubbed his hands down the back of his trousers.

'No! No, there's no mistake. It's all been seized. Everything has to go and the house comes down tomorrow.'

Alice breathed deeply, knowing that this was a moment when her practical common sense must prevail against the obdurate stupidity of the working class.

'Mr Mulligan, this is the third time you have been here. Last week you told me you absolutely had to remove my furniture from my home and I told you that you must be mistaken. The Morells are not generally confused with anyone else in this area. But there are the Murrays at Chumley Corners, and . . . ' her voice dropped slightly, 'I have heard that the Morgans at Five Oaks have been having financial difficulties.'

Mulligan was shaking his head and almost weeping.

'It's no use, Mrs Morell. It's got to go. You don't own it any more. You have creditors and the order was out to seize and sell your furniture six weeks ago.'

'I insist that you speak to my son!'

'Your son knows all about it, Mrs Morell. We told him and the sheriff's notice was put in your own hand yesterday.'

'Yes, well,' Alice paused, remembering a furtive little man who had slipped a letter or something resembling a letter to her when she had been pulling up dandelions. 'I recall a man – but there was no mention of furniture.'

'It's going, and it's going *now*!'

Mulligan signalled to his crew, who began trundling and dragging chairs and tables, mirrors and fire-screens through the rose garden.

It was nightmare and horror, and a giant swing throwing

her into a screaming chaos of wardrobes and inlaid dressing-tables, crystal lustres and Aunt Matilda's needle-point table-runners. The screaming was her own as she tried to push the men out of the rose garden, fighting to drag back a chair, crying as one rose bush after another was trampled. It only seemed a matter of moments and then they were gone. They had fended her off with her own furniture and destroyed her garden. Now she sat on a garden seat, her hair draggled over her face, her print dress torn in shreds. Every summer Barnsley Church had been scented with the perfume of the hybrid tea roses from Morell Manor. Now only the copper gold rose bore its flowers. Slowly she went over to it, reached up to pick the last sprays of blossom and carried them back to the seat where she sat with them in her lap.

If there was a time to follow Aunt Penelope into that magic world where everything was not as it was, but as it should have been, it was now. Alice tried to remember the second dance at the Hunt Ball when Henry Morell had toasted her from the doorway and . . . The sound of a door closing behind her made her look round and she saw Bessy at the top of the steps leading down to the driveway. She had two large suitcases, one tied round with a length of pyjama cord.

Bessy dropped the cases with a thud and stalked down to the garden seat. Alice shivered; there were times when the woman reminded her of a large, gnarled toad, but courtesies had to be observed.

'If you don't mind,' Alice said faintly, 'I rather think I'd like tea now. There is some fresh bread in the basket.'

Bessy stopped short in blank amazement, then she glared at Alice with dismal but nonetheless triumphant relish.

'*Tea*! Tea, she says! It's all gone – every stick of furniture in the house and tomorrow they're going to pull that down. That's what Mr Mulligan said – demolished – which means torn down, and you want tea!'

Alice looked wordlessly over to the house and could feel

24

its emptiness; even the curtains had gone from the bay windows. It had been a warm, friendly face that she had loved, now it had suddenly become a skull.

'And you should have been out of here last Friday. I read the notice to quit, you left it on the hall table.'

'Bessy,' Alice struggled to speak calmly and without undue emotion, 'Bessy, I do think a cup of tea would help us both.'

'You're off your head! Wanting tea at a time like this!'

'Alaric will be back very soon. My son,' she gestured vaguely, 'will attend to all of this.'

Bessy leaned forward and almost jabbed her finger in Alice's face. 'You have been sold up! All you have is a £20 note in your purse and not a penny in the house, and if I hadn't stopped them they would have taken your clothes from the cupboards.'

Alice closed her eyes, whispering, 'Alaric will know what to do. He's very resourceful.'

Bessy rocked with laughter. 'Alaric! Alaric! That pretty son of yours is probably in prison by now, if he isn't in Sue Padgett's bed – or someone else's. Never been known to refuse, your Alaric hasn't. The only thing he *has* always refused to do is pay!'

The enchanted world vanished. Alice was furious, but she could not find words expressive enough to describe her loathing and contempt for anyone who would dare criticize her son.

'Yes,' Bessy continued, 'most likely he's in prison, because that's where the idle rich belong. You're going to have to work like the rest of us. You won't be able to play the lady any longer. You and your kind – you're finished! Just like that garden! You don't belong.' She snarled at the broken rose bushes and trampled ground. 'I hope they bulldoze those roses and plant turnips!'

Alice wished she had the family Bible to lean on, as her grandfather used to do. She had never had occasion to give anyone notice before and felt that the Bible would help.

'Bessy, I regret having to do this, but you give me no

choice. I have tolerated much from you. And as for my not working – I never stop. But that's beside the point – the point is that I must give you notice!'

Bessy almost rolled on the grass laughing. 'Notice! I haven't been paid for the last six months!'

Slowly, and with great dignity, Alice opened her purse and drew out the £20 note, handing it to Bessy who snatched it and pushed it into a cavernous fold of her skirt.

'Bessy, please accept this and my son will send you a cheque at your new address.'

'If your son wrote me a cheque, I'd know what to do with it!' Legs astride and with considerable expression, Bessy gestured as though wiping her bottom with that promised cheque. She then snorted, stared at Alice with ineffable contempt and marched back to her suitcases.

*

Alaric had just returned to the table from changing a pile of chips into cash which he folded into his thin and dog-eared wallet. Already he had made £200 and this was only the beginning. Every time he rang the tuning fork he calculated the vibrations and wagered, and every time the wheel had stopped at his number. The sheikh was no longer chuckling, but staring at Alaric as though contemplating strange and excruciating tortures for him. Alaric smiled at him and reminded himself of the time when the Arabs had treasured Aristotle, days when the Christians of Europe were burning manuscripts as though they had come from the hand of the Devil himself. He felt a sudden twinge of compassion for the sheikh.

'He is rich, isn't he?'

The croupier's lips barely moved. 'Excessively rich, sir.'

After that, Alaric felt much better. He pulled out his tuning fork, rang it gently on the edge of the table and then called thirty-six.

As the wheel was about to stop at thirty-six, the sheikh

26

lunged across the table and tried to grab Alaric by the collar.

'You cheat! I saw you touch the table.'

Alaric blushed with anger and then turned white with outrage and mortification. He had spent months perfecting a difficult and scholarly mode of calculating tonic variations, and now to be accused of cheating like a common little snot who had palmed a card or changed the dice . . . It was too much! Then he remembered that the Arab had not had the benefit of a public school education, that he had not acquired a sense of morality under the dreaming spires of Oxford and therefore it behoved him to be tolerant. With considerable calmness, he tried to look down at the sheikh from centuries of superior culture.

'I cannot believe, sir, that you have accused me of tampering with the wheel?'

But the sheikh was almost frothing and one of his attendants was slowly pulling a knife from his belt. Even the croupier looked nervous and wondered if he should touch the alarm bell under the table.

'With these eyes I saw you! The eyes of the Falcon of the Desert are never deceived!'

The second attendant now also held a knife and motioned the croupier back from the table with it. The man had no chance to reach the alarm button. Alaric remained calm and determined to explain. He had great faith in education, even for the most primitive peoples, and a long tradition of imperialism had taught him to be tolerant of the tribal customs of savage races.

'I insist on you hearing me out! I was using a mathematical theorem derived from the Pythagorean Archytas. Archytas – Archytas of Tarentum! You must have heard of him!'

The attendant standing by the croupier spoke softly but distinctly: 'You are a thief! You were seen by his highness to touch the wheel.'

Now the sheikh leaned forward and passed judgement

upon Alaric Morell as though he were a common poacher getting six months from the local magistrate.

'The Falcon of the Desert is the justice of the desert . . .'

Nervously, the croupier tried to intervene. He had known many Arabs and most of them had warned him of Ibrahim ben Isfadil. The sheikh and his forebears had lived on a four-square-mile island of rock and sand six miles due west of Bahrein, drawing water from a single brackish spring and preying on neighbouring ships. Then one day the spring had gone dry and precisely forty-eight hours later a fountain of oil had gushed into the sky. A man who had counted his wealth in pats of camel dung was now the master of millions of petrodollars. The Arabs of the Ritz tolerated the sheikh, but encouraged him to confine his activities to the gaming tables. With luck and the will of Allah – as a senior Saudi had informed his entourage – the Sheikh Ibrahim ben Isfadil could be discreetly confined to the Ritz until his ocean of oil was safely siphoned into the bottomless well of the roulette table. Now the sheikh motioned to his attendant, who grabbed Alaric and pinned his arm behind his back.

'I am going to cut off your right hand! The hand of a thief is an abomination. And after that . . .' His eyes travelled downwards and Alaric remembered that look from a senior prefect at Eton who had pursued him through every dormitory in the school. 'When you have been cut, there will be a place for you amongst the women.'

There was a thin fillet of perspiration across the croupier's brow.

'Sir – your highness – it was a relatively small amount. If I may perhaps call the manager. I am certain this matter can be resolved.'

'It is not money – it is honour.'

Alaric had never intended to reveal the details of his system, but he saw no other recourse than complete honesty.

'All right. I'll tell you what the theorem is. You must know that Archytas solved the geometrical construction of

28

the line segment and . . .'

The sheikh nodded to the attendant holding Alaric. 'Cut off his hand now. I tire of his babble. His *right* hand!'

The first attendant moved away from the croupier and seized Alaric by his free arm as the second pulled back his sleeve and extended his wrist across the table. The sheikh slowly drew out his scimitar and raised it over his head. Alaric looked up and recognized it as a genuine Damascene blade, probably seventeenth century, although the engraving was unquestionably of a later date. Therefore, one would have to conclude the piece was a composite and . . . *he was going to lose his hand*! He tried to pull back, but the Arabs were holding him with practised strength, so he resolved on a feint and a rugby tackle, pulling back and then suddenly throwing himself across the table as the croupier tried to reach the alarm button. The collapsing croupier provided a temporary barrier to the Arabs as Alaric sprinted for a baize door that he hoped would lead to Jermyn Street.

A dim passage led to a flight of stairs. Alaric bounded up them three at a time, hearing muffled shouts behind him. There was a window at the top of the stairs propped open with a coathanger. As he dived through, Alaric knew this was exactly how Icarus had felt when his wings melted in the sun and he fell into the Aegean Sea. However, it was not water, but the dustbins in a small back alley into which he fell, landing on his feet, kicking the rubbish aside as he sprinted for the street ahead where he could see the comforting scarlet of passing buses. Alaric had always been good at games, and twice he had won the five hundred at Eton. Now, with a perfect stride, head balanced, he ran as though the honour of his house and his school and his right hand were at stake. Behind him, the Arabs floundered and fell amongst the dustbins, caught up in their flowing white robes.

Alaric was only panting slightly as he swung himself on to the 52 bus to Sloane Square. Then as he clambered upstairs, he thought of that blade descending and suddenly wanted to throw up. He sat back and wondered why the whole burden of the Morells had descended upon him. And his mother – what could he do with her? She was too old to get married, too naïve to cope with the real world. He could not bear to think of her ending like Aunt Penelope, a religious maniac, probably put away in some hideous national health institution where everyone wore strait-jackets and felt slippers. Why had Englishmen been trained as classical scholars for five hundred years and built an Empire, and why was he suddenly a freak? An elephant boy to be put in a cage and poked at by rotten little cads who took higher degrees in business or computer science. Alaric was almost crying with chagrin when he felt a hand on his. He looked up quickly and saw a middle-aged woman with butterfly spectacles beaming at him. Brusquely he pulled his hand away, saying tersely, 'Allergy. I'm allergic to bus dust.'

Only when he was in the second-class compartment of the train to Oxford did he really feel relaxed. It was full of tourists, Germans mostly, with bodies and personalities to match the back-packs piled on to the racks and between their knees. There was a wonderful sense of security in being wedged against a window by so much guttural humanity, complaining about weather and constipation and the need to begin every meal with prunes. He closed his eyes, remembering the smell of a football scrum, or the locker room after tennis when somebody had found the showers were not working, thinking of Greek athletes who had rubbed themselves with oil after a game and then scraped off the scum with a strigil shaped rather like . . . he paused, and opened his eyes to watch the scruffy outskirts of Oxford flash and vanish before his gaze. Fields, a dilapidated factory and some rows of washing, then a stretch of road and a stream of traffic heading north, and in that traffic a black Rolls Royce keeping pace with the train. There were three Arabs in it.

Chapter Two

It had not been easy to make tea, but there were a few odds and ends left in the refrigerator and at least the bread was fresh. Alice had dressed as carefully as though she were receiving the vicar and his wife, in a lace tea-gown with matching pastel shoes. The house was empty, even the curtains had been pulled down and sheets and blankets taken from the linen closet. The men had missed one towel on a roller behind the bathroom door and a few broken pieces of china in the pantry. She contrived a table out of an old packing case covered with a Kashmir shawl and placed two smaller boxes on either side of it. The roses were in a jar beside the teapot.

Alice sat waiting for Alaric to come home. It would soon be dusk and she hoped he had managed to catch the last bus out from Oxford. Still, he did have so many friends there and it was quite possible that he had stopped off at the college, and . . . but she was *not* going to cry.

Bessy had annoyed her enormously. For years now she had waited hand and foot on the old woman, who maintained she could not carry a tray because of her arthritis. It really was imposing on employers when the staff demanded breakfast in bed on Sundays and first read of the *Telegraph*! Alice remembered how much she disliked a newspaper with crumbs and jam on it. It was difficult to say exactly what Bessy had done in the house except make an occasional cup of tea. Alice had polished and scrubbed and done the laundry when Bessy said that lifting the sheets from the tub had hurt her back. There had been a time when Aunt Matilda was alive and Bessy could have been described as a servant, but after a while Alice found herself caring for the old woman and the house and the garden – and still the vicar would tell her how fortunate she was to have a servant these days.

Alaric would put everything to rights, she was sure of

that. The furniture would be returned and he would get a position teaching in a good prep school, or perhaps go into the city. He would marry and there would be children in the house and something would have to be done about the bathroom. For some years now the plumbing had crumbled into puddles of mud and rust and all bathing had been done in a tub before the kitchen stove. One thing she must not do was think of Aunt Penelope, or of Henry slowly unbuttoning her dress and then her camisole and kissing her between the breasts . . .

*

'There will be a bulldozer here tomorrow, Mother. The house is going to be torn down.'

Alice shook her head in disbelief. 'Alaric, those men were here by mistake. I'm sure it's the Morgans. I've heard such dreadful stories of their gambling and –'

'Once and for all, Mother. *We are ruined*! We cannot stay here.'

Alice shook her head. There were times when Alaric could be so obstinate. It was quite clear to her that the reason he was so bad-tempered was because he was hungry. 'Feed the brutes!' That was Aunt Matilda's recipe for dealing with difficult men, yet even though Alaric looked white and pinched, he seemed to be without any appetite. The ham sandwich lay untouched on his plate, despite her having found some watercress by the stream to decorate and cover the cracks in the old glazed platter which she last remembered holding a crown saddle of lamb. She had herself garnished each chop with a frill of white parchment so that it looked like a steaming tiara.

'You must eat, dear. And scones are much nicer when they're hot. It was so fortunate that I found a good cup and a half of flour in the old cocoa tin.'

'All we have are our clothes. I'm surprised they didn't take my cricket gear.'

'We must get in touch with Mr Grimthorpe. I can't abide

32

the man, but I'm sure you can manage him. Your great-uncle used to say that Grimthorpe wasn't a solicitor's shoelace, but –'

'Grimthorpe has kept us out of prison, Mother. There was the problem of your signing cheques after the court had declared that –'

'Alaric! I am trying to be very patient and if only you would eat something we should be able to discuss this rationally.'

She got up and walked to the bay windows, wincing a little as she looked out on the desolation which had once been the rose garden. If Sailor had been alive he would have harried those brutes from the property, but Sailor was dead and they had trampled on his grave. 'Turnips,' Bessy had said . . .

Suddenly Alice turned and smiled at Alaric, who was moodily reaching for another sandwich. 'Alaric, we can stay here and work this as a farm. I believe I could grow vegetables in that soil. Oh my dear, you don't remember when the Morell land reached as far as Wyvern End – and we grew the best sugar beets during the war, and Aunt Matilda's raspberries were famous!'

Something caught her eye at the end of the drive. It really did seem that a large laundry bag had flitted from behind the rhododendrons and across the laburnum. The light was fading and it could not have been a sheet blowing across the drive. There was no wind, not a single leaf trembling at the top of the tallest ash. Then another laundry bag dived suddenly behind the horse chestnut.

'We don't own this land. If we're not out of here by daylight, they'll bulldoze us too. We have exactly £210 and that is all.'

Another laundry bag had slithered behind the laburnums.

'How very odd!' Alice murmured.

'It is not odd, it is a fact – a fact that must be faced, Mother. We are symbols of social disaster. Neither of us is trained to make money. We're like a pair of stuffed peacocks suddenly told to fly. All I'm really good at is games and Greek. It's all over, Mother. I just wish we had some hemlock, then we could put that in the teapot and die decently like Socrates.'

'I never heard of anything so absurd. Alaric, why do you think there should be three laundry bags moving around the garden?'

With a strangled cry, Alaric overturned his box and rushed to the window. They were here – they had found him! He was sure he had given them the slip when he cut through the quad at Brasenose and climbed over a wall into Wadham, then took a devious route down to the bus stop. But they had found him and they would take his right hand and possibly . . . his thoughts sank lower and he almost fainted.

At that moment, there was a shrill whistle and Thomas the postman wheeled briskly up the drive. The Arabs disappeared amongst the trees and seconds later Alaric heard the roar of a disappearing car. They must have mistaken Thomas for a constable on his rounds. Alaric sank on to the window ledge as laundry bags and scimitars whirled madly in his head.

There was a thud as the post was pushed through the front door. Alice was carrying back a bundle of letters before he could really focus properly. She adored receiving mail, but most of it had been so dull in recent years.

'Bills!' She sorted them on to the shawl. 'I'm sure they're all bills, oh, and someone who wants to shampoo our carpets. This looks more interesting.' Turning over a long manila envelope in her hand, she carried it to the window so that she could read the inscription in the top left-hand corner. 'Who are Pettigrew, Marchant and Bliss?'

That question was an invocation to a greater muse than Lupin Tanner and the smiling goddess responded after her own fashion. Lupin refused to believe what people told her years later about Alice Morell and Alaric, preferring that her own story should end with a flight into oblivion, with Alice driven from her home and vanishing into the night.

And when some insisted on a sequel being told, in all fairness it should be said that Bertha Craddock insisted Lupin Tanner's version was the true and accurate one and all those other stories just rumour and romantic twaddle. However, it must also be noted that Alaric was oblivious of the presence of the goddess when his mother held out the letter at arm's length to catch the last rays of sunlight.

Alaric shook his head. 'Probably more lawyers. For God's sake, don't open it, Mother. I wish we had been arrested – at least we'd have a bed to sleep in tonight.'

Alice was already opening the letter. 'Lawyers – yes, you're right, Alaric. Gray's Inn, and it's . . . oh, dear heaven!' She clasped the letter between both hands, while tears poured down her face.

'Mother, it's all right, they can't do any more to us. They've taken everything. There's nothing worse that *can* happen.'

Without opening her eyes, Alice said slowly and with a rising note of jubilation in her voice, ' ". . . to see me at your earliest convenience, when you may be informed of something to your advantage. I have the honour to be, Madam, your most humble and obedient servant, Ambrose Twistleton Bliss." Something to our advantage, Alaric! You know what that means, don't you? It means money and inheritances and lost relatives and lotteries and money and windfalls, and, oh, Alaric! Always lots and lots of money!'

Alaric took the letter from her and he too suddenly found his thoughts exploding from those formal archaic phrases into a splendour of panelled libraries and endless tennis matches on summer afternoons with champagne and strawberries in iced glasses . . .

'The Irish Sweepstake! Mother, you took a ticket in the Sweepstake?' She shook her head.

'The football pool! That's it, isn't it? You've won the pools, Mother?'

Again, Alice shook her head. Then she paused and looked around the empty room, the cracked ceiling and the part of the floor you always had to avoid because of the dry rot.

'I shall be very sorry to leave here, but we must pack everything and leave for London immediately. Take the bike and phone for a cab from the Bennets' farm. Oh yes, and tell them that we'll pay for the eggs and milk as soon as we've spoken to Mr Bliss. If we hurry, we can catch the last train from Oxford.'

Almost without thinking, Alaric had gone and was pedalling furiously down the driveway. Suitcases – she must find some cases – and if she were lucky – and how could she not be lucky after such wonderful news? – then those brutes of removal men had not found the door behind the broom cupboard where all the trunks and bags were kept. Lighting a candle, Alice went down to the kitchen and opened the broom cupboard. It was empty. They had even taken her mops and the two buckets that Alaric had soldered again and again to make them watertight. The door into the luggage room was jammed, but she managed to prise it open and then she saw them – great steamer trunks, five feet tall, and massive suitcases of solid pigskin which were almost impossible to lift even when empty. Everything would fit into those! Over in one corner she saw something wrapped in a sheet. It was the shape of a hatbox, but when she opened it she realized it was Aunt Penelope's travelling-case, lined with blue satin, full of crystal bottles and bowls with silver tops. Ivory glove-stretchers lay beside a tortoiseshell comb and a hartshorn brush. She remembered Aunt Penelope sitting quietly by the fire one evening, nodding and smiling, then suddenly looking up and saying, 'One must always be prepared. He often comes in a railway carriage.'

Aunt Matilda had fussed and fidgeted, explaining to Alaric that Aunt Penelope was speaking of death, which could strike one down at any moment, and that one must always be prepared to meet one's Maker. After that it was difficult to get the little boy to take his pants down to go to the toilet, because he did not want to be caught by his

36

Maker with his trousers round his knees. She could do so much for Alaric now: he could live like a scholar and a gentleman and never work. 'Something to your advantage.' The phrase rang in her ears like victory bells from the Barnsley Church.

*

Alice had insisted on staying at Brown's, because the Dorchester was known to be so expensive. Occasionally Alaric had a twinge of doubt as his mother's castles climbed higher and higher into the clouds, but he had seen the letter and moreover felt sure that no Arab would find them at Brown's. The porters had been sullenly respectful as they dragged the leather cases up to a suite on the third floor. Alice had given her address as Morell Manor and when the clerk had asked for a credit card, looked so blankly astonished that the man had immediately apologized. Rumours of their wealth spread through the hotel when Alice graciously handed each sweating porter 20 pence as a tip.

The noise of Piccadilly traffic lulled Alice to sleep, and even Alaric appreciated the comfort of blankets without holes and hot water in the bathroom. Much as he fought against it, he was being infected with his mother's enthusiasm, so at ten o'clock the next morning he phoned Mr Bliss and made an appointment to see him that afternoon. He seemed bemused that there should *be* a Mr Bliss, and that there actually was someone who knew something to their advantage. He enjoyed the doorman tipping his cap to him and the way the receptionist had asked if he would like breakfast brought to his bedroom.

*

Ambrose Twistleton Bliss had never married, as a result of spending a considerable part of his early years as a barrister in the divorce courts. 'Women,' he would inform his brothers at the bar, 'are a luxury any rational man should learn to live without.' But he had sudden doubts about this theory of his life when Alice Morell and her son were

37

ushered into his dusty chambers. She was like sunshine and spring days and Mr Bliss hoped desperately that he was not too old to make a fool of himself. She had dressed formally for the occasion, her outfit completed by a navy blue pillbox hat with matching eye-veil. Possibly the reason Mr Bliss felt so young at heart was because everything Alice was wearing had belonged to Aunt Penelope and was at least forty years old. Alaric coughed, wondering why this dusty grey solicitor was staring so intently at his mother. He hoped the old man had not discovered that Alice had almost been convicted of forgery, having insisted on signing cheques in her uncle's name years after he had died.

Alice was quietly ecstatic as she looked at the piles of musty folios and wondered which one held her future. Mr Bliss was nervously shuffling piles of paper on his desk, glancing at her every now and then over the top of his spectacles and wondering if it was possible to fall in love at first sight, and what the rules were these days about marrying clients. He even liked Alaric. Alaric, on the other hand, was puzzled by the solicitor's silence and his mother's calm smile of blissful contentment. It reminded him uneasily of Aunt Penelope before she came out with one of her inscrutable remarks. He coughed again.

'My mother seems to think this may have something to do with a lottery, Mr Bliss. I've told her that I don't gamble – well, I did gamble once, but there were no tickets involved and I used a tuning fork and . . . perhaps my mother may have bought the ticket and forgotten all about it?'

Mr Bliss answered slowly, 'I wish I could say it was a lottery, Mr Morell. Unfortunately, very little to do with lotteries enters these chambers. No, no, this is an inheritance – in a manner of speaking . . .'

Alaric almost leapt from his chair with excitement.

'Then it's true! There *is* some money!'

'It is the estate of the late Joseph Tulliford.'

Alice frowned, then squeaked with pleasure as she recalled the name as though it had been one of the family dogs. 'Tulliford! Of course, I remember! Joseph Tulliford was a great-uncle by marriage; at least, I think he was a great-uncle. There was something we weren't supposed to remember about him but oh, Mr Bliss, you know what old families are like and you could never imagine how strait-laced my Aunt Matilda was!'

Mr Bliss spread out a large parchment sheet on the desk and Alaric recognized the family tree, with Morells going back to those ancient Morellinis, a Florentine trio of brothers who had served as advance spies for William the Conqueror. The names and the branching lines were a blur to him; all he could gasp out was, 'Money! How much?'

Alice laughed deprecatingly to Mr Bliss, who felt a passionate desire to hold her hand. 'You must excuse my son. He is the businessman of the family. I've never seen such a comprehensive family tree. I do believe that grandfather inked out portions of ours. Yes, now I can see that Joseph Tulliford married grandfather's sister Millicent. How very interesting! I wonder why he never mentioned her name.'

'Joseph Tulliford married Millicent Morell in England and took her out to Australia.'

'How very odd. He wasn't a convict, was he?'

'There are certain . . . pecularities about the will, Mrs Morell.'

Alaric was almost dancing with anxiety and anticipation as Mr Bliss guided his mother's hand across the family tree and down to her own name.

'Money! Could you tell us how much?'

Mr Bliss sighed: 'A *most* unusual will.'

'But there is some money?' Alaric knew now why every right-minded individual detested lawyers and why he had felt a moral obligation not to read law at Oxford. Alice was smiling reprovingly at him. Nothing could shake her joyful certainty that somewhere in heaven Joseph Tulliford was about to shower her with gold.

'In the north-west of New South Wales, there is the Tulliford estate known as Mockery Bend. It consists of forty thousand acres of most desirable well-watered grazing country, and there are $30 million in escrow.'

Alaric got up slowly and walked around the room, threading his way between piles of briefs like a sleepwalker. He could calculate reasonably well to a thousand, but beyond that the zeros tended to confuse him.

Alice was in a quiet rapture and spoke almost to herself, 'Yes, it was meant to be like this. I've always been such a fortunate woman – such a happy life, really, and now this. I don't deserve it, but I am so very grateful. I only wish it had come in time to save the Manor.'

Mr Bliss had never felt more acutely miserable in his life. If only he had expressed himself with less precision and more tact, if only he had met Alice Morell when he was a young barrister . . .

'I should explain, Mrs Morell. The will presents difficulties. Great difficulties. I do seriously apologize and regret having raised your hopes unduly.'

Alice leaned across and touched Alaric gently on the arm.

'There's probably some red tape involved, Alaric. Value added tax, something like that, but I'm sure,' and she smiled at Mr Bliss, 'I'm sure we have an excellent solicitor who will be able to look after everything for us. Mr Bliss is not Mr Grimthorpe of Barnsley, my dear!'

'The will . . .' and here Mr Bliss's voice assumed the peculiar flute-like quality he reserved for relating the most unpleasant facts, 'the will is unique in the malice of its intent. Joseph Tulliford married a Morell and there was issue of one son. It would seem that Mrs Tulliford was joined in the family house by her four unmarried sisters.'

'Amy, Louise, Victoria. and Hyacinth – I always wondered what happened to them,' said Alice, who adored genealogy and often contributed a detail or two to Lupin Tanner for her continuing saga.

'When Tulliford died, he left a matter of $100 to his son and the bulk of the estate to the women of the Morell line, provided they remained single. Now . . .' and he pulled out a handkerchief and blew his nose with extreme delicacy, 'Mrs Morell, I hesitate to mention this, but in legal fact it is Miss Morell, is it not?'

Alaric felt that ocean of guilt closing in upon him, but this time he was going to swim against it, he was going to reduce it to a puddle of piddling irrelevance.

'If you want to know whether I am a bastard, yes. I *am* a bastard. But I consider my father was an even bigger bastard for not marrying my mother!'

'Alaric! Don't be ridiculous! We had a perfectly gorgeous wedding at St Margaret's in the Meadows. It was unfortunate that –'

'That there was no marriage, Mr Bliss, because Henry Morell – the man who fathered me – had already been married twice: once in Switzerland, to a waitress, and later to a Blackpool boarding-house keeper. They were both alive and both regarded themselves as Mrs Morell. Henry Morell was a bigamist, and when he had gone through my mother's small inheritance, he dumped her in the South of France and left her for a Lebanese belly-dancer. Just before I was born, he died in a public toilet in Beirut, and I can't think of a better place for a bastard like that to perish than with one foot stuck in the shit-hole of a public lavatory!'

Alaric was astounded by his own vehemence, but he had never forgotten when a rotten little fag at Eton had found out about his father and spread the good news throughout the whole school. Fortunately, three of his best friends knew who their real fathers were, as distinct from their acknowledged parents, so the whole furore had died down in a matter of days.

'*Mrs* Morell,' Mr Bliss stressed her married title with deference, 'it is because of this slight irregularity that you are now the eldest female Morell – unmarried female Morell of the direct line.'

'And there was mention of thirty million, but I suppose there's some irregularity about that too?' Alaric said bitterly.

'The eldest Morell of the direct line can only inherit and

use the estate if the residual heirs are either married or dead.'

'So there's a queue, but Mother's at the head of it?'

Alice was bewildered and wondered if lifting up her eye-veil would help her to see more clearly. Mr Bliss was transfixed by her grey eyes and dark lashes.

'I'm finding this very difficult to follow. What – who are the others? Aunt Penelope is dead and Aunt Matilda was a Herriton before she married Uncle Theodoric; my own parents died in an accident when I was three, so there's no one except Alaric and he's not female and –'

'Your grandfather had a brother, Casimir, who left issue, Mrs Morell.'

'Oh dear, Casimir.' Alice remembered that Casimir's name had only been mentioned once in her hearing.

'He too went to Australia and left issue of a son who chose to settle in Brisbane.'

'Is my mother going to inherit $30 million or is she not?' Alaric felt like thumping the table with Mr Bliss's head, he was getting so irritated.

'Your mother is the eldest living Morell of the direct line, Mr Morell, but there are four cousins of the Australian line.'

Alice felt as though she were going to cry as one castle after another crashed silently around her.

'But there is some part of all that money for us, Mr Bliss?'

'Something? Well, yes, if you choose you can live in the house at Mockery Bend. Under the will it must be kept up as a habitation, but there must be no money expended on improvements, nor may you draw upon the funds in escrow or enjoy the rents. If you were the sole heir, it would all be yours to do with as you please but . . . four cousins, Mrs Morell.' He shook his head and sighed heavily.

'It all seems so unfair. Like being invited to dinner and told to bring your own food, or invited to a ball and told to pay for your ticket, or . . .' Alice was sure she could continue with a long list of the world's injustices, but felt she

42

had made her point.

The enormity of it all was dawning upon Alaric. 'My God, he must have hated his wife and the Morells.'

'I think that was the point of the will, Mr Morell.'

'My mother . . .' Alaric pointed to Alice, who was staring helplessly at Mr Bliss while he wondered if he could put his arms around her, 'my mother is a poor, elderly . . . widow. I cannot believe that anyone would want to harm her!'

Mrs Bliss was rapidly casting aside all the caution which had guided him since first he set foot in a divorce court.

'Mrs Morell, if I were you, I would not take any rash steps to secure this inheritance. The greater part of the property is rented out and –'

Alaric did not wait for the solicitor to conclude. He had already risen with considerable dignity and was walking across to take his mother by the arm. As he passed by the window, he glanced out and saw an Arab standing by the gateway to the court of Gray's Inn. He turned, went back to his chair and sat down again.

'But on second thoughts, why shouldn't we go to – to Australia?'

A small castle no larger than a cowshed was beginning to rebuild itself in Alice's mind as she looked up at her son with growing hope.

'Alaric, you really think . . .'

'Of course, Mother. Why not? Four old cousins who are probably on their last legs and as dotty as Aunt Penelope. They could be dead by the time we get there.'

'We're a long-lived family, dear.'

Mr Bliss felt that he had seldom met a more bumptious and unlikeable young fellow than Alaric Morell.

'Mrs Morell, this would be precipitate!'

Alaric shifted uneasily so that he could peer out of the window. The Arab was still there, but now he had been joined by another and both were talking and pointing in his direction. He moved back to his chair.

'There is nothing at all for us here in England, Mr Bliss.

We have lost our home in the Cotswolds. I cannot get a job and therefore, like many other stout-hearted English, I consider that the time has come for us to emigrate.'

The cowshed had now become a small-size villa in Alice's imagination as she smiled at Alaric, then turned to Mr Bliss.

'You did say we could live in the house at Mockery Bend, Mr Bliss. And it is in the country, so there will be flowers and sheep and cattle – oh, I'm sure I shall like it!' In her mind's eye there were already Cotswold sheep, those shaggy, dark-faced animals known as the Cotswold lions, spreading out in flocks of hundreds . . . and a garden of hybrid teas and hollyhocks . . . She was surprised to find that Mr Bliss had taken her hand and was squeezing it gently.

'Even though you no longer have family here, Mrs Morell, you do have friends. I – I would like to be of help to you . . . not merely as a lawyer, but as a friend.'

It was the only proposal Mr Bliss had ever made in his life, and he would never make another. Later, he always blamed Alaric for inquiring who would pay the fares to Sydney and whether there was a back entrance to the chambers and then whisking his mother from sight. All he recalled was Alice Morell assuring him that without her son she would be quite lost, and that but for his having such a good head for business, they would have been ruined years ago. He thought of Mark Twain's *Innocents Abroad*, and all those other colonials who had come to England to acquire culture and polish and how everything had changed. He felt as though he was thrusting two schoolgirls into a mining camp, sending two lambs to inevitable slaughter. If only he had held her hand a little longer, he felt sure she would have dropped on his shoulder and then he would have found himself a married man. As it was, the only indication Chambers had of his feelings was when he refused to contribute towards a wedding present for the secretary, observing that he was not going to subsidize legalized lunacy. They all said he was a born bachelor, but he never forgot Alice Morell.

*

By the time they had reached Brown's, Alice's spirits were quite restored and the villa had become a small mansion with stables and a greenhouse. Alaric tried to explain that they now had exactly £110 to their name and that he had just read on the back of the door that the cost of their suite was precisely £276 a night. Alice simply smiled and said she was sure that Mr Bliss would take care of everything. But Mr Bliss's clerk had not mentioned hotel expenses, Alaric insisted, simply that he would arrange to have them booked on the first flight to Sydney the following morning. Alice said she would just stroll round to Harrods to buy a lipstick and a bottle of cologne while Alaric attended to his packing. She left him shouting that they would not be able to leave the hotel without paying, that they would be arrested and that she did not have enough money to buy a box of matches, much less cologne. As she walked downstairs, nodding pleasantly to the hotel porter, Alice consoled herself with the thought that it had always been difficult to raise a son without a father.

Alaric punched the wall a few times, but found that he was only bruising his knuckles and then decided that nothing but a quick visit to the Greek vases in the British Museum would calm his nerves. He thought it worth the risk of another encounter with the Arabs. If fortune were with him – and he very much doubted it – they were still hanging around the gate to Gray's Inn. He felt his mother was like an albatross about his neck. Without her he would have jumped on a tramp steamer and been off to India or the China Seas. As a last resort he could always join the Army. But he had a duty to look after Alice. As he walked through the Roman galleries to the rooms of Greek pottery, he raged at the way that old solicitor had patronized her, how he had patted her hand as though she were an aged patient in some old-fashioned charitable institution. He accepted the fact that his mother was old, but there was

45

no need for Mr Bliss to help her out of a chair as though she were a chronic invalid.

Not even the eloquent kraters of the Platoxenos Painter could soothe Alaric, and the uniformed attendant at the door wondered if she should call for help when she saw him muttering savagely before one of the cases. Then he saw a tall white lekythos of the Thanatos Painter with a bowed Aeneas on one side bent low under the weight of Anchises, his father. The lines from Virgil began to roll through his head – the fall of Troy, Aeneas trying to rescue his family from the flames and at length carrying his father on his back to their divinely appointed home, the holy ground that was to be the city of Rome.

Once safe with a classical reference, Alaric felt relaxed and secure. It was true that he had only the haziest knowledge of anything that had happened in the world after his namesake had sacked Rome in the year 410, but once he could relate the fate of Aeneas to his own situation, he felt in command of events. Of course, he must carry his mother just as Aeneas had staggered half-way across Asia Minor with his father on his back, and in Australia he would build a new Rome – perhaps by going into banking or digging for oil – the possibilities were endless. All he had to do was remember his classics master at Eton who had glared down at the class from his podium, saying slowly, 'If you want to govern men, read Cicero. If you want to rule an empire, turn to Virgil!'

Even with the burden of his mother, Alaric now knew that he had the means to found an empire in the Antipodes. The attendant was about to ring the alarm bell when Alaric began to laugh, but as he had moved off in the direction of the proto-Attic grave stele, she decided to finish a particularly tricky row of her Fair Isle sweater and let the officious West Indian in the next gallery attend to the young man and his unseemly mirth.

Alaric chose to walk back to Brown's, holding the image of Aeneas and Anchises in his mind, refusing to allow anything but Virgil to direct his thoughts. But as he turned down by Marble Arch, he suddenly recalled the discreet list of prices on the back of the door to their suite, and knew with sickening certainty that no one ever left Brown's without paying. It was such a well-run hotel, with no lack of staff, particularly round the front door. There was nothing for it but to explain to his mother that they would have to slip out in the clothes they were wearing – and, if necessary, he would have to carry her on his back. He recalled the difficulties Aeneas had had with his father, and then braced himself. If Aeneas could reach Italy, he could make it to Heathrow with his mother!

*

Miss Muriel Hetherington of Harrods had been watching Alice closely for some time. She could enumerate without difficulty everybody who counted in society and on the fringes, and these days – as she would thinly state to her assistant staff – the fringes had more flounce than the frocks. Having been in Designer Gowns for the last thirty-six years, her staff never failed to appreciate the acid wit of that remark. She also prided herself on being able to place anyone by appearance and walk. Over the years she had learned to recognize the cantering rush of whinnying debutantes just before Ascot, the lurching stride of the Americans and the diving swoops and glides of the French. Foreigners she endured, but her real pride came from her knowledge of the English aristocracy. She knew every duchess by name, she could tell a marchioness from a baroness almost by instinct. Every day she read the *Court Circular* as though it had just been handed down from Mount Sinai on tablets of stone. Even the society reporters of the *Daily Telegraph* had sought her advice. Now she was mortified: she could not place Alice Morell.

A remarkably pretty woman with a fine figure and good legs, obviously athletic, so possibly down from the country, she thought. But the gown – twice, Miss Hetherington motioned back sales assistants who were bearing down on Alice with practised charm. It was the gown. Yes, either

47

she had just seen it in the Paris collections, possibly a Cacharel, or else she had a distinct recollection of a Balenciaga in the costume collection at the Victoria and Albert Museum. This was a gown of distinction, aesthetically simple, without any ornament or decoration except a fishtail pleat just above the knees. And the matching pillbox must have been made to order.

Alice could hear Aunt Penelope as she felt the soft grey carpet under her feet and her fingers touched velvet and sheer silks threaded with gold:

'Always let a man undress you, my dear. Women are so clumsy.'

Australia was beginning to sound strangely musical in her ears, like Aix-en-Provence with the swallows crying and calling at dusk, and Henry . . . the moments when she could feel him before he had even touched her.

'Madam would care to see the new spring collection?'

Now Miss Hetherington knew that the moment Alice opened her mouth, she would be able to place her. Appearances could occasionally – *very* occasionally – be deceiving, but voices never. Miss Hetherington's ears were like finely tuned radar saucers, sensitive to the faintest nuance of class or the lack of it.

'What on earth does one wear in New South Wales?'

Miss Hetherington paused only for the slightest fraction of a split second. The accent was perfect, the tone of vague bemusement was the quintessence of good breeding. She was now determined to find out the identity of this client (she had already ceased to be a customer) and before one of her assistants had the impertinence to call her aside and quietly tell her that this was Lady So-and-so, or the Countess of What-not. The affluent shabbiness of Alice's handbag and matching shoes convinced Miss Hetherington that she was speaking to old money in large quantities.

'New South Wales, Lady –?'

Alice laughed. 'There hasn't been a title in the family for over six hundred years.'

Gentry – old land – old family and money. Miss Hetherington was never mistaken when dippy duchesses came into Harrods in gumboots and tweeds that were ventilated with moth-holes. She could smell money like a well-trained beagle picking up the scent of a fox.

Alice felt it was so pleasant to have this quiet and sympathetic woman to confide in, a woman who reminded her in some ways of Lupin Tanner. Naturally, she did not make a habit of being familiar with tradespeople, but she felt there was a certain difference about this woman which put her at her ease like hot cocoa at bedtime.

'Alice Morell, of Morell Manor.' She extended her hand and Miss Hetherington touched it lightly, wondering frantically why the name Morell was not ringing chimes of recognition in her head.

'I am simply at my wits' end. I gather that my son and I have to fly to New South Wales tomorrow to inherit an enormous estate which has come down to me from a relation I've never even heard of, and my son is being as difficult as only boys of his age can be. I asked him what the climate was like and all he would say was, "Beastly!" Now, what does that mean? Beastly hot, or beastly cold?'

'I have been told that Sydney is hot when it's not rather coolish, Mrs Morell.'

'I knew it! It's going to be exactly like the Cotswolds.'

'Perhaps I could show you a little something that might suit?'

Before Alice had time to reply, Miss Hetherington had slithered over to a rack of Chanel suits. Then she did something which caused her a great deal of personal anguish. Through the lavender knit braided with black satin, she whispered to Miss Dedlock on the other side of the rack, 'Run a check on Morell.'

Unquestionably, if Harrods had not at that time been changing over to a computerized system of accounting, the mistake would never have been made. Names and credit ratings were being fed into the gaping maws of the computers and by mere accident a matter of sixty-five years was transposed. Now, against certain names there were discreet symbols which only the most senior sales staff could decipher. One of these symbols was a small circled crown and when Miss Dedlock told Miss Hetherington that Morell was a circle crown, everything became dazzlingly clear to her. Her instincts had been right: this was a lady favoured by royalty, and she had a very good idea which member of the royal family had been supporting her and why she suddenly had to leave the country. Inheritances in Australia! She laughed inwardly to think that anybody could hope to deceive her. Prince Charles had been known to prefer older women until his marriage, but now he was wed to Princess Diana, Mrs Morell might prove something of an embarrassment. So, like many others in the past, she was being paid off, and Miss Hetherington swelled with patriotic pride and the knowledge that the royal family had always been generous. Mrs Morell should have whatever she wanted. This was an occasion. It took her some time to remember when the last royal mistress had been outfitted at Harrods, but if Mrs Morell were being exiled to Australia she would go in style.

Upstairs in Accounting, Penelope Morell's name had vanished back into the computer, having signalled unlimited credit and all possible assistance from management. Nothing was actually *said*. Miss Hetherington had long learned to communicate with her staff by means of a quirked smile or a finger to the lobe of one ear; certainly her ability to speak without moving her lips would have been applauded by a professional ventriloquist.

So, within minutes everyone knew that Mrs Morell was leaving England in order that the future monarch might not be disturbed in the early years of his marriage.

'If only,' Miss Hetherington thought, 'if only that calculating Mrs Simpson had shown the same spirit of renunciation and loyalty!'

And immediately she sent for a selection of the latest furs in pastel mink to set off a blue beaded evening gown which had just been slipped over Alice's head.

Alice had long passed from bewilderment to a state of rapturous and uncomprehending delight. As one dress after another was held against her and deftly folded away, she managed to whisper plaintively 'I really can't afford anything. I only came in for a lipstick.'

And then Miss Hetherington looked at Miss Dedlock and they almost wept. This was just what England expected from a royal mistress, unwilling to accept so much as a paltry lipstick from the man she loved. The country would not show itself ungrateful to her. Miss Hetherington had now been joined by Miss Delworth from Cosmetics and Miss Portman from Ladies' Shoes and Handbags.

Alice no longer had the slightest idea what was happening. It was as though she had awakened in the middle of a Christmas pantomime, with a dozen fairy godmothers all vying with each other to shower her with gifts. Twice she had protested that she really could not afford anything and Miss Hetherington had sniffed delicately and said with tears in her eyes that Mrs Morell's credit was unlimited.

Everything had been selected for her and immediately carried from sight by a number of younger acolytes. Alice knew that very soon she would wake up and have to explain to Alaric that she had not exactly signed a cheque, but there had been some dreadful mistake which was not her fault. She closed her eyes and tried not to think of her son and how they would have to slip out of the hotel like thieves . . .

'Oh, Alaric! Oh, my poor boy!'

Alice's grief was in every syllable. After all, she had dedicated her life to him and really she had done so little for him. She looked up and saw Miss Hetherington and Miss Dedlock like two observers of the Transfiguration. Their hands were clasped, their breath came in short gasps. As this royal revelation unfolded about them, they felt as though a bright star had crossed the heavens to shine above Harrods. Neither could remember having heard of a recent royal bastard. No wonder this dear good woman was leaving England and taking with her the son who – had she not been a married woman – could have been their future king!

'Your son, madam?' Miss Hetherington's voice was hushed.

'I've only been thinking of myself – shoes, bags, suits, I can't even remember what I liked now – and all the time there's my son, and we're leaving for Australia tomorrow morning and how on earth can I get these clothes to the airport?'

Miss Hetherington moved backwards from Mrs Morell as though leaving the presence of royalty.

'Madam, I shall immediately request Mr Snutmole of Gentlemen's Outfitters to attend upon you. Naturally, if you will be gracious enough to let us have your flight number, everything will be packed and delivered to the airport in suitable travel cases.' She paused, hoping beyond hope that she would be able to see the replica of Prince Charles toddle in and rush into his mother's arms. No wonder the prince had taken so long to get married! It must have been heartbreaking for him to leave this modest, unassuming woman and their little son. And to think that now there was another small son in the Palace!

Mr Snutmole was reassuring when Alice told him that she knew Alaric would not set foot in Harrods, but that she did have all his measurements. Again the flurry of silk and linen cruise wear, Harris tweeds and grey flannels. Alice was a little hesitant about the linen suits, but Mr Snutmole assured her that he had personally dressed a number of Australian millionaires. He too shuddered slightly when he thought of the son of the future king of England being exiled to New South Wales . . .

*

'There is no need to worry, Alaric. All we have to do is make our way to the airport tomorrow morning and . . . leave all this here.' She paused, adding, 'But I must take Aunt Penelope's dressing-case and if you carry your

52

cricketing gear, everyone will think we're going off to a match somewhere.'

Alaric was too crushed to answer. He could accept the fate of Aeneas, and added to that the thought of being pursued by a pack of furious Arabs more terrifying than the Eumenides, the Furies who lashed harried mortals to the gates of Tartarus. Aeneas carrying his father was one thing, being hounded by the Furies was another, but nowhere in Virgil was there mention of Anchises being mad as well as old. He knew that his mother was changing into Aunt Penelope before his very eyes. Soon she would want him to push her in a swing. He did not even try to answer; Alice insisted they dine in the restaurant and Alaric followed her down without speaking.

The following morning, Alice stuffed a few clothes into Alaric's cricket bag and tucked some underwear in between the crystal jars of Aunt Penelope's travelling-case. Having breakfasted early, they sauntered past the receptionist and the hall porter shortly after nine o'clock. The doorman tipped his cap to them, called a taxi and grinned at Alaric.

'Make a century for your mother, sir!'

They took the taxi round the corner to Green Park Station, where they got out to the accompaniment of the driver's vociferous rage when Alice told him that 60 pence was more than adequate compensation for carrying them three hundred yards from their hotel. The train to Heathrow was jammed with foreign tourists, and Alaric looked enviously at their bulging suitcases and thought of his few clothes left behind in the wardrobe at Brown's. There was a Burberry he had inherited from his grandfather, which he had cherished like a favourite dog. Now that was gone with all the rest of his clothes. At least he had managed to stuff in his cricket blazer with his pads, and had refused to part with his college boater.

At Heathrow it seemed to Alaric that a vast barbarian horde was sweeping them along into a new age of darkness. With difficulty, they found the economy queue at the

British Airways counter and edged slowly forward. But the moment Alaric gave his name to the snippy little clerk, there was a sudden flurry of movement. He was standing there glumly, waiting to be told that anything he said would be taken down and used in evidence, when a suave and smiling gentleman appeared at his elbow.

'Sir – the first-class lounge is *this* way.' Then, smiling at Mrs Morell, 'Your luggage has been attended to, madam.' And as they followed his siren invitation, they saw twenty-seven cream suitcases wheeled past on a trolley.

Chapter Three

There had been only one terrifying moment for Alaric on the plane, when he thought he saw two Arabs seated at the rear of the economy class section. Then one of them got up to place a coat in the upper compartment and Alaric sank back with relief as he recognized a missionary nun dressed in white. He still could not understand why they were seated in first-class and being plied with champagne. Alice was convinced that it was a mistake, but if some people could make mistakes that meant having your furniture removed and your house pulled down around you, then it was quite possible that other people could have made a different kind of mistake and confused them with some rich dignitaries on a diplomatic mission.

Alice's raptures of excitement continued to climb as the plane descended in a wide curve across Sydney and towards Mascot. It was more beautiful than Provence, certainly it was a distinct improvement on the seedy Cypriot boarding-house run for the widows of Church of England clergymen where she had spent a number of summers. Alaric's fuddled good humour had lasted until the airport, when he saw the suitcases being packed into a small blunt-winged plane and realized they were his mother's. Then he became a little hysterical and assured her that Harrods would now be in touch with Interpol and they could expect to be arrested and flung into prison for the rest of their lives. To all of which Alice replied calmly that she had not given anyone a penny and she had not certainly signed anything.

From that moment, the enchantment seemed to dwindle as the pilot headed into the north-west across a red and grey landscape that shuddered in convulsive waves beneath them. Alaric looked down and thought of dying dragons or, worse yet, the Gorgons warming their metal hides in the heat of the sun. Alice smiled consolingly at him and squeezed his arm as he muttered under his breath and clasped his knees with white-knuckled hands. He turned away and stared bleakly out of the window into a dazzle of blue beating against the plane like fire shaken from the Furies' wings. Of course, he thought, it was not true that they were creatures of night; rather they came in sunlight and broad day, dissolving people and places to a white ash. Nothing could appease the Furies.

When they landed, the pilot genially assured them that it was indeed Gulgong, their destination and the closest air-strip to Hope's End and Mockery Bend. Lance Weston would be coming along any minute now to pick them up – 'a beaut bloke', reliable as the day was long. The pilot con-cluded his praises of Lance Weston somewhat limply, because other aspects of Lance's character kept coming to mind. He was dead sorry he had to push off now, but there was a dust-storm blowing out from the west and he didn't fancy being sucked into that. Alice barely heard him as she looked around in disbelief at the tin shed with a long grimy window and a screen door that would not close. The cream suitcases were stacked in a mound and there was nothing else in the shed. Outside, the plane rose almost vertically into a sky that was now the colour of old blood; around them stretched a landscape that looked like Mars, with rocks and stunted trees shrouded in red dust.

'Foolish man,' Alice said faintly. 'He must have mistaken the place.'

Alaric only moaned, turned his face to the corrugated iron wall and felt the scorching breath of the Furies. He stood with arms folded and eyes closed, trying to compose Greek hexameters very slowly while the wind tore at the tin roof with a thousand clawed hands.

*

Twice Lance Weston decided to turn back to Hope's End, but he thought of the fee Barnhouse had mentioned and decided to push through the dust-storm. Barnhouse was a useful friend – a big name such as the Sydney solicitor was not to be turned down when he asked someone like Lance to drive across to Gulgong and pick up a party of two for Mockery Bend. Amongst other interests, Lance ran the taxi service in the area; he also owned the freehold of the Shearers' Arms in Hope's End and had an interest in a garage at Belton. These were the businesses he declared for taxes, but there were others, more lucrative, ranging from two-up to illegal immigrants. And the latter were always transported in his taxi and private limousine service. He was making money hand over fist and had even bought a few acres of land, where he raised some sheep and fancied himself as a squatter in his own eyes, if not in anyone else's.

Lance's problems began with his name, which was not Weston but Esposito, and unfortunately everyone in the area knew it. 'Lance the Wop', 'Lance the Dago' could not even remember the Abruzzi where he had been born fifty-three years ago, but he did remember vividly working sixteen hours a day in his father's fruit shop in Bankstown. It was there, at the age of fourteen, that he discovered there were only two things he wanted from life – money and sex. The money came slowly, but his prowess with women was fabled by the time he was twenty and had assumed mythic proportions as his victories were recounted through the local Leagues Clubs, where Lance's weekly score was given odds like any of the major football teams.

At that point in a brilliant career, Lance got Phyllis O'Brien in the family way. O'Brien ran the Golden Barley with two gigantic calloused fists which had brought him within challenging distance of the heavyweight title of Australia. At which point he was immediately paid to retire by certain concerned interests and settled down in the Golden Barley, where he did all his own chucking-out and fixed every bar fight in seconds. Phyllis – red-haired, freckled and smart – was her father's pride and joy, a girl who knew precisely how much water to add to the beer and who could juggle two sets of accounts faster than her father could remove a brawler from the premises. O'Brien's first idea was to kill Lance, but when Phyllis said she would then hand over his books to the nearest tax inspector, he consoled himself with the fact that Lance was Catholic and bought the young couple a pub at Hope's End, telling everyone that the only other females in the area had long tails, pouches and hopped, and that if Lance wanted to chase them he was welcome. How could O'Brien have foreseen that Hope's End would become a flourishing small town with shapely legs and jiggling bottoms, and all of them finding their way either to Lance's limousine with its plaid fold-out mattress, or to a small air-conditioned flat above the garage in Belton?

Two miles from the airstrip, the dust was so thick that Lance almost drove off the road, but he switched on foglights and kept going. It would do no harm to hand Barnhouse a favour, and he had to admit he was curious to see this Mrs Morell and her son, particularly if it meant taking a rise out of Jos Tulliford. Tulliford, the Burton brothers, Crockford and the rest were the silver-tailed squatters and the ones who never seemed to forget that Lance was an Esposito. He grunted and sighed and thought back over his life – he had a few thousand squirrelled away and the kids were off his hands, not that they had given him much pleasure. Two sons had become priests, as though to atone for their father, and the only girl had married a public servant in Canberra. What he wanted now was something he could not really define, yet it made him restless. He would have liked to be on equal terms with Crockford and his kind, to be in the top drawer instead of in the till, but he was not really sure that was the whole of it . . . Let it be said now that if Lance had not been fifty-three, and if he had not been born in the Abruzzi, it might never have happened. As it was, he pushed open the screen door, spat out a mouthful of dust and then the beatific vision was vouchsafed him.

Wearing a pale blue dress, she was standing by a small white mountain, and something shook his heart. There had been statues like that in every church, in grottoes at the side of the road, and one above his bed as a child which first gave him a taste for blondes. But this was stirring him to the sound of trumpets and a thousand voices singing of love and devotion to fair ladies and blessed damozels leaning across the bar of heaven. It was Dante and Beatrice, Petrarch and Laura, it was Don Quixote prepared to do battle with giants for Dulcinea's sake. Swords clashed, shields rang and he was driving back all the armies of the world in her name. It was then that he saw the boy and reality edged its painful way into his vision like the serpent into Eden.

'Are you the person supposed to meet us here?' Alaric tried to keep his voice down, but it was almost breaking.

Then she, the vision, came towards Lance and he felt as if a fountain of light had suddenly exploded in his head.

'I'm Mrs Morell and this is my son, Alaric. You must be Mr Weston, come to our rescue!'

She could have been chanting a hymn composed in Poictesme or on Brendan's Isle. Lance coughed, thought of spitting again, decided against it and contented himself with nodding and shuffling. And this was Lance Weston who could talk a girl's pants off faster than she could put them on; Lance, who regarded women as a rat does a hunk of Gruyère cheese; Lance, the best-known stud since they

58

put Bernborough out to grass. He shook his head and tried to remember everything he had heard about the Morells, but nothing fitted this lady. The boy was a mystery too. Was it simply that Lance had fallen in love? And could that be enough to explain what happened to him on Wednesday afternoon at twelve minutes past two? Or was it Saul on the road to Tarsus, Bunyan in his prison cell, Anthony in the desert? All one can really say is that Lance Weston was a changed man from the day he looked at Alice Morell and carried twenty-seven matching cream suitcases out to his station wagon.

It was impossible to see through the side windows of the car as the red dust billowed and twisted around them. Alaric lay back with his eyes closed and tried to concentrate on Aeneas carrying his wretched, complaining, undeserving old father, who should have been left in the bonfire of Troy, but he kept hearing his mother's voice and the whip-cracking drawl of the feral-faced little abomination at the wheel.

'I still don't reckon you should be coming out here, Mrs Morell. This Mockery Bend – it's no fit place fer a lady like yerself. Now, why don't you put up at the pub with the missus and me? You'd be comfortable there.'

'Mockery Bend is the home that I've inherited, Mr Weston.'

'Yeah, well, there's always been a lot of talk round these parts concerning the Tulliford will, and I do recall some saying that there was a Morell tried to live there once, but she – Mrs Morell – she wasn't like you, she was round the twist!'

Alice laughed. It was astonishing that everyone seemed to think she expected a palace and powdered footmen, when all she wanted to see was a red-brick manor house with a tall chimney leaning askew. Every now and then she could glimpse the country through the surging tides of dust and her heart sank a little, but she knew how quickly land could change, often from one field to the next – sour, dank soil by Wyvern Bend, for example and the rich loam of Elder Crossing – and it would be like that at Mockery Bend.

A sudden desperate thought had taken hold of Alaric. What if he deserted his mother and ran away, anywhere, without that burden on his back? Then he heard the school chaplain intoning the lesson: 'No boy is ever expected to love his parents. There is no reason why he should love his mother. What he must do is laid down in the Commandments – honour thy father and thy mother – and that means do your duty by them even when you cannot like them.'

The station wagon pulled to a halt and Lance rushed round to open the door for Alice. She stepped out slowly and almost fainted. The dilapidated ruin might once have been a house, but now it looked more like the decaying carcass of a dead animal. A straggle of trees ran down to a stony creek, beyond which the parched grass lay buried under the red dust.

'Mr Barnhouse did send out a man to take the padlock off the front door, but I reckon that's all anyone's done out here fer a long time, Mrs Morell.'

Alaric was standing beside his mother and she reached out and took his hand. 'Well, it's not quite what I expected, dear. But it *is* a house.'

'Mother,' Alaric said weakly, 'we have to go back to England. We can't stay here.'

'I think we should examine the property first,' Alice said firmly. She coughed and choked on the dust and asked Lance if it ever rained.

'Hasn't for six months,' he replied and then, without quite knowing why or who had put the words in his mouth, added, 'You could try praying.'

'What a good idea! We'll do that this evening.'

Years later, Lance liked to say that the heavens opened over their heads as soon as Alice looked up. Of course it wasn't like that at all and the drought continued for another three weeks, but he was close enough to the truth. Alice did pray that night – frequently and emphatically – and even-

60

tually it did rain.

Alice led the way up the broken steps and across a sagging, cracked veranda. The front door opened at a touch. Inside the walls were peeling and sacking covered what seemed to be furniture. There was dust over everything. Only the spiders seemed to be at home, spinning webs from one corner to another. Alice stood back and saw a dusty square of sky through the ceiling.

'It's a roof, almost a roof, over our heads,' she said softly.

Lance was shaking his head in disbelief. 'You can't live here. Nobody's lived here.'

With quiet fury she turned on him and Lance almost fell through the door.

'This is *my* property. This will be *my* home. I shall make it a home for my son and for me. I'm not afraid of a little dust and that hole up there will be patched and sealed before we have dinner. I never heard of Joseph Tulliford until a few days ago, but that bitter vengeful old man is not going to drive *me* away from here!'

Even Alaric was startled by his mother's vehemence.

'I have come here to claim my inheritance. I lost one . . .' and here she tried not to think of all those diamond bracelets slipping through Henry's fingers, 'but I most certainly shall not lose this. We Morells have been persecuted for generations and I have been bullied by grandfathers and uncles and old aunts, simply because my parents fell off a cliff while collecting gulls' eggs, and I am not going to be driven off my land by anyone again.'

Alaric felt there was a certain incoherence in his mother's argument, but he approved of the general sentiment. As for Lance Weston, it was as though Joan of Arc had risen up before him in shining armour and called upon him to carry her standard into battle. From that day he was pledged to her service and had she demanded any deed of chivalry from him, he would have charged off to slay droves of dragons.

Of course, this was not the way he described what had

61

happened when later that evening he was in the Shearers' Arms. He sprawled against the bar, spitting on his forefinger and polishing the beer spigot to an unaccustomed lustre.

'Funny old girl – got a son with her. I don't think she's as mad as people make out.'

He watched to see the effect this was having on his cronies, who gathered there regularly to check on his latest score.

'I thought I'd give her a hand, get her settled in because it'll be like a poke in the eye with a burnt stick to that skinflint Jos Tulliford. He still thinks he has a right to that land. Yeah, and it'll give a shake-up to Syd Crockford and the Burton boys to know there's a Morell at Mockery Bend. Another of our finest families has arrived in style to take up residence amongst us.' He laughed and raised his glass, waiting for any sign of interest, then decided to stress Alice Morell's age.

'I wouldn't say she was on her last legs . . . exactly. Rather a nice old duck really, white hair and a crooked hip. Just between ourselves, I don't reckon the young feller is her son, more like a keeper, if yer know what I mean. He did hint to me that she gets violent at certain times of the month. Pity about her harelip . . . I tried to talk to her, but it's terrible difficult understanding her. She slobbers a lot.'

Lance grinned as Whitey Macguire blanched and asked for a stiff whiskey. No, he didn't think the boys would be making unnecessary trips out to Mockery Bend. He could do more than talk barmaids into bed.

That night Phyllis was startled to find Lance at home for tea. He was unusually quiet, and after two helpings of curried sausages and mash he sat back and belched like a well-fed ferret. Alarm bells were going off all around her, warning signals flashing every time she looked at him. She had lived with Lance's reputation for so long that she almost took a pride in it; certainly she only displayed a flicker of interest when a friend told her that Lance had raced off to meet a visiting hockey team and its instructor.

This evening he was different and she was worried. Lance represented a thirty-two-year investment for her which had always paid handsome dividends and, as she told her well-meaning friends, he had never brought a girl friend home and never touched the housekeeping money. But he was picking his teeth now as though trying to dig out the right words and that was unusual too – generally Lance Weston had more conversation than a commercial traveller. His eyes were . . . she could not describe how they looked, almost as if . . . and she went out to the kitchen and nearly threw up. She decided then that it was time to ask questions.

'Lance? Is there something you want to tell me?'

'Maybe.'

Feeling the muscles in her throat tighten, she said three Hail Marys quickly under her breath. Then she tried to sound casual, but her voice squeaked unnaturally: 'Got a problem?'

'Sort of.'

'Female?' He shrugged in reply.

'Is she pregnant?'

'Struth, no! She's a *lady*!'

'They get pregnant just like the rest, Lance. Now, I hope you don't have anything on your mind like divorce – which is contrary to our faith – or anything foolish like that, because I don't mind what kind of a woman you make me, just so long as you don't try to make me a divorced woman, because if that's what you do have in your thick skull, then I am going to the phone and I shall call my father, who may be an old man but who can still choke you with his bare hands, and then I shall call Father Mulveeny who will curse you and –'

'Phyllis, I want you to meet her!' Lance said imploringly.

'If I meet her, I shall first spit in her eye, then I shall most likely wrap a chair round her head and stamp on her so hard you'll be spending the rest of your life pushing her about in a wheelchair!'

'Phyllis, I want you to meet her and help her, because

she's a lady and she doesn't mean nothing to me like that.'
He pulled out a crumpled sheet of paper from his hip
pocket. 'She gave me this list and I thought you could help
get some of these things together for her. Fer Gawd's sake,
it's Mrs Morell and her son and she is determined to stay
out there at Mockery Bend. She needs sheets and towels
and . . . yeah . . . buckets and soap and bleach and . . .'
He paused, at a loss to read Phyllis's expression. 'Oh,
Phyllis, she's like nothing you've ever seen.'

Phyllis felt as though she had been drowning and
someone had just thrown her a lifebelt – no prospective girl
friend asked for six tins of Bon Ami. She concealed her
relief admirably, raising her eyebrows and sucking her
front teeth audibly.

'A lady, eh? I don't know, Lance. They do say you've
had one of every kind. Maybe this is an original!'

He was really angry. 'I don't want you saying anything to
her about – well – I don't think she'd appreciate loose talk. I
intend to help her get settled, because it's going ter throw
Jos Tulliford into a flat spin when he finds out she's here.
Besides . . .' his voice almost trembled, 'it was kind of
upsetting to see her out there in all the muck and dirt, trying
ter move furniture round with her son.'

Phyllis folded the list slowly and looked at Lance expres-
sionlessly.

'I'll be out there first thing in the morning. But if she
means to make a home there, she'll need the heavy work
done by a man. I hope you're not pushing this off on to me.
I'd like to think you're going to pull your weight in getting
this poor soul settled. It's time you thought of doing a few
acts of charity in your life.'

That night, Phyllis said, was better than the time when
they were snowed up in a motel for three days. But, as she
smiled at herself in the mirror the next morning, there were
few women smarter than Phyllis O'Brien. She sighed
happily and wondered where in the world there was a man
with Lance's staying power – better than a team of

bullocks. She started packing a trunk straight after breakfast.

*

For three days Alice had scrubbed, until Phyllis said it was making her feel ill to see a woman work so hard. The dust had been followed by rain and now the countryside was a quagmire of ochre mud, but the wood-stove was working and water running from a tank on the roof. Alaric tried to think of the labours of Hercules as he nailed boards and hammered down lengths of corrugated iron where the old shingles had rotted away. Phyllis had brought out a collection of worn print dresses, because Alice refused to open a single one of the twenty-seven suitcases until the house was clean. The two women worked together as Lance carried in supplies and told Alaric how to glaze windows and fit wire screens. He could not say that he had actually taken to the boy, but he did find him easier to get along with than his own sons, who had always wanted to duck off somewhere for a quick prayer when there was any work to be done.

Occasionally Alaric glanced at his mother and shuddered. Somehow he had to get her out of this purgatory and back to England. Every time he saw her she was in another hideous smock with her hair tied up in a rag, plastering walls or nailing up shelves. He decided to put on his boater against the sun, and go up on to the roof again to continue with his hammering. There, at least, he did not have to contemplate his mother looking like a drudge and listen to the nasal twang of Phyllis Weston and her equally unpleasant husband.

It all came to him in a blinding flash. He knew it! He could solve everything! The resolution of the problem was simpler than Archytas's tonic equations. Archimedes might have discovered the principle of his name in a bath, but Alaric found his on a tin roof. Suddenly he wanted to stand up and dance, throw his boater in the air and turn a somersault. Instead, he lost his balance and slid awkwardly down

65

on to the verandah where Alice was just handing Lance a cup of tea.

'Darling! I was going to call you! You're just in time for tea.'

Lance had learned to drink lemon tea as though it were ambrosia. At first he had gagged: now he almost preferred it to beer, provided Alice's hand was on the tea-pot.

'It all came to me up there. For weeks now I've been trying to work it out. Now I've got it!'

'I agree,' Alice replied absently. 'It is time we opened our suitcases and looked like civilized people again.'

For the last three days she had been promising Phyllis that she would open those mysterious cream suitcases. And now, Alice felt she could pause for a moment to look at herself in a mirror and put on a dab of lipstick. Mockery Bend was still not a house, but it could be described as a habitation. Phyllis came out from the kitchen wiping her hands and complaining.

'I would sooner have cleaned out a pig-pen. Those lawyers in Sydney should be shot, expecting decent human beings to live in this kind of muck-hole.' But, as she looked around, even she felt a distinct pride in what they had accomplished, and every night she thanked Alice Morell for what had happened to Lance. Just to think that she had got on her knees and scrubbed a floor with . . . Phyllis was at a loss to know quite how to describe Alice . . . with a lady who was C. of E. and spoke of the Queen like she was a distant relative. Just watching her drink a cup of tea was an education. If only that snotty-nosed daughter of hers and her stuck-up husband could see her hobnobbing with English aristocracy!

'Mother! Will you please pay attention? I have the solution to this nightmare. I can take you back to England!'

Phyllis almost snarled at him. 'You were up there too long in the heat, sonny.' The last thing she wanted was to see Alice Morell leave Mockery Bend, but Alice was leaning forward now with eager anticipation.

'Alaric, I knew you had a head for business. What is it, dear?'

'Wills,' Alaric said slowly, 'can be contested. Wills can be broken.'

Lance came round the verandah with a bag of tools and shook his head. He was getting quite attached to Alaric, even though the kid was a little soft at times.

'There's one thing you've forgotten, Al, my boy – where there's a will, there's relatives. In this case, four cousins!'

'But my mother is the direct heir, Lance. What I plan to do is go to Sydney and talk to the executor, this . . . this Barnhouse chappie.'

'Cavalry Barnhouse,' Lance said with hushed breath, 'is no bush lawyer. I've had a few dealings with him and he's smart.'

Phyllis had sat down on the verandah steps and was beginning to feel a little queasy.

'You never want to tangle with lawyers, Alaric. They get rich making other people miserable. The only time you talk to a lawyer is when you can't see the sky for steel bars. My old father used to say that and he was right.'

Alice was looking down at the creek where a herd of russet-brown cows had come to graze after the rain. She had never seen finer dairy cows and said thoughtfully, 'I'm sure whatever you do will be for the best, Alaric. You know how I've always relied on your judgement.'

Alaric knew exactly how Moses had felt when he came down from the mountain and delivered the Commandments to an unbelieving and ungrateful people. Phyllis was frowning at him as though he had said or done something to offend her, his mother was audibly counting the cows, and Lance was staring at her in a way he would have found offensive if he had not become so accustomed to it. However, it was galling to see his mother pitied by this wretched little man in quite such a public fashion.

He decided to begin again, very slowly. 'The way to break the will is to offer to buy out your cousins, Mother.'

67

'Lance,' she said, 'do you think you could bring me out some rock salt tomorrow?'

'There's plenty of salt in the kitchen,' Phyllis said, adding tartly, 'What you need real bad is some curtains and if it says in the will that this place is supposed to be a habitat, then it doesn't make for good habits to live in a house without curtains – if you get my meaning.'

No one seemed to have heard her.

'Would you please pay attention to me!' Alaric was shouting.

'Darling, we're all very interested, but I don't see what we can use to buy anything from anyone at the moment. There isn't a Harrods around the corner.'

Alaric took a deep breath. 'I am quite sure that Mr Barnhouse will be delighted to have the estate wound up satisfactorily. Lawyers often need laymen to help them find their way out of all the legal technicalities. They tend to get bogged down in detail, you know.' Then he paused. 'Why do you need rock salt, mother?'

Alice's eyes widened. 'Because it's so useful to have around the house. Heavens, Alaric, no well-run household is ever without a supply of rock salt. It's even more necessary on a farm.'

Alaric still felt uneasy, but continued, 'Now, the way to break the will is to buy out your cousins. There's thirty million at stake, for pity's sake. All your cousins have to do is give up their claim to the estate in return for a share of the money and then we could all benefit. It simply means cooperating in order to break that damn will. Good Lord, if the Greek states had only learned to cooperate, there would never have been a Peloponnesian War!'

'Five into thirty million – that's a very satisfactory slice of pie,' Lance said.

'Forget it!' Phyllis brushed the idea and four cousins aside.

'I am going,' Alaric announced, 'to Sydney, where I shall show this Barnhouse fellow how to negotiate a settlement.

Mother, I shall go and pack.'

'Such an impetuous, brilliant boy!' Alice said as she followed Alaric into the house.

Phyllis sat glumly staring over the sodden, steaming countryside, cursing Alaric and all his bright ideas. Out of the corner of her eye she could see Lance staring after Alice like a famished dog watching its dinner disappear from view. For over thirty years she had been praying for something that would keep Lance on the straight and narrow, and at last all those novenas had been answered with fringe benefits. There had been that long pause at the other end of the phone when she told her daughter that she was helping the Honourable Mrs Henry Morell to settle in at Mockery Bend, she had added the 'Honourable' because if cabinet ministers could use it, she saw no reason why a real aristocrat like Alice should not have a handle to her name. And what comforted her soul like a good act of contrition was knowing that Alice was completely unaware of what was going on. There was Lance grovelling round her feet, and yet it was only with some difficulty that she had been persuaded to call him by his first name. Not that she seemed inclined to have him address her as Alice. It was a perfect arrangement and Phyllis didn't need any fancy shrink to tell her how and why it was working. She was a religious woman who also knew a lot about sex and nobody needed to tell her what had happened to Lance. She only wished her two sons had found their vocations in the same way.

When Alaric came out he was superbly dressed in a cream suit to match his travelling valise, and was carrying his college boater. It was so long since he had worn new clothes; everything had been handed down in the male line with suitable alterations for waist and height for so many years that he now felt as though he had abandoned an old skin. And Alice . . . Lance stood up and gaped.

'I didn't want to say good-bye to Alaric in that old – that very comfortable and useful smock you lent me, Phyllis – so

I opened the first case and took this out.'

This was a powder-pink linen with a white belt and matching sandals.

'Oh Phyllis, we're going to have such a marvellous time looking through those cases. I can't remember what I bought at Harrods now.'

But Alaric wanted to be on his way; the sooner he had the will settled, the sooner Harrods would be paid. This time he no longer felt like Aeneas with Anchises on his back, but like Jason off to find the Golden Fleece in Colchis. It was a comforting thought to know that Jason had left his mother Alcimede at home.

Lance and Alaric disappeared across the rise and Phyllis rushed in to examine the cases. She was thunderstruck as one gown after another was lifted from tissue paper, with every accessory wrapped alongside it: shoes, handbags, perfume and matching underwear. By the time everything had been examined, it was time to light the kerosene lamps.

Phyllis was absently stroking a shaded pink mink. 'I – I swear to God I've never seen clothes like this, not in the Members' at Randwick – nowhere, Alice. And I . . . me lending you those old cotton things.' Her voice rose. 'And you wearing them without a murmur when this is what you're used to! Oh, blessed Jesus – I feel so ashamed!'

'I've never had things like this before in my life, Phyllis.'

'You are a woman of mystery, Alice.'

Alice laughed until the tears came. She had always known that she was extravagantly normal, and to be regarded by this kind freckled woman as a creature of romance was too utterly killing. She wondered what on earth they would make of it in Lupin Tanner's hairdressing salon . . .

At that precise moment Lupin had reached the epic's pitiful climax where, deserted by Alaric, Alice struggled on alone through a frightful storm that washed away roads and tore up mighty oaks. Lupin experimented with a number of endings: struck by cars, murdered by gypsies – until she settled on one that moved her audience to gasping sobs. In a brackish fen outside Cambridge, Alice stumbled into a bog where her calls for help were drowned by thunder. The storm passed, the moon came out and one pale hand was raised above the ooze like a crumpled flower. It seemed to bid a last farewell to the moon, then sank from view, and Alice Morell was never seen again in this world.

Lupin was indeed contemplating an *Alice in Heaven*, but decided against it. If Milton couldn't pull it off, she didn't fancy trying herself; besides, she enjoyed unhappy endings. Bertha Craddock had been received back in favour and would nod lugubriously when Alice was sucked down into the mud. She joined Lupin in scoffing at a fanciful tale brought back to Barnsley by Mrs Wimsy Toffs, which said that Alice Morell had come into a fortune and flown off to Australia to enjoy it.

'Some people,' Lupin said pointedly, 'cannot abide the truth, which is always painful and upsetting. However, in her life, she had made it a rule to prefer the truth to lies.'

Alice hung up a grey silk Chanel suit and resolved not to think about Morell Manor again. She would not, she told Phyllis firmly, live in the past like Aunt Penelope or Uncle Theodoric, recounting his stories of the blitz on London and how his firewatching unit had saved St Paul's and the Houses of Parliament in the same night. Alice had the beginning of an idea, and this did not require a Harrods dress but a good five pounds of rock salt. She smoothed back her hair and wondered why it was no longer falling around her face in wisps. For some reason she seemed to be looking much better groomed since she no longer visited Lupin Tanner once a week.

'Tell me,' Alice said, 'who owns those beautiful cows I saw on the other side of the creek?'

Phyllis was fingering a cocktail dress of ivory silk and, for a moment, she did not answer.

'Such beautiful cows, Phyllis. And isn't my land supposed to extend to the other side of the creek?'

'I reckon so. Oh Alice, how can you talk of cows when you have clothes like this? Just the feel of this silk is like having a man stroke you where it does the most good.'

'But the cows . . .'

'Oh, that's Syd Crockford's prize herd. Dairy cows are real difficult to raise in this part of the country and that's some special breed he imported from France. He reckons he gets milk from them that's half-way to being butter when it hits the pail. I wouldn't swear to that, but I do know that the only taste Syd Crockford's got is in his mouth. Stuck-up little twit! Everything Crockford owns has to be the biggest and the most expensive. Now those cows have won dozens of prizes at the Royal Easter Show and –'

'That may be so,' Alice said, 'but they happen to be on my land.'

*

Lance drove for some time without speaking. He did not mind admitting that he found Alaric a very weird kid. And he wasn't sure if he was straight. However, he thought that if he stayed the night in Pott's Point at the Marie Rose private hotel, this would be a real education for him. He had frequently passed a night there himself and left so tired the next morning that he could barely walk to the car.

'How are you fixed, Al – bread, moolah?'

'I don't think I have more than a fiver, Lance.'

'I'll lend you twenty. And just by luck, I have a limo going down to Sydney with four Asian gentlemen who . . . who came in by boat recently up north. They are going to visit relatives in St Mary's. Ask Wilf – he's on the wheel – to drop you off at the Marie Rose.'

It would not hurt at all, Lance thought, to have another white face up front with his latest shipment of illegal Indonesians. He must remember to tell Alaric to keep on that hat of his in the car.

Alaric was at the bow of the mighty ship *Argo*, urging his rowers on to Colchis and the Golden Fleece. Soon he would be able to place a sizeable share of the Tulliford estate in his mother's hands and return to Oxford to continue his research in the Ashmolean – perhaps take a D.Litt and spend the rest of his life on Hieronymus of Cardia, who was the main source for Diodorus, and if only Jane Hornblower had not misread the *Fragmente der griechischen Historiker* he would . . .

'Did you hear me, Al?'

'Ah yes, Lance. The Rose Marie Hotel.'

'Ask for Mildred. She's the proprietress. And if she's not there, then Beryl is on reception and there's Amy out the back and Winnie – if you get Winnie, you won't complain.'

'You're acquainted with all the staff?'

Lance paused. He was never quite sure if Alaric was taking a rise out of him, but a sideways glance at Alaric's gentle profile and slightly abstracted gaze convinced him that the kid was just soft.

'Mind you, I don't hold out any hopes of you getting anything from Cavalry Barnhouse. That man is a legal machine.'

'Lance, I have yet to find the man who is totally impervious to reason. The case will be resolved, the will can be settled and then I can take my mother back to England where she belongs.'

Not so many years ago, towns in Italy went to war to defend a holy relic, a femur of St Ambrosius. Now Lance felt as though a pagan was planning to steal the last vial of holy blood in existence, a priceless treasure which God had placed in his care. He jammed on the brakes outside the pub and told Wilf to shove Alaric into the front seat of the car. Then he thought of Cavalry Barnhouse and his momentary irritation disappeared. Sending this kid to cope with a lawyer like Barnhouse was like throwing a tadpole to a grouper.

Phyllis agreed with Lance as they drove back to the Shearers' Arms together. She knew all about the Marie Rose and Lance's intimate acquaintance with Mildred and the girls. She was a little afraid that Alaric might not get out of the place in one piece, but she shrugged – it was never too late for a boy to learn the facts of life and if she were lucky, Alaric would fall for one of the girls, marry her and settle down in Sydney.

'Yer see, Phyllis, I reckon it's the best place for him to spend the night on account of – well – I wouldn't like to think of that kid turning gay. His mother's got enough to trouble her out there at Mockery Bend.'

'I wanted to talk to you about that, Lance,' she said firmly.

Lance's hands tightened on the wheel and he stared straight ahead into the darkness. If Phyllis wanted to bawl him out over Alice Morell, then she was asking for a one-way ticket back to Bankstown via the nearest family court. He was not going to be pushed around and ticked off by a woman who seemed to think she had a collar and chain on him. He had his rights and . . . he paused in his unvoiced monologue to listen to Phyllis, who seemed to have been talking steadily for some time.

'And I can't get out there every day, Lance. But it's different for you. You're travelling between here and Belton all the time. And I can't see that it's going to be such a trouble for you to call in on her once a day. After all, you have a kind of duty to her. If I were you, Lance, I'd start thinking of past sins and try to make up for them now. You know what Father said last Easter – once a year isn't enough to save you, Lance, and don't think a few Hail Marys and my prayers are going to help you. You've got to do something yourself, otherwise you'll burn, Lance.'

Unable to believe what he was hearing, he coughed and cleared his throat as she continued.

'I don't want to hear any whingeing from you, Lance. Somebody has to keep an eye on Alice Morell, and I can't manage to get out every day. That's all I'm saying. She needs supplies brought out and she reckons she wants a fence repaired. I hope you don't expect me to be out sinking posts, do you? I don't see why you can't take a couple of those Chinks out there. No reason why they shouldn't see a little of the bush before you drop them off into somebody's noodle factory.'

If they hadn't been driving through a stretch of prickly

pear, Lance would have pulled over to the side, taken Phyllis out and made love to her alongside the car. As it was, he breathed deeply and started playing with her knee. And Phyllis smiled and leaned against him. She had discovered the key to a happy marriage and she could lock Lance up any time she felt like it now. As for Lance, he had sworn eternal devotion to Alice Morell and would never be unfaithful to her by even looking at another woman. In this condition of courtly love, wives were a necessary convenience which did not disturb the purity of service to the perfect ideal. Lance's allegiance was unswerving, but it was Phyllis who enjoyed the benefit in bed that night. And it was Phyllis's reward that Lance still did not know what had happened to him, although somewhere a smiling goddess recorded that Lance Weston of Hope's End had become in spirit a troubadour in the lists of love.

*

Alaric saw very little of Sydney's western suburbs. He was aware that the Asians had been put down in the middle of a used-car yard, then he tipped his hat over his eyes and thought pleasantly of how he would one day translate the love letters of Aristaenetus; it really was time they were better known. Absolute rubbish, all this current furore over Heliodorus, when Aristaenetus had so much more to offer the general reader.

The limousine made an abrupt turn off McLeay Street and nosed down an alley. Wilf pointed to a neat corner row house at the end of the alley and told him there was a side entrance.

He mumbled his thanks and pushed open an unobtrusive gate into a covered walk that led up to a Moorish grille door. There he rang a clappered bell and found himself in a small foyer under an enormous branched chandelier which seemed to extend from one wall to the next.

Then he saw Mildred, a red-head with flowing curves and slanting dark eyes who reminded him of the entrancing Turkish girl whom he had coached for a part in the *Bacchae*. It was weeks before she learned to rattle her thyrsis, and even then he was spending more time in her college room than his own until she acquired the basic movements.

Mildred almost fell over her rococo desk when he came in, and hefted Beryl aside with an elbow in the ribs that sent her tottering and complaining into the back office. Mildred explained that the hotel was booked out with a convention but, since he was Lance Weston's special friend, she could make up a bed for him in her own small flat at no cost whatsoever.

Since Lance had only given Alaric $20, he was overwhelmed by the generosity of this warm and handsome woman. After dinner – served in her sitting-room – she offered to wash out a shirt for him, and then, without his quite knowing how, they both ended up in the same bath with Mildred washing him from the toes up. They had very little sleep and at one point, when Alaric was giving Mildred a long Phoenician kiss, Beryl and Amy hammered furiously on the door, demanding that Mildred stop moaning and screaming so that they could concentrate on their own clients.

Alaric thoroughly enjoyed himself and Mildred was ecstatic, promising him trips to the Barrier Reef and Ayers Rock (she was not quite sure of his age), anything so long as he stayed with her for ever. Eventually they did fall asleep, with Mildred's head between his thighs. Alaric woke first with a sudden start. He was Jason in quest of the Golden Fleece and who was this dishevelled, voluptuous woman lying on her face with golden-brown buttocks heaving gently as she sighed in her sleep? But the Golden Fleece was in Sydney, guarded by Cavalry Barnhouse, and here he was sprawled in bed with Medea. He remembered his shirt on a hanger in the bathroom and went to collect it and the rest of his belongings. Mildred never stirred, only sighed more deeply as though she were having small, delightful orgasms in her sleep.

Everything was dim and silent in the foyer of the motel as he dodged under the chandelier. Then he heard voices and

76

two bedraggled men staggered from a hallway.

'You been on an all-night special too, kid?'

Alaric merely smiled and asked if the motel provided breakfast.

The two men gaped, looking at Alaric admiringly.

'I wish I was as young as you, kid. You need a lift anyplace?'

In less than an hour Alaric had been given breakfast at a McDonald's and dropped off in front of the building that housed Cavalry Barnhouse's legal empire. He looked up at the towering steel and wondered where the Golden Fleece was kept behind that multitude of reflecting glass windows.

*

Lance had been puzzled when Alice Morell took the parcel of rock salt from him as though he had brought her a crate of caviar.

'I still don't know what you'll need all that for, Mrs Morell.'

She smiled up at him and her grey eyes were the colour of dreams.

'Dear Lance, you and your wife have been so good to me. But I can't rely on friends all the time; I must learn to look after myself.'

Lance felt as though he wanted to cry, but he just shook his head and choked.

'I am going to have a farm here,' she went on. 'That was my intention at Morell Manor, but there was a wretched mistake about the land and we had to leave . . . rather suddenly. Now, I may not own Mockery Bend, but I am a tenant with a legal right to this land and I intend to work it.'

For a sudden wild moment Lance thought that Alice intended planting rock salt and growing some strange English crop he had never heard of. All he could answer was that she had nothing to work the land with – no seeds, no livestock.

And then Alice laughed and looked across the stream at the cattle grazing on her land.

77

Chapter Four

The lobby of Cavalry Barnhouse's firm was decorated in late Imperial Roman with a heavy emphasis on bronze. A purple velvet staircase led to the second floor and a number of brooding, saturnine eagles were posted at strategic angles to overlook the clients. The message was plain – law was oppressive, omniscient and very expensive. Alaric was not impressed, frowning slightly at the conjunction of incongruous styles and marvelling that anyone in his right mind would confuse a Hapsburg eagle for the Roman bird. His superb education had at least given him the ability to stand bare-foot among millionaires and despise them for their poverty. On this occasion the platinum-haired receptionist, who resembled a Roman matron of the old school, had priced his silk and linen suit to the last dollar and noted the matching Italian silk cravat.

'I would like to see Mr Barnhouse. Would you tell him that Alaric Morell is here?'

The receptionist breathed deeply at this profanity.

'You do have an appointment, Mr Morell?'

'No. But I feel sure he will want to see me. I have come to arrange the settlement of the Tulliford estate for him.'

At this, Mrs Belle Perkins felt that her twenty-six years spent in loyal defence of the front desk of the largest and most respected law firm in Sydney were being brushed aside like a second in all the centuries of eternity. And the brushing was being done by a golden-haired, grey-eyed boy with an accent that sounded as though it had just been cut from the middle of a fruit cake.

'Mr Morell – Mr Barnhouse never, *never* sees anyone without an appointment. And he is fully booked up for the next five months.'

Alaric beamed at her with the genial understanding of a member of the upper sixth for a particularly dim first-former.

'Quite so, with the common run of clients, no doubt. But you did appreciate what I just said, didn't you? I am here to settle this whole wretched business of the Tulliford will for Mr Barnhouse.'

Mrs Perkins gasped, then rose abruptly and ran across to an adjoining door. She dared not risk using the phone or the intercom, for she knew that this was somebody who had to be dealt with by a secretary, or an associate – perhaps even a junior partner or the police. Meanwhile Alaric made himself comfortable on a divan-like settee and rested his elbow on an arm-rest that resembled a gilded and scowling sphinx. He had already noted with disgust that the firm's taste in journals was on a par with its decor. Not an *Encounter*, not even so much as an *Illustrated London News* in sight.

He began to review the past night's events and smiled as some of them started to tingle from his mind to other parts of his anatomy. It was quite apparent to Alaric now that he had spent the night in a brothel, but his two friends at breakfast had assured him that the girls were as clean and crackling as new dollar bills. They had marvelled at his lasting the distance with Mildred, for no man had ever been known to get up and walk away from her, but as Alaric patiently explained, he had received training for an affair like this. An Oxford Blue in cricket meant you always commanded a straight bat, and that was necessary for a satisfactory innings at the wicket or on the mattress.

Word had passed from Mrs Perkins to one of Mr Barnhouse's secretaries, and one after another a succession of pretty young women now found reason to walk across the lobby to other offices. Alaric watched them pass with considerable pleasure – slim, shimmering legs under tight skirts – and his thoughts began to drift back to an enchanting picture of dancing Maenads on a vase by the Brygos painters, while Shadwell's song lilted into his mind: 'Nymphs and shepherds, come away . . .' He began humming it softly under his breath, 'Nymphs and shepherds, come away, come away, come away. For this is Flora's holiday . . .'

He had last sung this with five of his friends on a secluded little beach of the Isis where they had punted down from Oxford for lunch. Sally, Jo and Beth immediately decided they were nymphs, threw off their clothes and began dancing naked like the Three Graces. They had all joined in and after everyone had collapsed in a riotous heap of thrashing limbs in consequence of trying to form a Priapic circle – with no one quite sure who should be face to front, or front to back – they suddenly heard raucous laughter coming down the river. Everyone dived for towels or the bushes except Gerald Spedding; he placed a towel over his head and stood with arms folded as three punt-loads of American tourists came round the bend.

'I don't know how you chaps are recognized in Oxford, but I'm known by my face!'

Recalling that, Alaric laughed aloud, and that laugh decided Barnhouse to see him. Nobody entered his lobby in a mood of levity, no one ever laughed. Barnhouse had received rapid reports of Alaric's astonishing good humour, his appearance of affluence and then his laughter. If he could laugh, Barnhouse thought, it must mean he had something tricky up his sleeve and Barnhouse did not appreciate surprises. His square jowls sank into his collar and his eyebrows came down in a black line which had made eminent counsel quail before now.

The Tulliford will had established Barnhouse's fortune, and his father's before him. Not that a penny had ever been misused; rather had they brooded over it like a generation of dragons guarding a golden treasure. Their management of the estate had been admired internationally and drawn clients in a never-ending stream, all hoping to feast from the same gilded trough. The will was a sacred trust which had represented both fortune and burden, for Barnhouse had once dreamed of becoming a barrister, of storming down Macquarie Street in flowing silk to beat down juries and hector judges with abstruse points of law. Instead, the will had made him a solicitor who took some pleasure in hiring barristers who almost doffed their wigs to him, and as for the rest, well . . . he sometimes felt he could put out his hand and control the destiny of the city through his clients: millionaires and mobsters, bishops and bankers, they all felt their affairs would prosper when they had paid Cavalry Barnhouse his exorbitant fees. It was his boast that' when he retired he would pass on the Tulliford estate to his son, having doubled its assets in his lifetime.

Every year he travelled to America on behalf of clients, and when he was in Texas he had addressed the local bar association on the subject of the Tulliford will. He had told how his grandfather had drawn up a will for an angry old man and now, under the good stewardship of his firm, it was an estate of $30 million. This was no Dickensian slur against lawyers, no Jarndyce *versus* Jarndyce dragging its way through Chancery in *Bleak House*, but an example of how good commercial lawyers could transform little into much and fulfil the teachings of the Master as in the parable of the talents. For a lawyer, an estate was a sacred trust. At that point the Texan bar had risen and clapped and roared its approval like a pack of seals when the keeper arrives with a bucket of fish. Barnhouse's parable had a simple resolution: no man, woman or child should have control of his or her own money; only a legal firm had the foresight and the sagacity to manage money wisely for other people and increase it tenfold in the process.

Barnhouse stared bleakly at Alaric and recalled having seen similar types when he was last in Oxford trying to persuade a client's daughter not to marry a Sri Lankan psychologist. He motioned silently for him to be seated, then contemplated him across an implacable ocean of polished cedar.

Alaric flinched and Barnhouse chuckled inwardly, imagining the boy to be already terrified by his presence. He compressed his eyebrows more tightly and brought them down a little lower, but Alaric had only reacted to a room which resembled something from Hampton Court with a touch of the Brighton Pavilion thrown in for colour.

81

He listened in baffled outrage as Alaric blithely proposed a settlement of the estate, suggesting an agreement between the cousins and the happy release of Mr Barnhouse from his duties as executor.

'My boy, a will is a living force in the law and society. Joseph Tulliford lives on in that document and his wishes must be respected. Besides, there have been other attempts to break the will and all have failed. It was drawn up by my grandfather.'

'Nonetheless, Mr Barnhouse,' Alaric said patiently, 'the will is not just.'

'My boy, people seldom have justice in mind when they consult lawyers,' Barnhouse replied icily, thinking fleetingly of the merits of retroactive abortion, 'I very much doubt if old Joseph Tulliford had any notion of justice *per se* when he spoke to my grandfather. No, a man can make a will in any way he pleases and for any reason he wants, provided he doesn't break the law of the land. Now, sure as hell, there's nothing in law that says you can't hate your wife and her family. There are some who would say that's a definition of natural law!'

Alaric was not amused. He was here to help Barnhouse and the solicitor was being as obstinate as only stupidity allied with a legal education could make a man. He would try again.

'Mr Barnhouse, I propose seeing these cousins – my aunts, shall I call them – and suggesting a fair division of the estate.'

Barnhouse grinned at the naïvety and primal innocence of this fresh-faced youth.

'It won't work. They hate each other!'

Alaric felt a number of appropriate classical quotations would fit the occasion, but resisted the temptation. He knew instinctively that Barnhouse would react to Latin as he would to Sanskrit. So he decided to humour the fellow.

'Mr Barnhouse, if you would give me the names and addresses of the extant heirs, I will go and talk to them myself.'

At that moment a secretary came to the door and whispered urgently, 'Mr Barnhouse, you're due in court!'

There seemed to be a stirring throughout the building, a low hum of voices, the rustle of innumerable sheets of paper being collected simultaneously.

'Mr Morell, a man's life depends upon me this morning. A man who has been cruelly and unjustly accused of having murdered his wife and his three children. That man is waiting for me to instruct his counsel and save him. You will appreciate, therefore, that I do not care to waste that man's time and life by chatting to you about the improbable likelihood of your even meeting your remote relations.'

Doors were flung open and a throng of attorneys and clerks carrying files, tomes of law and padlocked brief-cases burst into the room. Alaric now learned why Clarence Barnhouse had earned the soubriquet of 'Cavalry'. The whole cavalcade jostled behind him, there was a second's pause, then with outflung arm he signalled the charge and led the attack upon the enemy.

Alaric was almost flung off balance as the horde pushed past him. As he collapsed into a chair, he wondered if there were room enough in court for a judge and jury when Cavalry Barnhouse arrived with his troops.

'Excuse me,' came a soft voice at his elbow, and Alaric looked up at a dimpling nymph.

'I heard you asking about the Morell heirs. Well, I know I shouldn't tell you, but there is one here in Sydney. She's married, but I reckon she could tell you where her sisters are.' And a slip of paper was pressed into his hand, on which he read: Mrs Betty Morell Carpenter, 47 Royal View Road, Killara. Underneath, in smaller letters, was the name Mary Lou Myerson and an apartment number.

*

The cows were jostling and pushing Alice to lick the salt in her outstretched hands. Liquid brown eyes, velvet soft noses surrounded her. She was trying to decide how many she could lead back across the stream and up to the fenced run which Lance's Vietnamese helpers had repaired for her. She always spoke to animals as though they were rather more intelligent than people and the cows seemed to understand her perfectly.

'I do want to explain to you girls that I'm not blaming you for trespassing. You simply haven't been properly looked after.'

One particularly rotund cow bellowed mellifluous assent.

'So, I'm going to have to confiscate some of you as a warning to whoever is supposed to own you. Now, follow me, girls!'

Four of the cows responded as though they were members of a hockey team being rallied for a fresh defence and followed Alice and the salt across the creek and up a winding track to Mockery Bend. Every so often she would give them another lick of the salt until she had them safely penned in her own yard. She looked back across the stream and then at the four cows she had already enticed home.

'You really need six,' she thought, 'for a reasonable butter and cheese dairy. Yes, two more and that should be sufficient warning to Mr What's-his-name to keep his cows off my grass.'

She was half-way across the creek with the two cows, her skirt tucked up around her hips, when she heard an extraordinary noise coming from the direction of the trees. She paused in midstream, then decided to go forward. Whatever it was, it was on her land, and Alice's ideas of property were distinctly feudal and derived from her grandfather and Aunt Matilda, who had even shown a tendency to confiscate children who strayed on to Morell Manor and hold them for ransom.

The noise was a growl and a panting whimper. Alice wondered if there were any dangerous animals in Australia, then she looked at the two cows who were reaching out greedily for the salt.

'Well, if you're not afraid, there's no reason why I should be.'

84

Trust a cow for good plain common sense, she thought.

The sound was coming from a thicket of scrub by the edge of the creek. Slowly she made her way towards the spot and parted the branches. A blue cattle dog tried to lunge up and take her by the wrist. She saw that the dog's hind leg was in a trap, saw caked blood under the steel and a fragment of bone. Obviously it had been caught some distance away and had dragged its way down to the stream for water. It was very close to death, but determined to fight with its last parched breath. Gently, Alice put out her hand for the dog to smell. He tried to pull himself back, snarling. She had seen dogs mutilated and torn after a fox hunt, but never one like this, and a fury rose within her as she saw how the teeth of the trap had closed around the leg. It was as though Sailor, her old labrador, had come back to her. She had never realized until then how much she missed having a dog.

'You poor old chap! Oh, poor fellow – you're going to let me have a look at that leg, aren't you?'

The only response was another weak panting snarl, but Alice was not deterred. She shook her head as though she were addressing a recalcitrant child.

'This is very foolish of you when I'm only trying to help.'

And as she spoke, her hand was stroking the dog which now seemed more bewildered than alarmed.

'You are a good fellow – and a very intelligent fellow too. Did you ever hear of Androcles and the Lion?'

Now she had hold of the trap and with all her strength forced the teeth apart. The dog had stopped growling and was staring at her, not flinching, as gently she eased the broken leg free.

'Of course, you're not a lion and I'm not Androcles, but it's a story I used to tell my son when he was a little boy. I wanted him to grow up loving and caring for animals. Well, one day Androcles met this lion in the jungle. The lion was roaring and growling because it had a thorn in its paw. Now, I know you're in much more pain than the lion, but then a dog is a much braver animal than a lion!'

At this point the dog began to whine more in bemusement than pain. In all his short life he had never been spoken to like this, nor had any other dog of his acquaintance.

Slowly, Alice put one hand behind the dog and eased him forward. He was lighter than she expected. There was a slight struggle but no attempt to bite her, and all the time she continued talking.

'Androcles took the lion's paw in his hand and pulled out the thorn. Years later, Androcles was thrown to the lions in the Roman arena because he was a Christian. People were perfectly beastly to Christians in those days, but the lion – *his* lion – recognized him and protected him from all the other hungry lions. And now – we're going back to the house and you won't even think of trying to bite, will you?'

She had the dog in her arms and was walking up the track when she saw the cows standing, patiently waiting for her. She turned and smiled gratefully at them.

'Thank you for waiting.'

First she gave the dog water and then fetched bandages and a splint for the broken leg. She set about the job professionally, talking brightly to the resigned and puzzled animal. He barely whimpered when she cut away the matted fur, cleaned the break and applied the splint.

'You were very lucky not to lose that leg. As it is, the bone's only chipped. Oh, I wish I knew who'd set that trap!' Next she set a bowl of bread and milk in front of the dog, who gulped it down and almost choked.

'Not so fast! I wish I could get a vet for you, but I don't think I could afford it. Of course, it will be different when Alaric comes back with all the money from the estate, but that could take time. No, we'll just have to hope that fracture heals. My grandfather's hounds used to have worse breaks than that after a hunt and we'd patch them up on the kitchen table just like this. But . . .' she paused, 'you don't even have a name, do you?'

The dog looked up at her, while Alice stroked his dusty,

dry ear and wondered what colour he was under that coat of dirt and blood.

'I shall call you Lion. And you may call me Androcles.'

She sponged Lion clean, admiring the steely blue of his fur, then let him dry in the sun. That night he slept beside her bed, opening his yellow eyes whenever she stirred, and Alice dreamed she was picking roses with Aunt Penelope while Sailor chased imaginary rabbits.

'It's easier to train a man than a dog,' Aunt Penelope had said and laughed softly at some secret memory. Alice shook her head and frowned; whenever she remembered Aunt Penelope, it was as though she had been inveigled into that secret world of assignations and champagne and Maseratis. What she must do, Alice told herself firmly, was concentrate upon making Mockery Bend a flourishing dairy farm with perhaps . . . yes, honey on the side.

*

Alaric heard the house before he saw it. He had caught a train from the city and then found himself pleasantly lost down leafy shadowed streets in Killara which reminded him of some parts of Wiltshire. After receiving directions from a kindly woman trimming her hedge, who insisted he should have a cup of tea with her, Alaric found himself in Royal View Road, a spanking new development which had once been an old ten-acre property. It looked like a cardboard display in a shop window to him: lawns of a brilliant chemical green, every bush in flower, all the trees with immaculate branches like mannequins showing off the new length in sleeves. But the noise from Betty Carpenter's house was like a freight yard, a rock concert and a zoo combined. A vast, rambling ranch house, it vibrated with every kind of sonic disturbance. There was a clutter of toys on the lawn, cars parked as though they had just avoided collision on a slick road. It was even more difficult for him to absorb the contents of the kitchen, much less hear what Betty Carpenter was saying to him.

She came swaying towards him behind an enormous belly which made her look like some primitive earth goddess fecund with the fruits of a new season. Alaric blinked and thought of dark Eleusinian mysteries and fertility rites requiring blood and grain and a considerable amount of pain from the worshippers. He was almost lifted off his feet and swung over that belly as Betty embraced him, laughing and crying. But still he could not hear what she was saying.

A television set over the sink was blaring out the latest news on detergents, a cat had taken refuge on top of it after having been disturbed while eating from the unscraped dishes on the sinks – and louder than the TV and radio were a pair of six-year old girls pulling apart a rag doll in the corner as they punched each other simultaneously.

Betty screamed, 'Oh, let me look at you! Oh, I can see the likeness!'

Alaric did not dare to inquire about the likeness to what or whom. The dirt and clutter resembled an opulent fowl-house. Underneath the kitchen table a baleful two-year-old was eating a chunk of chocolate sponge, most of which was on its face and through its hair. As Alaric stared, it deliberately pushed a lump down one ear and then began to scream, presumably because it could not taste anything.

'They're all so glad to see you, Alaric. Imagine! Their English cousin!'

Three teenagers had rushed through the kitchen, yelling. Meanwhile the chocolate child had managed to shove some cake into its mouth and was silently swallowing.

Alaric had begun trying to explain about the will and his mother, when two small boys hurtled past and flung open the fridge door with such force that he felt himself belted half-way across the room. At this point Betty laughed, shrugged and pointed outside.

The tree house was twenty feet up a massive eucalypt tree and Betty explained as Alaric pushed her slowly up (wondering when a newborn baby would drop on to his head) that it really was the only quiet place to talk. He hunched back against the far wall of the little shelter with his knees under his chin, wondering if the thin planking would hold Betty's weight. Far below there was a muffled roar like that of peak-hour traffic in a large city.

Betty was obviously in her thirties, but she was dressed like a flower child of the sixties with lank blonde hair hanging round her shoulders and a smear of mismatched mascara over her dark grey eyes; indeed there was something about her eyes that immediately made him think of his mother. He had come in quest of the Golden Fleece and found himself up in a tree house, listening to a story which made Jason's battle with the Harpies seem like a game of croquet on a vicarage lawn.

'You've got to think of this as your home, Ally, love. I know everyone round here calls it "Kiddie City", but as I always say when the neighbours complain about the noise, it's their kids as well as mine. And they would love to have you here – the kids, that is. I also think you might take some of the starch out of my snooty neighbours.'

'Please, Aunt Betty, don't – don't lean over the edge like that!'

'Oh, lovey, you shouldn't worry about me! I always come up here when I want to have a quiet talk to Bert – that's my husband – or someone.'

Alaric was considering what she had already told him about her sisters. 'You're quite convinced they wouldn't share the estate?' he asked.

'*Share?*' Betty threw back her head and laughed and Alaric could not help noticing the creases of dirt in her neck. 'Share?' She hooted and rocked with laughter. 'You haven't met my dear sisters. When I was little,' she paused for effect, 'they used to try to kill me!'

Alaric was now convinced that he was up a gum tree with a pregnant lunatic.

'Augustine, she's the second oldest, once tried to poison me with a chocolate frog. She injected arsenic into the cream centre. Fortunately I broke it in two, one piece fell on the floor and the dog snapped it up and rolled over stone-dead.'

Alaric shook his head in disbelief. 'Are you trying to tell me that your own sisters tried to . . . to murder you, Aunt Betty?'

'All the time. Once when I was on my own at the beach, building sand-castles, Gerda took a crowbar up to the top of the cliff and tried to start an avalanche. I could have been crushed to death or buried alive.'

'But – but why?'

'It's perfectly natural, Ally. As soon as we could walk we heard about the will and the money and Mockery Bend, so we all grew up trying to bump each other off. Our parents sent us to different schools, but it didn't make any difference. Honoria went to Ascham, Augustine to Rose Bay convent where they hoped the nuns would calm her down, and Gerda went to Frensham because she was very athletic, but it didn't make any difference. You should have seen the Christmas cake which Flodie – she went to Sceggs – sent to Honoria. It had a shrapnel bomb in the middle of it!'

'My mother is so different. She's quiet and gentle and very ladylike. Of course, she's elderly now.'

'She might have been just like the rest of them if she'd heard about that thirty million earlier.'

'No – she's, well, not precisely helpless – but I've always had to look after her, Aunt Betty.'

Betty shrugged. 'I wouldn't waste my time going to see any of them, if I were you. As soon as I turned sixteen I got married . . . well, I was almost sixteen when the baby came. And don't get me wrong! I did it to stay alive. Mind you, I've never regretted it for a minute. Bert's a wonderful husband. He travels in baby foods –'

Alaric was beginning to like Betty despite all his better judgement. She was so artless and vulnerable and yet strangely contented with her chaos of children.

'At least your sisters must like you now, Aunt Betty.

After all, you can't inherit the estate if you marry.'

'They hate my guts! They haven't talked to me since I married Bert. They reckon I threw in the sponge.'

'Gerda, Flodie, Augustine and Honoria.' As he said their names, he could not conjure up a mental picture of four juvenile murderesses.

'And a nastier, meaner bunch you never met in all your born days, Ally. Each one twisted up worse than the next by that damned will. Old Tulliford never liked his wife and he hated her even more when her unmarried sisters came to live with them and ganged up against him. That's why he wrote the will the way he did. He was intending to keep the Morell women single and at each other's throats. Well, it didn't work out like that with me. Bert loves kids as much as I do, but I told you he was in baby foods, didn't I – and I don't care if I never see my sisters. Particularly Gerda . . .' She leaned forward and her voice became a hushed whisper. 'You know what they call her, don't you? "Gerda, the Ghoul of the Golf Course." It's true! It's in all the papers! Well, let me tell you how she developed that swing of hers!'

Alaric listened, almost paralysed with shock. He kept thinking of how Medea had maliciously told the daughters of Pelias to chop up their old father and boil him in a cauldron in order to restore him to his youth. The witless girls followed the recipe to the letter and ended up with a smelly stew which even the dogs refused to sniff.

'Gerda's been playing professional golf all over the world, but she's down on the South Coast now and everyone is terrified of her!'

Alaric felt in despair. Jason had never been presented with obstacles like this. Brazen bulls, a few dragon's teeth – what were these by comparison with his murderous aunts? Involuntarily, a tear crept shamefacedly down to his chin. Betty saw it and heaved a gulping sigh.

'I – I must do something to help my mother, Aunt Betty. I wouldn't say she's irresponsible, but she can't cope with things. Years ago I suppose she could have got married again. But what chance did she have, with my grandfather on one side and her uncle on the other? They would never have supported me and given me an education if she'd remarried. And now she's old, and all she has is me . . .'

Betty would have liked to adopt Alaric on the spot.

'My mother's always led such a sheltered life. For a long time now I've had to be the practical member of the family.'

Betty's grey eyes darkened. 'If you want to protect your mother, then there's only one solution.'

'Exactly! I know it! I have to get them all to agree to share the inheritance.'

Betty shook her head calmly and the baby inside her kicked in agreement. 'No, Alaric. You have to *murder* them. Kill the lot of them, before they kill your mother. I'll get Bert to lend you his shotgun. It's all right, love, it's licensed.'

Alaric sat bolt upright and felt the flimsy wall behind him shake and tremble.

'You're joking, of course.' Then he paused, remembering how he had always preferred badminton to boxing. 'I'm not a very physical person.'

'Well, that's a pity! Because they are very physical – and very experienced. They spent years trying to kill each other and they all became experts. Every night when I went up to bed I wondered if I would ever come down the stairs the next morning alive – or in one piece. I always used to give the dog something from my plate before I ever touched my dinner. We had eleven dogs! That was Augustine – she learned Latin so that she could read the labels on the poison bottles. I think the only reason I survived was because I was the youngest, so really they were just using me to practise on. Mind you, they do seem to have calmed down a bit lately. They just pray for heart attacks, cancer, strokes . . . . normal things like that.'

Alaric felt that he was Aeneas once again, feeling the weight of Anchises on his back, struggling to find a resting-place for them both.

'If only it weren't for my mother!'

Betty's heart was melting rapidly and she could hardly speak.

'Oh, Ally, you're a love; you really do care for your mum, don't you?'

'I . . .' Alaric was not going to join his aunt in a puddle of maudlin sentiment. 'Yes, I am deeply attached to my mother.'

'Oh, a boy who loves his mother! Now, that's really something and it just shows that there is real goodness in this country. Do you need any money?'

'Well . . .' Alaric did not quite know how to explain that after paying for the train ticket to Killara, he had less than $11.

'I can give you whatever you want, Ally. Bert gives me a thousand every time I deliver.' She patted her belly proudly. 'And I deliver regular every eleven months. Just about due for the next thousand, I'd say. Trouble is, love, I never have time to spend any of it. But if you are so downright determined to see your aunts, then I'm going to bank-roll you.' She leaned over and gave him a sloppy kiss, which reminded Alaric of his grandfather's favourite hound when it was frothing after a long run.

'But I still reckon you should take Bert's gun with you — or he's got the sweetest little revolver you ever saw, but I reckon you should stick with the shotgun; I just re-membered the revolver isn't licensed. You've got to be legal, you know.'

Alaric was shaking his head vigorously. Betty sighed, then suddenly moaned and clutched her sides.

'Ally, you better get me down real fast or I'm going to deliver up here. That thousand dollars is coming real fast!'

*

Lance was deeply troubled. He had fended off questions at the hotel about his making a daily trip to Mockery Bend, by saying that Cavalry Barnhouse was paying him to keep an eye on Mrs Morell. Not that she was real crazy, but it was cheaper to let her live out there than keep her in one of

93

those fancy institutions with tame shrinks. At least that had kept everyone away from Mockery Bend, and Phyllis had been equally tight-lipped. But now there were six of Syd Crockford's prize dairy cows in Alice's fenced run and half the countryside out looking for them, with Crockford swearing blue murder and threatening to shoot the cattle thieves when they were caught.

'You see, Lance, since you come out here every day, and Phyllis almost as often, I can get you to take my butter and cheese in to Hope's End and sell it for me.'

Lance was beginning to learn that the code of chivalric love required more than devotion; occasionally it called for the complete abdication of reason.

'My Aunt Matilda came from Chesire, so I know how to make excellent cheese, and since I learned to milk and run a dairy when I was a child, it will be no problem managing six beautiful, well-behaved cows.'

'Mrs Morell . . . Lance barely knew how to begin. 'There is a problem.'

'Not really, Lance. I found the old dairy, and those splendid Chinese – or were they Cambodian – boys you brought out here last week cleaned and whitewashed it for me. Long ago, there must have been a large dairy herd here. The cheese pans were in the loft and –'

'Mrs Morell, the problem is that you don't *own* those cows!'

Alice had already cast Lance in the role of faithful retainer and she was becoming quite fond of him.

'Lance, you don't understand the law, that's obvious. Now, you said yourself that those cows were on my land, eating my grass. Well, that's trespass. I could have taken the whole herd, but I only took six. I consider I've been very restrained and far more forbearing than my grandfather would have been under the circumstances. I could quote the law to you if you're interested but . . .' she paused, not wishing to embarrass Lance with technical matters of property and tenancy law that were beyond his understanding.

94

In his mind's eye Lance could still see Crockford hammering the bar counter in the Shearers' Arms and telling the crowd what he planned to do with the thieves when he caught them – it began with throttling and ended with disembowelling. All he said to Alice now was, 'Syd Crockford has spent years building up that herd. You could say it's been a hobby with him.'

'Oh, I saw their breeding when they first came down to eat my grass, Lance.'

All over Hope's End there were placards about the missing cows. There had even been a small paragraph in the country section of the *Sydney Morning Herald*. The local sergeant of police had appeared on TV and warnings and rewards were broadcast hourly over the radio . . . while here they were, lined up along the fence, placidly chewing their cud and almost smiling at Alice.

Lance remembered how long it had taken him to get a footing in this area, and he was not still classed anywhere near the top families. It was all right for Crockford to drink in his pub and sound off to the locals, but he hadn't forgotten how Crockford had turned him down flat when he tried for membership of the Hope's End Racing Club, the select little group which ran the picnic races. Tulliford had said on that occasion that he was of questionable character; as for the Burton brothers – Lance spat and rubbed the spittle into the dirt with his boot-heel. Still, they all passed the time of day with him, and after he had bought some land he had been invited to a few functions. Now he could be run out on a rope – he knew the penalties for cattle theft. Then he watched Alice stroke the nose of each cow in turn, while a huge blue cattle dog hobbled after her. There was something familiar about the dog too; he knew he'd seen it before, but could not quite place it. When he tried to call it over with a whistle, the dog just bared his teeth at him, looked up at Alice and wagged his tail.

Now Alice was smiling at him, and Lance would have got into his truck and brought her back the rest of Crockford's herd if she had asked him.

'So I can count on you to take my butter and cheese into town, Lance?'

Lance would have given his life for her.

Chapter Five

Alaric wrote a long letter to his mother with a great many parentheses and subordinate clauses, explaining that he was on his way to Wollongong in order to negotiate a settlement with Aunt Gerda. He thought of concluding with the line from Ovid: *'Ardua molimur: sed nulla, nisi ardua, virtus,'* but did not think she would be able to translate the Latin, even though she must appreciate its aptness.

Just before the ambulance arrived to rush Betty to the hospital, she thrust a cheque for $500 into his hand and told him that if the baby was a boy she would name it after him. Alaric thought of the chocolate child under the kitchen table and shuddered; nevertheless, he was grateful for the money and decided that after the estate was divided he would insist that Betty receive a share.

The letter was posted and he was walking back towards the train station, considering how far Sappho and Alcaeus could be said to share the same traditional rhetorical forms, when a truck pulled up alongside him and the driver inquired his destination and offered him a lift. The red-haired, tattooed fellow in a blue singlet gave Alaric a gap-toothed smile and told him he should buy a lottery ticket. When Alaric murmured some uncomprehending response the driver told him that by pure luck he was taking the Wollongong road. Alaric was overwhelmed with gratitude. He had no idea what expenses awaited him at the country club where his Aunt Gerda was star contender in the South Coast Women's Golf Championship.

Late that afternoon he was barely conscious of the pulsating diesel engine and thinking of Jason rowing between the Symplegades with grinding rocks crushing down upon his ship. He was about to order the rowers to double time when he felt a hand on his crotch. Glancing sideways, he saw that the truck driver was beginning to breathe heavily, the eagle on his chest almost bursting into flight. It was all very irritating because Alaric had been enjoying his reverie.

The truck driver winked and began to dribble. 'How's about we stop off along here an' you and me get together?'

Poor chap, Alaric thought – and to try it on with someone who had survived being a sex object at Eton and Oxford! Why, he had fought successful rearguard actions against experts, and now this uncouth, smelly, panting gorilla wanted to climb into his trousers. However, to refuse without giving offence was always the hallmark of a gentleman, and Alaric decided to deliver the traditional speech that a responsible sixth-former gave a new boy caught in the act, one serving as a deterrent against masturbation, sodomy and other unspeakable acts known only to de Sade and the junior forms.

'I've been thinking the same thing myself,' Alaric said. 'I kept wondering why you hadn't asked.'

The hand tightened on his crotch and Alaric knew he would not be able to fight his way out of this one. He sighed heavily. 'Oh dear, I suppose I should tell you why I'm going to Wollongong.'

'I bet you've got a real beaut big steelworker waiting fer yer there?'

'Only my aunt.'

'Yer *aunt*?'

'Yes, she'll let me stay with her. You see, I had to leave Sydney in a hurry.'

'Yeah?'

The truck was slowing down and Alaric knew he must make his point quickly. 'I was having an affair with this marvellous boxer and then he found out . . .'

'Found out what?'

The truck had stopped by a sandy stretch of road.

'That I had AIDS. He said he was going to kill me. I tried to tell him it wasn't true, but the cancers are all over my . . . my you-know-what. I can feel them now, burning and itching.'

He did not have to continue, for both the driver's hands were now firmly on the wheel and all he could hear was a muttered invocation to a number of saints with whom Alaric was unacquainted. He noted with considerable satisfaction that this fellow was more easily convinced than any number of beady-eyed, sophisticated little first-formers he had had to discipline in his time. It was time for *l'envoi*.

'The frightful thing about it is that I have this terrible urge for sex. I – I just can't control myself!'

Alaric reached over and grabbed the gorilla's balls and the truck driver shrieked and almost fell out the window. Tremulously he shifted over to the very edge of the seat, saying, 'That's a real funny noise coming from the generator. You hear it?'

'I may have, now you mention it,' and Alaric fluttered his lashes appealingly.

'I better pull in at the next garage and get it all checked out. You'll be able to hitch a ride here without any trouble, mate.'

When Alaric last saw him, he was spraying the front seat of the truck with an aerosol disinfectant. Several unexciting hours later, Alaric was reading the sporting pages of the *Wollongong Gazette* in a small motel near the South Coast Country Club.

Everything Betty had told him about Gerda seemed confirmed by what he read that night and all that he saw next morning at the fourth hole. The three main rules of golf are first, that you do not move when a player is making a stroke; second, that you do not talk when a player is making a stroke; and third, that you do not stand directly behind the player or behind the hole when the player is making a stroke. Gerda Morell always managed to break those three rules within the first half-hour of play.

Alaric first saw her backside as she peered along the putting green, her buttocks erupting from the grass like a great puce toadstool. On her knees with her nose to the grass, Gerda Morell could have been taken for a prehistoric lizard getting ready to spring. Slowly she rose and groped for a ball in a subterranean pocket of her pants, and as she reached down into that dark and secret place she held the club between her teeth. She was playing against Mildred Coffinspray, the Victoria champion, a tall, rangy woman with a mottled complexion that was gradually beginning to darken as Gerda paced slowly round the green with the stick clamped between her jaws. A handful of spectators were watching Gerda with the same attention given a professional wrestler about to ricochet from the ropes. Alaric had placed himself strategically behind a portly Singapore tourist clad in a pineapple-patterned sarong. It was obvious to everyone that Mildred was reaching breaking point, nervous tics made her look as though she were winking at a dozen different men simultaneously, while her head jerked back as if attached to a broken spring. She took a deep breath, walked to her ball and was just about to swing when Gerda sneezed like a train disappearing down a tunnel, then noisily wiped her nose with the back of her shirt-sleeve.

Mildred's lips pursed, she looked up for a moment with eyes closed and again addressed the ball. This time Gerda waited until Mildred was in the middle of her swing, then she farted. Mildred dropped her club and burst into tears. The crowd hissed. Gerda stalked across the green and put her grizzled face next to Mildred's:

'Mildred, if you're trying to psych me out, you better hire a professional or piss off. I've played balls next to rattlesnakes before this and you're not going to put me off my game now!'

As Mildred cowered back, confused by this unexpected assault and the enormity of the accusation, Gerda deftly

99

kicked her own ball back into the rough with her heel and, as she moved forward as though to threaten Mildred with her five iron, a ball slipped down the back of her left pant leg and rolled into a convenient spot close to the hole.

Mildred was imploring the crowd to help her, screaming for a referee, anyone to come and save her from the 'Ghoul'. Only Alaric, peering out from behind the pineapples, had seen that ball dropped down by the hole. Gerda was now brandishing her iron and threatening to chase an hysterical Mildred off the green.

'I never said a word!' Mildred wailed. 'No one ever dares say anything to you, Gerda! I'll never play against you without an umpire!'

'You swore at me,' Gerda shouted.

'I never opened my mouth!'

'I thought it was a flushing john! Didn't you think it was a flushing john?' She turned to the crowd and glimpsed Alaric's white and horrified face.

'Look what you're doing to the kids, Mildred! You're a terrific role model for young players, aren't you?'

Mildred collapsed, sobbing, and Gerda grinned wolfishly at her.

'Now,' she said, 'I'd like to try sinking this ball in silence.'

Gerda was declared the winner of the tournament amidst booing that almost drowned out the announcer's voice. Alaric pulled back his shoulders and remembered that Perseus had managed to kill the Medusa by not looking at her. He must remember to keep his eyes on the ground when discussing the will with Gerda.

*

Even Phyllis was beginning to feel uneasy as she looked at the cows and admired Alice's cheese-making. She agreed with Lance that there was something very familiar about the dog, but she couldn't recall where she had seen it either. Fresh posters about the missing cows had been pasted up all over Hope's End, offering a $500 reward for information about their whereabouts, and Crockford had appeared on

100

television, his red face exploding on the screen like an angry boil. She sighed and hung the last of the Harrods outfits in a tall dark wardrobe they had lined with white paper. If only it were not for those blasted cows, everything would be just perfect, Phyllis thought. But cattle theft was a serious matter and if Crockford thought Lance was implicated – which he was – he could lose the pub or be blackballed in the area. And how could she explain *that* to her daughter in Canberra?

Alice brought in Alaric's letter and some of Phyllis's worries seemed to vanish. 'He's met his Aunt Gerda, Phyllis! Oh, and he's going to talk to her about the will tomorrow. Isn't that marvellous?'

Phyllis looked from the cows outside to the long rack of designer dresses and shook her head. For the first time in her life she had to admit she was baffled.

'Nothing figures, Alice,' she said limply.

'Oh, but everything's working out splendidly, Phyllis. Come out to the kitchen. We can have some tea and Lion is waiting for his biscuit.'

Phyllis saw the cows again from the kitchen window and felt panic replacing nervousness. She had tried to explain what cattle theft meant to Alice before, but Alice had only laughed and told her she did not understand the law. Still, she felt she should try once more.

'Alice, this is the bush. People here don't live the same way they do back in England. Now take Crockford, he is the most vindictive little shit that ever drew breath.'

'Well, Phyllis, we can't all be perfect. And I do appreciate this is not Barnsley. By now I would have had a stream of visitors in to call. All the neighbours and –'

'That's it, Alice. Your direct neighbours are Jos Tulliford, the Burton boys and Syd Crockford. Now tell me who you'd like to see first – Crockford or Tulliford?'

'Not Mr Tulliford.' Alice stiffened and her hand tightened on the tea-pot. The very name of Tulliford was anathema to her.

'Then think about Syd Crockford, Alice, who is still out

looking for his cows.'

'I should be delighted to meet Mr Crockford and explain the law of trespass to him, Phyllis.'

Lion sat up, Alice balanced a biscuit on his nose and he tossed it in the air and swallowed it.

'Trespass here doesn't mean what it seems to mean to you, Alice. Now look, the only reason Crockford hasn't been out here is because he now thinks that Tulliford may have his cows, and he doesn't want to get on the wrong side of Tulliford.'

'Good heavens, why not? If he's a Tulliford, I find it difficult to believe he has a right side.'

'Well, Tulliford is not only richer than everyone else round here, he also happens to be a bachelor, and if you had four unmarried daughters like Crockford then you'd go easy with your accusations.'

Alice seemed only partly interested in what Phyllis was saying and far more concerned with patting Lion.

'Do tell Mr Crockford to call and discuss the matter of the cows with me if he's still concerned, Phyllis. I shall be more than happy to enlighten him on these legal matters.'

She sighed as she remembered how often she had heard grandfather explain to the local constable why he had been forced to appropriate a neighbour's livestock when it had strayed on to his property.

Phyllis gave up and drank her tea silently. She could understand how Lance had fallen for Alice. It wasn't just her looks – and now that she had started dipping into the Harrods wardrobe, she was a stunner – it was a quality of sympathetic remoteness about her which seemed to set everyone dreaming down strange paths. Phyllis shook her head; it was one thing knowing what had happened to Lance, but surely it wasn't affecting her too? She prided herself on her sharp wits, but after talking to Alice Morell everything became misty and yet oddly comforting. Odd lines kept drifting into her head . . . she had caught herself humming something under the shower the other morning which went, 'Can you hear the horns of elfland calling?'. . .

102

She really must take a hold on herself and face a few facts. For example, what would her local chapter of the Children of Mary say if it became known she had been hobnobbing with a cattle thief? Then she thought of Crockford on TV the other night, bulging with rage, and she wanted to giggle. Fancy popping one over Syd Crockford. Fancy . . . but when other facts came to mind it no longer seemed quite so funny.

'If I could have some flowers. If I could only grow roses again like the lovely old teas at Morell Manor, I really think I could be very happy here,' Alice was saying. 'You have no idea what plans Lion and I make for the future when we sit here at night. Alaric will settle the will and then we shall have enough money to rebuild this house and have a real farm.'

'Alice,' Phyllis touched Alice's hand gently, as though trying to pull her back to reality, 'there are four cousins and they're all as fit as fleas. You can never make anything of this place until they're dead.'

'My dear, you don't know how persuasive Alaric can be, and what a head for business that boy has. You'll see, he'll get Gerda to sign anything he wants.'

*

At that moment, Alaric was crouched in some bushes by the sandpit. Gerda trampled in, saw her ball, cursed, then looked round stealthily and promptly buried it like an alligator concealing its eggs. After some furtive scuffling, she threw another ball from that cavernous pocket of hers out on to the fairway, shouting, 'Found the little bugger! Thought it was in the sand, but it landed on the straight!'

On the putting green, Gerda first trod on her opponent's foot, then took after her caddy when she called for a baffy and he handed her a five iron. She was about to break the club over the shrieking caddy's head when a brawny man in the crowd shouted, 'Gerda the Ghoul! Cut it out!'

The crowd murmured and then voices were raised everywhere asking 'who'd brung her', and advising her to pull her head in. Holding the caddy by the collar and almost choking him, Gerda walked across the green to the burly heckler. The unfortunate caddy managed to break free just as Gerda confronted the man of brawn. There was silence and she looked him up and down, then poked him with her club.

'How would you like me to shove this iron up your arse, mate?'

The man vanished and Gerda looked round for the caddy who was racing back to the club-house yelling for help. It was then Alaric showed the heroic spirit of Jason confronting the Hydra, or Perseus challenging the Medusa which turned men to stone. As Gerda screamed for the 'cretinous little turd' to come back and pick up her bag, Alaric stepped forward and, fixing his eyes firmly on her nail-studded purple leather shoes, politely offered to substitute for the missing caddy. Gerda was so dumbfounded that she agreed on the spot.

The more Alaric came to know Gerda, the more she reminded him of a large black-haired, warty toad which had just climbed laboriously from the depths of the Styx where it had been feeding on the flesh of dead men. Every day on the driving range where she was practising for the Ocean Side Open, he would try to reason sweetly with her. but in vain. Gerda seemed determined to make the boy suffer, to humiliate and torment him. Nothing about her reminded him of his mother except the gimlet eyes the colour of polished steel bolts, and he tried hard not to meet that piercing gaze which made his blood run cold. Gerda lived by a code which made the more stringent forms of social Darwinism seem capricious. She would, Alaric thought dismally, have made the Spartans look sloppy.

Another ball flew a full one hundred and sixty yards from her six iron, and Gerda gloated.

'See that? Jack Nicklaus couldn't beat that for range.'

'Aunt Gerda, if you and your sisters agreed to a settlement . . .'

Gerda held the stick between her teeth, which made it a

104

little difficult for Alaric to understand what she was saying.

'Survival of the fittest. And I'm the fittest of that bunch!'

'Aunt Gerda – reason would insist –'

'Never heard of reason, kid. All I know about is winning, coming first, being top, always the best. Second is dead in my book.'

'But your sisters could outlive you.'

'Impossible. They'll drop like flies without any help from me. Take Flodie with her crackpot antiques; she's been on happy pills for years. One day she's going to open a bottle of Tylenol and . . . another middle-aged woman dies of an overdose. Then there's Honoria, an alcoholic and a junky. As for Augustine, she has a very weak head. She took to religion and when she's not fasting, she's flogging herself. I do not think,' Gerda concluded with satisfaction, 'that there is a decent health habit amongst the lot of them.'

Alaric hesitated, suddenly feeling a thread of fear touch his mind. 'And – and my mother?'

At that moment he felt like some unwary traveller who has chanced to look into the Medusa's face and knows the coldness of stone spreading out from his heart. Gerda grinned as she reached down for another ball.

'I don't think your mother's going to last in this climate – not out there at Mockery Bend. Of course, Augustine may have sent her a special box of her chocolate creams by now. She always made a speciality of those. And I could decide to pay her a visit one of these days!'

Alaric had a vision of Gerda nailing his mother to the ground with golf clubs, while he stood by, turned to stone, unable to help her.

'Honoria and Flodie both specialized in bombs and detonating services.'

She reached up and stretched and Alaric saw the muscles rippling across her shoulders. Her eyes narrowed as she looked across the golf course.

'No, I've always had a dream. I'm going to inherit Mockery Bend and turn it into the best golf course in the world. A real test for the best players in the game. Nothing pansy, no putting greens like fairy rings. Sand traps around every green – real traps with quick sand, and a water hazard with whirlpools. This game is getting flabby, Alaric. I'd like to see Mildred and the rest of the "lady" golfers on my course.'

'I'm sure there'd be enough for a golf course if the estate were divided,' Alaric said plaintively.

'There are no second places. That was the lesson I learned when I was four years old and Honoria was running my bath – with an electric hair-dryer.

'My mother is the most reasonable of women!'

'Is she?' Again the wolfish grin displaying yellow teeth, chipped from holding too many golf clubs. 'Reasonable, eh? That's why she'll be the first to go. Now, the Ocean Side Open – that's a real challenge. Mildred's held the cup for the last three years, but you saw how I disposed of her in the prelims. Next week that cup is going to be mine.'

She paused and stared at Alaric, who felt like a bird transfixed by a cobra.

'Provided you do exactly as you're told, Alaric. Remember, I'm your aunt – sort of – so this is family and you have a sense of loyalty to me, haven't you?'

Alaric could not answer, he could only stare mutely at her brogues.

'And if you don't do exactly as you're told, your darling little mummsy won't recognize you when I've wrapped this round your skull.' And she playfully tapped his head with a pitching wedge.

*

The cows had been milked, the cheese pans checked for temperature and Alice had just stepped out of her bath-tub and rubbed herself down with a mignonette cologne. Lion sat watching her, his large yellow eyes reflecting total admiration. As she reached for a towel, he suddenly put his head in the air and bolted through the door. While she dressed, Alice thought how well his leg had healed; there was only the slightest limp when he ran. Possibly he had gone out to check the cows for her. There were times when she felt so tired, but at least she wasn't carrying trays to Bessy or listening to her everlasting complaints about not being paid. She rather liked being alone, remembering Aunt Penelope and the wonderful stories she had told before she drifted into a land from which she sent only brief messages.

A number of those messages were in Alice's mind now as she opened her wardrobe, wondering when she would ever be able to wear the silk and pastel chiffons or the long shaded mink in its cotton wrapper. Once, swinging gently under the apricot tree, Aunt Penelope had chuckled softly – more like a crooning sigh than laughter – then had looked straight at Alice and said, 'A lady is always dressed at first.'

When Alice repeated this to Aunt Matilda, she was given a lecture on the importance of a lady always finishing her chores by ten in the morning and being dressed and ready to receive callers by ten-fifteen. Lupin Tanner's reaction had been quite different when she told her; the comb span in parabolic loops and baroque tyres as responsive currents flew through the salon. Sometimes, in church on Sunday morning, Alice would read the 'Song of Solomon' and think that the commentaries at the bottom of each song about Christ's devotion to the Church and Christ revealing his love for the faithful were rather like Aunt Matilda's interpretation of Aunt Penelope's messages. But now it was almost eleven o'clock and she was still not dressed, so she carefully selected a blue linen skirt and lace blouse, arranged her hair and walked out into the sun on the veranda.

Lance never arrived with the same helpers, which puzzled Alice – one week he brought out three Vietnamese, the next time four Indonesians, none of them able to speak English. But they worked well and already Mockery Bend was beginning to look alive, as though it had thrown off generations of decay and started to grow, just as a fallen tree will sometimes put out branches.

Alaric's last letter had been full of hope and with such

107

interesting news about the golf tournament and Heindorf's theory that women may at one time have participated in the Olympic Games. She had particularly appreciated his description of the winedark sea north of Wollongong, and that all the walking around the greens had reminded him of Plato's insistence on exercise as being part of the training of the moral man.

If only she could plant some flowers by the veranda and set out a rose garden! Down by the creek she had already discovered an old orchard with one massive, gnarled apple tree. Pruned, it could well yield fruit next summer. She was about to turn and go back into the house when she heard a crowing and cackling, and a rooster and four hens appeared at the end of the driveway, neatly shepherded along by Lion who was dodging from side to side, his blue-slate fur glittering in the sunlight like polished metal. The rooster turned and tried to make a stand, wings flapping, a raking spur close to Lion's nose, but the dog simply went flat to the ground in front of the bird, edging closer; his gold eyes were fixed on the rooster, which gave one defiant shrill of challenge and then scuttled away from that terrible yellow gaze.

Alice ran down to help him, clapping and guiding the little flock towards the cow-yard. She knew the cows would not trample the birds and they would be safe there until she could make them a proper run. She closed the gate on them and turned to congratulate Lion.

'Oh, you clever chap! Where on earth did you find them? Ah yes, of course, you must have heard them when I was getting dressed and realized they were trespassing. What a splendid, intelligent fellow!'

The dog preened and smiled, stiffened, listened again and then dashed off down the track towards the stream.

'Such a wonderful dog!' Alice had not been able to recognize the breed, but she felt sure he must have a long and distinguished pedigree. And Aunt Penelope was quite wrong: he had been no trouble whatsoever to train.

Indeed, the dog seemed to know instinctively what was needed on a farm.

She walked over to the cow-yard, where heads had barely been raised to greet the newcomers. She could recognize these chickens immediately as Rhode Island Reds – such good egg layers, and these were magnificent birds. The rooster was already claiming his territory, his crest no longer standing upright like a battle flag. Alice began calculating rapidly; with eggs and her cows, possibly a small vegetable garden (she really must not hanker after flowers) why, she would be self-supporting by the time Alaric had settled the estate.

Half an hour later Lion arrived with another hen in his mouth, carried so gently that not a feather was bruised, and she knew by the rolling flourish of his bushy tail that he expected a reward. The biscuit had been balanced on his broad nose and swallowed in a single gulp when Jos Tulliford reined in to a sudden and startled stop.

Jos detested Mockery Bend and everything it represented in his life. As a small child, his father – a dour, grizzled man – would ride out here with him and point to the house and the land around it as a symbol of life's injustice and the particular iniquity visited upon the Tullifords by a perverse and sadistic will. Mockery Bend was the reason why he had not gone to university, Mockery Bend had kept him from every pleasure and opportunity as a boy. His father had hankered after the estate and he too felt that it was like a giant mouldering albatross hung round his neck.

Naturally, he had heard the stories in the town about the harelipped lunatic at Mockery Bend, the arrival of another 'Mad Morell' in the neighbourhood. One of the Burton brothers had even been rash enough to inquire if he had paid a call on his cousin yet, receiving in reply a bleak stare which produced an awkward silence and an immediate change of subject. Jos Tulliford was a justifiably bitter and chagrined man. He was a millionaire, but his millions were as nothing compared with what *should* have been his if only

109

his grandfather had made a rational will. And every time he met Cavalry Barnhouse in Sydney, he had the grim pleasure of hearing how the Tulliford estate had increased by another five or six million thanks to Barnhouse's capable management.

Jos was caught off guard by the radiant fair woman, but promptly tagged her as a companion or keeper of the resident lunatic. But the dog . . . the dog licking its chops and staring at him! That was his champion cattle dog, bred from the best Queensland blood-lines, and here it was, not even recognizing him and obviously waiting for another biscuit to be put on its nose. So many emotions of surprise, disgust and bewilderment crowded upon him that he could barely speak. All he could manage was a muffled, 'That's *my* dog!'

Alice looked up at him in surprise – a tall, brown-faced man under a wide-brimmed hat. His horse was a light sorrel that showed lack of correct grooming, but it had a good head and she liked its expression. Having accepted the horse, she examined the man more critically. He was about forty or thereabouts and he seemed very disturbed. She smiled and put out her hand,

'Good morning, I'm Alice Morell. I didn't quite catch your name? What were you saying?'

Jos ignored her outstretched hand and pointed to Lion who had slunk behind Alice and was now sitting at her heels, snarling silently at him.

'That's my dog!'

'Indeed? How interesting!'

Alice had inherited a strong sense of property and she was beginning to regard this man as a trespasser – one not to be confiscated but driven off by the local constable, if there were such a visible embodiment of the law in the neighbourhood.

Tulliford did not permit any animal to snarl at him and he reached for the rifle slung at the side of his saddle. Alice was outraged. This was . . . it was shooting out of season . . . shooting on her property, and she could hear

110

grandfather citing a dozen different statutes which would have given a man six years for even attempting what this man obviously had in mind.

'Put down that firearm! Don't you dare try to use it here!'

There was such authority in her voice that Tulliford faltered, and that moment's hesitation was to change his whole life.

'The dog's gone wild. He's mad – he should be shot.'

'The dog is no madder than you, sir. Stay, Lion!' She motioned to the dog, who looked as though he wanted to take Tulliford by the throat. Even the horse began to shift uneasily and he decided to dismount. The name . . . she had mentioned the name of Morell.

'I'm Jos Tulliford.'

'I might have known.'

'Did you say –'

'You ignored my introduction, Mr Tulliford. Alice Morell.' And this time she did not offer her hand.

'I . . . I heard you'd arrived here.'

What the hell had people been saying about harelips and crooked hips? This woman was . . . but he would not continue that thought and concentrated instead on his dog and her madness. Lunatics, he knew, came in all shapes and sizes; it was quite possible for a 'Mad Morell' to look like a vision of blue and white sky with sunshine for hair and . . . she was unquestionably mad. And since she was so obviously unbalanced, he decided he must reason with her before he shot the dog.

'Mrs Morell – that is my dog. That's Blue, but judging from his behaviour and the saliva he's probably got distemper.'

Alice laughed scornfully, mentally approving the tone of her laugh; it was just the note Aunt Matilda contrived when confronted with an irate tradesman demanding payment.

'Mr Tulliford, that dog is in excellent health and probably saner than you are.'

'He's gone wild. I raised Blue from a pup and if he's taking on to me now as if I was a stranger, then he's as mad

111

–' '. . . as you,' he wanted to add, but remembered that lunatics have to be humoured.

'That dog is not Blue, Mr Tulliford. His name is Lion and that is what he answers to. You're confused about your dogs.'

At this point Lion crouched down, snarled and seemed ready to spring. Tulliford lost his temper and raised his rifle again.

'Mr Tulliford! I've warned you already! If you shout at my dog once more, I shall be forced to remove you from my property.'

He looked down at her in amazement. 'You – are going to force me to do *what*?'

'Leave this property. Are you deaf as well as obstinate?'

'Would you mind telling me how?'

Alice could not help pitying the man for his stupidity. Aunt Matilda was fond of quoting Amelia's description of Othello, 'Ignorant as dirt,' when referring to people who claimed she owed them money. It was appropriate, but Alice decided to take a gentler tack with this towering fool.

'I shall simply request you to leave as a gentleman. And if you don't, Mr Tulliford, then I shall have no recourse but to regard you as a lout and a bully.'

Tulliford was more confused than he had been since the day he tried to read the Tulliford will. He sensed that he was losing ground, that those clear grey eyes had measured his defeat, but the Tullifords were a stubborn breed.

'Now listen, Mrs Morell, that is my dog and by rights I should have blown him off the landscape by now.'

'Mr Tulliford, I found that dog with a broken leg, lying down by the stream where he'd crawled to find water and die. He must have dragged the trap with him. Certainly he had tried to chew his leg free of it. He was starving and dirty; it was quite clear that he'd never been fed properly, never been washed.'

'*Wash*! That's a working dog!'

Alice's nose wrinkled very slightly. 'Even a working man needs to wash occasionally.'

112

Tulliford stepped back a pace and began to explain, 'I lost Blue a month ago.'

The dog obviously heard something amongst the trees, because he vanished in that direction. The horse watched him, but Alice and Tulliford were too intent on each other. She looked up at him sternly.

'Did you look for him?'

'Of course I did.'

Alice's voice was dry with disbelief. 'Most assiduously, I'm sure. And no doubt if you'd found him with a broken leg from a trap you had probably set yourself, you would have shot him – to put him out of his misery?'

Tulliford felt he could deny at least part of the accusation.

'I have never set a dingo trap on my land.'

'Or mine?'

Tulliford knew why he had remained a bachelor since his one reckless venture into marriage at the age of twenty.

'All right, if you're so set on giving that crazy mongrel a home, you're welcome to him!'

Alice smiled. 'You're too kind, Mr Tulliford.'

'But he'll turn on you. An animal that doesn't respect his master deserves to be shot.'

'Respect has to be earned,' she said firmly, adding, 'You don't have much feeling for animals, do you?'

He was preparing an answer, but his horse kept ambling towards Alice and trying to nuzzle her outstretched hand. Twice he had had to shove it back.

She sighed. 'I can hardly believe we're related – almost cousins.'

He was about to swing up in to the saddle when suddenly he saw the cows and the chickens, and almost fell from the stirrups.

'My God, those are Crockford's cows! The little twit accused me of stealing them!'

Alice replied with considerable dignity and every assumption of authority: 'I'm holding them here by right of trespass. If needs be I shall invoke livery of seisin, but I fancy that simple trespass is sufficient.'

Tulliford staggered like a man dazed after a long fist fight and leaned over the fence to the cow-yard. He had to hold on to the railing as he stared in complete disbelief.

'Those are *my* chickens!'

Alice had joined him, saying pleasantly, 'Rhode Island Reds, aren't they? They also trespassed.'

Tulliford stood back and pointed at her with a trembling finger. 'You – you called me a lout! You . . . you are nothing but . . . but a –'

'Yes, Mr Tulliford?' Alice inquired sweetly.

'A thief, a lowdown, common thief!'

He flung himself on his horse and rode at full gallop towards the track. At that moment Lion came up from the creek, carrying another squawking chicken in his jaws.

Tulliford rode blindly back to his property and even three straight whiskeys failed to clear his head or settle his nerves. This Morell was his cousin, and she was a cattle thief, and what in the name of hell should he do about it? Then he remembered that Lance Weston had been making daily calls on a harelipped, hunchbacked lunatic, and he saw that golden hair in the sunlight again and the line of her breasts under a lace blouse. He smashed the glass and decided to deal with Weston first. Mrs Morell was his cousin after all.

*

The ocean stretched out to the horizon, a stiff breeze whipping the flags of the tournament. Alaric was bowed low with misery and the heaviest bag of clubs ever carried by a single caddy. He felt like Odysseus in the cave with Cyclops, or Theseus making his way down a labyrinth of bones to meet the Minotaur. Aunt Gerda was two strokes ahead of Mildred Coffinspray and exultant. Her last massive drive had sent her ball over the rise and towards the cliffs. She began a long loping run, growling at Alaric over her shoulder.

'Quick, you fool! We've got to get ahead of those turds!'

114

If the gods had any pity on suffering man they would speak to him now, Alaric thought. His back felt as though it would break, and a terrible threat sat in his head like a squat, dank toad.

That morning at breakfast, Gerda had been unusually jovial as she described the humiliations and sufferings in store for Mildred. Then she had paused, prodded him with a fork and said that she never indulged in sex during a tournament, but that night . . . and she had prodded him again with the fork. When Alaric looked up now and saw those massive, turnip-shaped buttocks striding ahead, the bulging legs covered with a curling mat of black hair, he wanted to drop the bag and run. But there was the estate, and his mother – that helpless burden. His grief was unbearable.

Gerda was muttering and cursing the wind that might have blown her ball off course. Alaric tried to remember a special prayer that Odysseus had made to Aeolus, father of the winds, and the gift he had been granted in a leather bag. But he was dizzy with fatigue, barely able to keep pace with Gerda. She stopped abruptly and he almost collided with her.

'That bloody wind! Look at the ball!'

The wind had indeed taken Gerda's ball and it was caught in a tangle of scrubby brush hanging over a precipice of cliff.

Gerda nudged him, and hissed, 'Grab it, you fool!'

Alaric's fatigue vanished with the horror of that suggestion.

'Grab it, Aunt Gerda? That's against the rules! This is a tournament. You'd be disqualified and disgraced!'

Gerda was almost berserk with rage.

'Get it, you ass-holed little boy scout!' She glared around and saw a straggle of spectators coming over the rise.

Alaric dropped the bag and retreated, saying defiantly, 'I won't cheat, Aunt Gerda!'

Gerda began a wild, stamping dance of fury, screaming, 'You rotten little pimping parasite! And to think I was going to take you to bed with me tonight and give you the best fuck of your life. Why, I'd like to screw your cock off, stuff it in your ear and spit on it! Now! Get that ball!'

'No!' Alaric shouted over the rising wind.

Gerda snatched the bag and pulled out a number one iron. She waggled and swung at the ball, but the force of the waggle and the wind were too great and she toppled, fell forward and floated down towards the Pacific Ocean like a gigantic multi-coloured bird. The wind rose up and drowned her last shrieking cry as Alaric fell on his knees by the golf bag and thanked the responsible god.

Chapter Six

Tulliford called first at the pub and asked for Weston, but the barmaid told him he was over at Belton. When he drove in to Belton he was told that he had just missed Lance by a matter of minutes and should try back at the pub. The garage mechanic phoned Phyllis, who put on a mauve and green satin housegown which seemed to have an instantaneous effect on her husband these days, and prepared to receive Tulliford. He had never been upstairs to the flat and Phyllis was determined to make the most of the occasion, as she hitched up her bra straps an inch on either side and spat on her holy medals so that they gleamed against her freckled skin. Over the years Tulliford had treated her like a lump of landscape and never seemed quite sure whether she was Phyllis, Flora or Flossie. She never enjoyed being snubbed by the local gentry, but this afternoon she felt that a number of accounts were going to be settled in her favour.

After a few stiff courtesies Tulliford asked to see Lance, and Phyllis told him that he was out of town arranging to bring in some legal Asian farmworkers.

116

That, thought Tulliford, was a cool way to describe Lance's sideline of smuggling Asians down from Queensland. Phyllis decided to get to the point and keep it there.

'Jos, I don't imagine you're here to inquire about Lance's health, or mine for that matter. I'm sure you want to talk about Alice?'

Tulliford jumped faster than a frightened rabbit and Phyllis rejoiced that God might not have given her looks, but he had not exactly left her behind the door when brains were handed out. She breathed deeply and the Child of Mary chinked pleasantly against Our Lady of Lourdes.

'You know, Jos, unlike you I was brought up a good Catholic and always taught that family came next to Godliness.' She thought of her old father in a Strathfield nursing home, boring everyone to sobs with the story of how he could have been heavyweight champion, and sniffed. She visited him regularly even if he didn't recognize her, and she made sure he went to confession and attended mass every single week. As for her children . . . two sons were priests and a daughter was married to a high-up in the Department of the Interior. Again she breathed deeply and Our Lady of Fatima tinkled against St Francis. She felt a sense of righteousness coursing through every vein and continued, 'Now, I'm not accusing you of anything, but I would say – speaking frankly – that it was un-Christian to ignore a cousin who had the misfortune to be poor and helpless.'

He tried to answer, but Phyllis had spent some time rehearsing her act and was determined to play it through to the final ovation from Lance, who was in the bedroom with his ear pressed to the door.

'That poor soul arrived here without a friend and if it had not been for Lance who took pity on her – and who has never forgotten that he was raised by the Marist Brothers – she would have starved out there. God knows that son of hers has tried, but he's down the coast now so everything's been left to Lance and me. And together we have tried to

117

make that dump a home for her.'

Phyllis thought of the days she had spent scrubbing with Alice and almost wept. 'On our knees, scraping off years of accumulated dirt, and she never flinching or complaining of broken nails like every barmaid you ask to rinse out a glass. And you, Jos Tulliford, what were you doing all this time? No doubt hoping she'd starve and die out there and the cows would save you the price of a burial. I must say,' and all the holy medals chimed together, 'it's not Christian. But then, you were never of the faith, were you?'

Tulliford had attempted to answer twice, but Phyllis swept on like a mighty flood. Still, he did have a trump card.

'Phyllis, could you tell me why Lance has been out there every day, as I'm told? Now, you appreciate that he has a certain kind of reputation with women and –'

Phyllis tried to look seven feet tall, but didn't quite make it.

'There is nothing I need to know about my husband, Jos. If you're asking me whether he's making it with Alice Morell, then I suggest you ask her.' Phyllis pounced.

Tulliford thought of those grey eyes and faltered . . .

'Exactly! Lance does have a reputation with women, I would never deny it, but simply because he's an expert with women means that he can recognize a true lady when he sees one. Maybe you were never lucky enough to meet up with many ladies, Jos. All I can say is that I am proud to call Alice Morell my dear, good friend.'

Lance rolled over behind the bedroom door and almost choked with silent laughter. For years he had prayed for a moment like this – years of being patronized by Tulliford, Mr Holier-than-Thou, the man the whole Country Party was clamouring to elect as a senator – and now he was getting the kind of come-uppance you had nightmares about.

Tulliford shifted ground uneasily, unable to imagine Lance and Alice in the same bed. 'There's still the question of Crockford's cows, Phyllis. And my chickens.' To

118

mention the dog seemed excessive at this moment.

Phyllis grinned. 'I didn't know you were standing up for Crockford these days, Jos. Still, if you're so keen on the little snot, why don't you just drive off and tell him where to look? Speaking for myself, I'd be inclined to let a smart businessman like Syd Crockford find his own cows.'

Tulliford thought of the last argument he had with Crockford over leasing land at Mockery Bend and remained silent.

'As for your chickens – I wouldn't grudge any cousin of mine a few miserable chickens that might provide her with an egg for dinner. She has precious little else to live on – apart from what we take out to her from a sense of charity.'

The word 'charity' stung Tulliford, and with a few muttered messages for Lance he turned and made for the door. To feel that he was under an obligation to that randy little ferret made him writhe. Abruptly he turned and said that if Lance wanted to enter a horse in the Hope's End Invitation Mile, he was free to do so. Then he left.

Lance burst out of the bedroom, grabbed Phyllis and threw her on to the settee. They were still gasping when Lance began to laugh again.

To all outward appearances the Hope's End Racing Club was the most democratic of institutions, but it had not become one of the major racing clubs by espousing an equine egalitarianism. After all, it was held on Crockford's property under the auspices of the club, which was restricted to the local squatters and their friends. The main race was by invitation and if many hoped to be called, few were chosen to run that celebrated mile. Phyllis had never even been asked up to the house or to the dance in the Crockford's wool-shed. And, as she told Lance, if she couldn't be treated the same as those stuck-up bitches from Toorak who drove up for the weekend, she could always find plenty to do in the pub.

Lance pulled on his pants, pinched Phyllis deliriously and guffawed, 'Love, we have made it in Hope's End! If Tulliford wants me to enter a horse in the Invitation Mile, I have to be a member. My God, it's taken twenty-eight years but we are *in* at last!' He paused and was silent; quietly, and almost in a tone of reverence, he whispered, 'That is a most remarkable lady at Mockery Bend.'

Tulliford drove back to his property at a killing speed and wondered what on earth he had accomplished. He had always despised that little runt Lance Weston, yet now he had invited him to be a member of the Hope's End Racing Club. Admittedly he was stung when Phyllis accused him of being uncharitable, but he had taken his fair share of abuse in life. Thinking what the reaction of his fellow members would be when he nominated Lance Weston, he was almost sick over the wheel. He could only hope that Lance would refuse since he had no suitable horse, but doubted it. So, for reasons that he did not really understand, he was sponsoring Lance for the Club, while Crockford's cows were still at Mockery Bend together with his chickens and his dog; he wondered how much else he had left out there.

Alice wept when Phyllis brought her the papers, open at the sports page. There was a photo of Alaric and a long account of how he had almost flung himself over the cliff in an attempt to rescue his aunt. Mildred Coffinspray had made a short statement to the effect that golf would be a different game without Gerda Morell, but most of the reporters had concentrated on Alaric and his heroism. When asked his future plans, he had simply said that he was heading for Sydney to visit his Aunt Flodie.

Phyllis was impressed. 'One down, three to go,' she said. Frankly, she had never thought that Alaric would get out of the Marie Rose alive, but here he had managed to bump off one aunt and almost get a medal in the process. That, Phyllis thought, was smart, real smart.

'He was always such a brave, good boy,' Alice said tearfully.

Phyllis decided she should bring up the subject of Jos and learned that the cousins had not parted as friends. It was time to talk openly about her husband, before Tulliford came back with any awkward revelations. But she was not quite sure how to start. Alice must know that Lance was crazy about her, yet she always had this air of dreaming innocence that made you wonder how she ever came to have a kid.

It came out awkwardly enough: 'I had real problems with Lance before you came here, Alice.'

Puzzled, Alice looked up from her fifth reading of Alaric's heroism, but she was accustomed to hearing tenants' domestic problems and proceeded to adopt a sympathetic expression.

'Yeah, he was a devil with women,' Phyllis went on.

'Really?' Alice was genuinely surprised. She could not imagine that ferrety little man with his beady eyes climbing into any woman's bed.

'Now,' Phyllis said, 'it's like our honeymoon all over again!'

'How very nice for you,' Alice replied and began reading the newspaper account again.

'You don't understand, Alice. It's all been because of you!'

Alice folded the paper and looked quizzically at Phyllis. She could not recall ever lecturing Lance on his marital duties.

'He's discovered a hopeless passion and that's keeping him on the straight and narrow.'

'Phyllis, are you implying that your husband is in love with me?' It was difficult for Alice to keep a serious face as she said this, but a long tradition of beneficent snobbery trained one never to laugh at servants' problems.

'Love you? He worships you!'

'That's really very touching, Phyllis.'

Phyllis felt as though the conversation were taking place on Mars with one of the local residents. Nothing she had said seemed to shock or disturb Alice in the least.

'I don't think you appreciate how much he cares for you, Alice, and because he has this hopeless passion he's been great with me.'

'I'm sure he has, Phyllis, and I'm so glad he's making you happy.'

My God, thought Phyllis, she takes the worship of a man like Lance Weston as her right! However, she had to go on . . .

'Now, I would appreciate it if you gave him a kind word to keep him in hopes, so to speak. Alice, do you know what I'm talking about?'

'Oh yes,' Alice smiled. 'There are some men, philanderers generally, who find an object for their dreams, but the important thing is that the dream should never become a reality. It's rather like a religious vision and the way that can change a person, although I've never been impressed with the religious side of it. That comes of being brought up as an Anglican – we do feel so uncomfortable with enthusiasm, you know. Of course, I appreciate that Catholics – well . . . perhaps your family was Irish, so you couldn't really help it.'

It was as though Alice could hear the bells from the little Provençal chapel that night they had made love in the perfumed air, or that other time when Henry kissed her under Aunt Penelope's apricot tree with the smell of ripening fruit above their heads and his hands holding her breasts. Why should she suddenly think of that now? Alice shook her head and tried to concentrate on Phyllis and her problem. Of course, Lance was infatuated with her; everybody was in love with someone or something. And was loving the unattainable any less rewarding than loving a memory? She had memories as sweet as any of Aunt Penelope's and Lance had a hopeless passion. Who could hope to receive the reality of love in this world? To live with dreams and to be satisfied with them seemed perfectly natural to her.

Phyllis never raised the subject again. Instead she asked about Alaric and his Aunt Flodie in Paddington.

*

Alaric did not attempt to hitch a lift to Sydney; instead he took a train and arrived at Central Station shortly after noon. He had an address in Paddington – a street off Jersey Road – and he decided to walk there. It was rather colder in Sydney than Wollongong and he was glad he had packed a cashmere overcoat. As he crossed Oxford Street and made his way past the Barracks, he was accosted four times: twice by elderly gentlemen, once by a prostitute and once by an army sergeant. He walked on, oblivious to them all, feeling that since he had successfully disposed of the Medusa he could now concentrate on the Golden Fleece.

Flodie Morell's antique shop was in a secluded row of terrace houses with more period bric-à-brac in the way of ironwork and door-knockers than the most frivolous Victorian could have envisaged. Every veranda looked as though it was being choked by paper doilies. Alaric shuddered as he pushed open the door. He knew who it was in the slanting light from the stained-glass bow window – Circe the enchantress, a mountain of silver curls sparkling in the light of a fake Tiffany. Long sweeping lashes over stone-grey eyes, and a bosom . . . there Alaric gasped and almost dropped his valise. He had never seen such breasts, erupting from her dress like volcanoes of throbbing, burning flesh. Only a fertility goddess, Ceres, the mother of corn and harvests, could have carried such immortal images of ripe promise.

She was seated at a bar on a high stool that exposed a thigh struggling to match her bosom with its deep curve, a goddess dressed like a barmaid. If only she had not been wearing pince-nez on the edge of her nose and turning over a brass door-knocker with long, silver lacquered nails, Alaric would have bowed his head and worshipped her.

Falteringly, Alaric introduced himself, but she did not look at him, simply turned over the door-knocker as though searching for a hallmark.

'It's Provençal,' he said timidly, 'late eighteenth century. You can tell by the shape of the bracelet on the wrist.'

Flodie slammed the knocker on the counter and stared at

123

Alaric.

'Little Alaric Morell! How fortunate your father carried the family name.'

Alaric did not answer. He knew that you had to tread very warily indeed with goddesses, who often made a point of insulting people in order to test their humility. He was not going to be found guilty of hubris on this occasion.

'I'm Flodie Morell. Antiques, love. I'm in antiques.'

She waved her hand and Alaric saw a jumbled tier of restored Chippendales, gilt mirrors, chipped cherubs and cracked card tables. As she breathed, the whole shop seemed to be filled with her breasts.

'You have some remarkable pieces, Aunt Flodie.'

'A myriad choice articles to suit every taste.' Her stone-grey eyes were cold behind the glint of her spectacles. 'Tell me, did you kill her?'

'Who?'

'Gerda.'

Alaric was horrified and too aghast to answer. Flodie continued in the same cool, measured tones.

'She almost murdered me once. Tried to push me into a concrete mixer. And I can't tell you how many times she shoved me in front of trucks and buses. Very brutal, Gerda. Not like Augustine . . .'

'My Aunt Gerda,' Alaric said stiffly, 'killed herself. It was an accident.'

Flodie looked at him with amused contempt.

'Yes, and some accidents are more accidental than others, aren't they? Well, you can stay here if you want to, Alaric. I gather you have some foolish notion about sharing the estate between my sisters and your mother.' She looked around. 'I could do with some extra help.'

When she did raise her voice it was like a siren in the night. On this occasion it was directed at a curtain against the wall.

'Moggs!'

There was a shuffling shamble in the distance and a man parted the curtain and lurched out. The humanity was

124

barely discernible, the creature seemed barely sentient. It was as though someone had shaken an enormous bag of dust and wood-shavings into the rough semblance of a body.

'This is my nephew, Moggs. On the wrong side of the blanket, I might add.'

The shape did not move or answer, but Alaric quailed as two blood-red eyes fixed him with a look of pitiless hatred. This was how Cyclops came to Odysseus, Alaric thought. This creature was not only a murderer but a potential cannibal.

'I think you should know, Moggs,' Flodie continued in her silvery voice, 'that my nephew Alaric is here with the probable intention of killing me. He's just managed to dispose of Gerda. So you will keep an eye on him, won't you?'

Flodie adjusted a jeweller's glass and began examining a dented silver christening mug. It was not easy for her, since one long curling eyelash kept finding its way under the glass and into her eye.

The change in Moggs had been miraculous. He was actually grinning, and his feet moved clumsily to a silent dance. As one dusty arm went around Alaric's shoulder, the boy gasped from the strength of it, and from the breath reeking of turpentine and wood-glue which was in his ear.

'I'll take you to your room myself. Don't worry, mate, I won't let her touch a hair of your head!'

Alaric looked back and marvelled again at those two pearl-white globes resting lightly on the bar counter. Moggs's arm was around him and guiding him to a small attic bedroom, where he pushed Alaric gently over to the window and closed the door behind him.

'How – how did you do it?'

'Do what?'

'Kill her.'

Alaric was beginning to feel a tide of indignation overwhelm him at these continuing and unjust accusations. Why, even the Wollongong police had congratulated him on his bravery, while Mildred Coffinspray had cried and thrust a $100-note into his pocket. He could almost believe himself that he had tried to save Gerda's life; certainly he had done something that was morally of greater significance – he had saved her from cheating.

'Better death than disgrace.' He could hear the commander of the Cadet Corps at Eton now, as he tried to encourage the boys to enlist for service in Northern Ireland. And to be accused of murder by this hulking elemental was more than he could bear. Stiffly, he replied, 'I do not wish to discuss the subject further.'

Moggs shuffled his strange dance again, touched his nose with a dirty forefinger and winked.

'Got the picture, son. The greatest picture ever made.'

It did not take Alaric very long to realize how Flodie ran her business. The antiques were constructed by Moggs in a shed at the back of the shop; the actual selling took place across Flodie's bar – a private bar, as she was quick to inform Alaric, where a few select patrons of the arts would be invited to imbibe.

Flodie examined a large ring that looked as though it had just fallen out of a Christmas stocking. She twisted the glass, squinted and handed the ring to Moggs.

'Genuine opal!'

Moggs barely glanced at it. 'Mexican jasper.'

'In the right setting,' Flodie sent her voice down steel wire, 'in the right setting, it's opal. See to it, Moggs.'

Muttering, Moggs shuffled off with the ring, and Alaric continued dusting the bric-à-brac.

Flodie removed the jeweller's glass, adjusted her lashes and fixed him with a contemplative eye.

'You're such a pretty boy, Alaric. I'm sure I could get a handsome price for you. There's quite a boom in ornamental boys these days.'

She laughed, but her laughter was drowned out by a snore coming from a large, bald man asleep in a crimson padded chair by the bar. Flodie shook him gently by the elbow, then pinched the back of his neck. 'Mr Fortindale, I

126

can see how you've grown attached to that magnificent Chippendale. You've been admiring it off and on between drinks for a week now, haven't you?'

Mr Fortindale looked up blearily at Flodie, smiled and nodded back to sleep.

'I understand perfectly, Mr Fortindale. How could you possibly be happy until that chair is really, truly yours?'

Flodie went to the bar, pulled out a cheque book and almost guided Fortindale's hand across it. She examined it carefully, tucked it between those luminous spheres and screamed for Moggs.

'Moggs! You can drive Mr Fortindale and that chair home. And handle it carefully. I don't want anything to happen to an *objet d'art* of that value!'

As Moggs staggered out with Mr Fortindale under one arm and the chair in the other, Alaric felt his aunt was in such a good mood that he should broach the subject of the will again. Every time he had mentioned it before, she had laughed and told him not to be a silly boy, or else made disconcertingly personal remarks about the cut of his trousers. But he had assured his mother in his last letter that he was making great progress towards a settlement.

'Aunt Flodie, I want to discuss my mother and the will.' Flodie began to circle round a grouping of chairs, patting the seats as though they were people.

'I think I'm going to make a feature of you in the shop, Alaric. I have a number of clients who might well be very interested in you. Mr Tumesant, French, very charming – I think he'd find you quite enchanting. Of course, you'll have to know something about furniture.'

'You are a woman of business, Aunt Flodie. Now, surely you can see the benefits of dividing the Tulliford estate and –'

'You must be able to sell effectively as well . . . please the customers, Alaric. Tell me, do you know the difference between a Chippendale and a Hepplewhite?'

Suddenly, Alaric felt at ease. He perched on the edge of a table, stretched out his legs and felt as comfortable as though he were back in his tutor's room at Merton, sharing a pot of tea and a plate of toasted crumpets while discussing the vagaries of some recent criticism of Theognis. Nothing comforted Alaric more than theory, and over the years he had taken an interest in furniture.

'You must understand, Aunt Flodie, that I am not a connoisseur.'

Flodie smiled and raised eyebrows of the texture of steel springs.

'However, I always like to think of Chippendale as the Bach of furniture design and Hepplewhite as the Mozart, but often the differences between the two are so subtle that it requires an expert to make a determination. Yet I must confess, Aunt Flodie, that I really prefer the lyre-back Sheraton – Sheraton does seem to combine the best of Hepplewhite and Chippendale. I've always found his Egyptian motifs and brass strings fascinating. But the enthralling aspect of the Egyptian motifs is their derivation from . . .'

'Brass strings!' Flodie could feel her membership of the Antique Dealers' Association of Australia being stripped from her, her reputation as an art dealer trampled and her business hurled headlong into bankruptcy by this golden boy with velvet eyes. Clearly, he had been sent by his mother to destroy her, but Flodie smiled as she remembered how she had outlived all her sisters' efforts to murder her.

'Ah yes, brass strings. Well, in this business you have to learn not to confuse the client with too many facts.' She paused. 'Instead of working out here in the shop, I think you'll be happier in the back – helping Moggs with the restorations.'

Alaric was determined to pin her down. He could feel the Golden Fleece slipping through this woman's hands like mercury.

'Aunt Flodie, the will –'

'I shall undoubtedly be the heir, Alaric. Augustine is a chronic asthmatic apart from suffering from religion, while

128

Honoria is an alcoholic.'

Alaric was insistent: 'There is my mother.'

Flodie smiled thinly. 'So there is. Frankly, I'm surprised she's still with us. But if she doesn't have an accident, I'm sure she'll marry someone. She sounds like that walking incubator Betty to me.'

'My mother has never married. I mean – she wasn't allowed to – my grandfather wouldn't let her . . . not after the first marriage. She remained single so that I could be educated at Eton and Oxford. I'm sure she must have had a couple of offers when I was growing up; now she's scrubbing floors at Mockery Bend, cooking on a wood stove and boiling clothes in an iron copper. No servant would endure what my mother is doing now. And nothing will change for her unless I can settle this estate.'

'Ah, yes – the famous marriage that resulted in you, Alaric. Well, I have never married, and not for want of offers like your mother. Men have always found me irresistible,' and here the globes rose and fell like twin full moons. 'But I wasn't born to please one man. Besides, I intend to have Mockery Bend and all that goes with it.'

'Aunt Flodie, you could share!'

'I am going to build a French *château* with reflecting pools, and there I shall enter into the spirit of Diane de Poitiers and surround myself with period beauty.'

All of the Morells, Alaric thought, had a weakness for dreaming, and he was delighted that he had not inherited that failing.

'If my mother is prepared to divide the estate, it would seem –'

Flodie's voice was a razor. 'You poor little half-wit. What makes you think she's alive now?'

*

For want of a horse, Alice had taken to riding Blossom, her favourite among the cows. As a child she had learned how to ride and guide cows and now she was getting accustomed to the ambling gait again. Lion had barked and dashed up to the house, so she knew the post was waiting for her in a box by the main road. Blossom stood placidly while she mounted and moved off slowly to a nudge from her knees. Alice hoped she would not have to brush too much hair from her peach-coloured pant-suit when she'd collected her letters. Lion had vanished on business of his own and all she could see was a blue flash of sunlight as he crossed the rise and headed south.

The first batch of cheese was waiting for Lance to take to town and she did hope that he had remembered to bring out the flower seedlings she had ordered. The bed was dug ready for them by the front steps – surely Sweet Alice and a few geraniums would grow there? It was such a strange climate – the middle of winter, yet the sun was beating down and the country needed rain. She tried not to think of her rose garden at the Manor and that particular yellow tea with a perfume which filled the drawing-room.

Blossom ambled to a stop and Alice reached down into the post-box. She had never managed to meet the postman. Once she had glimpsed him from a distance and waved, but he had spun his truck into a skidding turn and driven off at top speed. Generally, Lance brought out Alaric's letters. She was sure there was something in the box now – not only one from Alaric, but a large, fat, interesting envelope. She was just about to open it when Lion came back over the rise with a large squawking hen in his jaws. The letters were dropped on the mailbox and she urged Blossom back to the pen where the rooster was already crowing his welcome to a missing wife.

She reached down and opened the gate; Lion dropped the chicken, sat down and clearly expected a biscuit. Alice laughed, closed the gate and told him he must wait until she had fetched the letters.

They were in her sight on top of the box when a breeze came up, lifted them in the air and dropped them. And at that instant there was a blinding flash and a crack of thunder. A confetti of paper showered down and the earth all around was smoking and charred. Even Blossom

130

stopped short and Lion edged forward, whining.

Alice was still staring when Tulliford galloped over the rise, and he too skidded to a halt. He had reached the point now where he would not have been unduly surprised if a brace of unicorns had trotted down to greet him from Mockery Bend. But this was like an archetypal myth rising up into his consciousness from unimaginable depths: a blonde woman astride a cow, her bare feet in gold and white sandals, her hair held back with a creamy-white bandeau. A trembling coldness shook him and he felt himself shiver in the sunlight. He had been planning to visit Alice today, to explain once and for all why Crockford's cows must be returned and to arrange for her return to England. But here he was confronted by something as strange as a dream of fable or romance. Half an hour ago he had been mounting his sorrel when he saw the dog which he no longer recognized as his own jump the chicken run with one of his fowls and head off towards Mockery Bend. This time he was going to shoot the mongrel before he cleaned out every bit of poultry he owned. Yet, at this moment he felt as though he had strayed into a dream and it was all he could do to speak.

'I saw him take it! He jumped my fence like a kangaroo!'

'My letters have just exploded,' Alice said numbly.

Tulliford had dismounted and walked over to Alice's chicken run. He pointed at one particular bird and turned to her furiously.

'It's still wet from his jaws.'

Alice ambled over on Blossom, and Tulliford trembled again as though a myth was bearing down upon him with mystery and romance at every step.

'Are you sure, Mr Tulliford? It may have decided to have a bath. It does look as though it's trying to dry itself in the sun.'

She was pleasantly surprised to find that she was now looking down at Tulliford from the height of the cow's back.

Tulliford looked up at her and shook his head in disbelief. 'You are cleaning out the whole countryside. You have got to go, Mrs Morell!'

'Mr Tulliford,' Alice said firmly, 'I have just had a most distressing experience. There was a letter from my son this morning and either it, or another, exploded.' She felt the need to be very precise with this man. 'Now, I suggest we discuss this in the coolness of the house.'

She jumped off Blossom's back and pushed the cow into the yard. Tulliford felt as though the whole order of nature was being changed before his eyes. Nobody rode cows except in a rodeo – and then only for a matter of seconds before being thrown into the sawdust. Yet here was this woman brushing herself down, closing the gate, patting the dog – that dog which he was intending to shoot before he left – and inviting him to have a discussion with her.

He appreciated a part of what Phyllis Weston had said to him and was not going to be accused of behaving in an un-Christian fashion. Now he had a solution to the whole problem which he was preparing to put to Alice Morell fairly and squarely; afterwards he would shoot that damned dog which was snarling at him silently.

At least, Alice felt, she had been able to meet her cousin on equal terms.

'When you go to turn off a tenant, go on horseback with a riding crop,' was what grandfather used to say. But she didn't feel that quite applied as Tulliford stretched his long legs under her table. She wished now that she had been riding her dapple pony, or her uncle's black gelding. Aunt Penelope's voice was in her mind as she carried in a pot of tea and sat down opposite Tulliford. One morning Penelope had come to the top of the steps and watched the Barnsley hunt ride out, nodded, smiled, then whispered to Alice,

'So important for a lady to be well mounted.'

Alice poured the tea in silence, remembering how Aunt Penelope had chuckled softly and drifted off to her swing and those secret adventures in a rapturous countryside. Tulliford's hand was on the table and Alice felt a sudden urge to reach out and fondle it, but she handed him a cup of tea instead.

Tulliford was trying not to look at her. Something about her eyes disturbed him. Besides, he had disliked and distrusted women ever since his seven-week marriage which had cost him a fortune to get out of. Only Cavalry Barnhouse had shown a considerable profit from that little episode. Fortunately his wife had found a Mexican millionaire, so the alimony payments ceased, but he still remembered Barnhouse's legal fees. One thing he had promised himself – he was never going to supply that loud-mouthed leech with any more business.

Alice was trying to explain about her letters and Tulliford tried to swallow the tea, wondering if she were certifiable or just hopelessly eccentric. However, he was convinced that he now had a fair and equitable solution to the whole problem. He put down his cup and looked at Alice, who smiled.

Tulliford coughed and said, 'It's this business of cattle theft. God knows what Crockford will do when he finds out his cows are here. Next thing, I'll find you've got *my* cattle in your back yard.'

Alice thought it futile to try to explain trespass and seisin and right of free warren to him. He seemed impervious to any legal argument. She sighed and Tulliford quickly looked away.

'Mr Tulliford, I am trying to earn enough to keep myself. I did not have a very extensive education: a governess when I was young, finishing school at a small establishment in Corfu. All I know is how to run a farm –'

'That's it!' Tulliford almost shouted, although he was not quite sure what *it* was.

'Your grandfather's will was barbarous, Mr Tulliford. But I'm not going to be persecuted and punished for something a Morell long-dead may have done – or not done.'

'How do you think I feel about the will?' Tulliford had brooded over the will ever since he could think. His father's last rambling words had been to curse the injustice of it and

133

revile Barnhouse for drawing it up and making it all possible.

'My father was an only child. He was the natural, rightful heir to his father's estate. Instead, he was cut off with the bare minimum the law would allow, simply so that *his* father could get even with his wife and her sisters. How do you think he felt? If he hadn't been lucky, bought some land near Darwin and struck silver, he would never have been able to buy his way back here.'

'Then since we both feel hardly done by, don't you think we should try to be good neighbours – at the least, Mr Tulliford?'

'Good neighbours!' Tulliford almost choked. 'When you're stealing my chickens with the help of my dog?'

'Your dog – and your chickens – chose to live here. And I think that animals have some rights, don't you? I can assure you that when my grandfather confiscated some of his neighbours' livestock, it was because those poor animals had wanted to escape from their brutal owners and live with us.'

Tulliford felt the whole purpose of his being there was evaporating – a point had to be established, a fixed point from which there could be no divergence.

'All right, we're not going to talk about poultry. What I'm here to say is this: it is quite impossible for you to stay here.'

Alice was beginning to get very angry with this obtuse man.

'First you want to shoot my dog –'

'Mrs Morell, I am going to shoot *my* dog – forget the dog. The point is that you cannot make a living from six cows and a few chickens.'

'Oh, but I am!' Alice was overjoyed that it was only his concern for her which made him sound so grim. She remembered Henry Morell once saying to her, 'You're in trouble. You're going to have to wear this!' And then handing her an engagement ring. Henry had the same

134

sandy-brown hair as Tulliford. All she needed to do was explain how splendidly she was managing.

'I've just made my first batch of cheese. You can try some if you like. Lance comes out every day and he delivers my eggs and milk to the co-op. He says he can find a speciality shop in Sydney that will take my cheese. And he's offered to take –'

'For God's sake, Alice, Lance is a married man!' He was quite unaware that he had used her first name.

Alice laughed. 'I know he is! Phyllis is almost my best friend – next to Lion, that is.' She leaned down and patted Lion, who was lying comfortably across her sandals. 'I'm Lance's hopeless passion.'

Tulliford was baffled. 'You're his *what*?'

'Phyllis says it's so much better than all those bunny girls and barmaids, and so much less expensive.'

Tulliford shook his head in despair.

'Oh come now, Mr Tulliford, you've heard of Don Quixote, haven't you? I'm Lance's Dulcinea.'

Tulliford felt that any moment he would begin tilting at windmills himself if he didn't manage to return to that one fixed point.

'You may – you may *just* be able to survive here, Mrs Morell, but you can't make a life for yourself – not out here – not on your own. It's unnatural and dangerous, and because I'm your nearest relation I feel responsible for you. At least people have said I should be –'

Alice replied so quietly that he could barely hear her, 'I've often had to be alone in my life, Mr Tulliford.'

'Your son should be here, instead of charging round the countryside killing off his aunts.'

Alice was outraged and would have stamped if Lion had not been across her feet.

'My son tried to save his Aunt Gerda's life! It was in all the papers and he was referred to as a hero by some very discerning journalists. At the moment he is working in my cousin Flodie's antique shop, trying to negotiate a settlement.'

'He should be here! Looking after you!' Tulliford shouted.

'I do *not* need a keeper!'

'That is a matter of opinion.' Under his breath, he muttered, 'Exploding mail!' Then he continued aloud, 'I don't seem able to make you understand what a serious matter stealing livestock is in these parts.'

'I am only trying to make a living.'

'Mrs Morell, you cannot stay here on your own. It's not safe for you – or anyone else,' he added.

'I have Lion for company.'

Tulliford felt the table shake as Lion wagged his tail vigorously under it.

'Perhaps . . . perhaps it's the loneliness that's made you think so crazy. I mean – how about if I take you to the picnic races so that you can get the feel of real people?'

Races? Alice thrilled at the very idea and for a moment she could not speak.

'I daresay you dislike horses?'

'I adore horses,' Alice replied.

'Well, it's next Saturday. I'll be over to pick you up at nine.'

'I'm always very punctual,' Alice assured him.

At the top of the steps, he turned and said almost gently, 'We'll be able to have a good long talk then about your leaving here and going back to England. It's the loneliness that's turned your head.'

He had forgotten his intention of shooting the dog and was not to know that half an hour after he had left, Lion came back with another chicken and deftly dropped it into the run. Gloomily, Tulliford rode back to his property, his memories neither pleasant nor comforting. He could barely remember his wife, and the women he had known since had left him angry and dissatisfied that they should fall so far below his ideal. That ideal had never been a clear image and since he regarded it as unattainable, he had

136

never bothered to define it in practical terms. Why then did the mythical figure of a woman astride a cow come before his eyes like the emblem of some ancient religion which his ancestors had followed? He kneed the sorrel to a gallop and closed his mind to everything except the track ahead.

*

Alaric was convinced that Moggs was less than sentient, but he had grown quite fond of the lumbering fellow. He had begun to think of him as Briareus, the hundred-handed Titan, because of the extraordinary delicacy with which he could repair an intaglio or mosaic. Moreover, there was a deep and abiding bond between them – they both hated Flodie's guts! As they polished and glued, they would invent possible tortures for her, and when Alaric spoke of the lingering boat death of the Persians, Moggs went into a frenzy and began a shuffling dance around the room.

'You mustn't think I've always been like this,' he told Alaric. 'I was a proud man once, standard bearer for North Bondi Surf Club. Oh, I was six-foot seven in me bare feet then and when I led the team up the sand with the flag streaming above our heads, I was a giant among men, a regular hero. "Alf Moggs!" the girls would scream "Alf! Alf for ever!" But I kept my eyes straight ahead and the flagpole never wavered in me navel.' Then, often in mid-sentence, the mighty Briareus would fall silent.

Once, after they had slowly dropped Flodie into a pit of hungry tarantulas, Moggs said in a whisper, 'You know she's the human beast, don't you? You read *Revelations* and you'll see she was prophesied. Something rotten like her doesn't turn up by accident!'

'The Scarlet Woman in a Blakean or Biblical sense?' Alaric inquired politely.

'No,' Moggs shook his great shaggy head and a shower of sawdust fell on the table. 'No, the great dragon with seven horns.'

Sympathetically, Alaric handed the friendly Titan a

137

chisel and said, 'Moggs, you don't have to stay here, do you? I'm sure a workman of your skill could find a job anywhere.'

Moggs put up his head and wailed like a wolf when the moon is full: 'I am bound to her in servitude!'

Alaric was continuing to polish a walnut veneer table when he sensed that there was something behind him. He looked up and found his face buried in those spheres of soft flesh. After examining the table with pursed lips, Flodie thrust a chair-leg in front of him.

'There!' she said.

Alaric was nonplussed and could only muster a weak, 'Ah?'

Flodie seemed irritated and shook it in front of him.

'A leg – of a chair?' Alaric said hopefully.

'Louis Quinze,' replied Flodie.

From his bench, Moggs muttered, 'Louis can't and Moggs won't either.'

Flodie closed her eyes and the great globes rose and fell like ocean tides.

'Obviously part of a matching set of six drawing-room chairs. I can see them . . . the elegance . . . the élan . . . the ésprit de corps – and the shadow of Madame de Pompadour casting a soft radiance over them all. Touched by the rustling silk of her robe, those chairs became immortal!' Her tone dropped to a steely precision and she handed the chair-leg to Moggs. 'Six chairs, Moggs.'

Moggs bellowed, 'From that?'

'I have given you the model and the inspiration. They will be covered in beige satin with the teeniest gold fleck.' Then she swung round to confront Alaric: 'You must rub harder to bring out the grain, dear.'

'Not too hard, or you'll crack the veneer,' Moggs whispered.

Floddie carried her bosom before her to the door.

'I need that table for Mr Porteous tonight. Now, I simply must do something with this wretched Mrs Wilkerson. She

138

can't make up her mind about the Tiffany. It's going to take another two martinis.'

Moggs dropped his chisel and waved his arms in a frenzy.

'Fakes! Fakes! All of them! And when she gets that estate, she's going to build a fake *château* at Mockery Bend and fill it with fake furniture just like this. One chair-leg and she wants a dining-room suite. I tell you, Alaric, there's only one way to deal with her!'

He rushed over to the corner of the room and pulled back a tall screen, whereupon Alaric screamed and clutched his right wrist. They had followed him from London! He had not been able to escape the Maenads! Now they would take his right hand!

'No! Get back!' He tried to thrust back an enormously tall Arab standing in the corner, screamed in terror and fell over in a dead faint.

Chapter Seven

Alaric revived slowly, then he almost fainted again as he saw the figure in the corner. Moggs had found some brandy and Alaric drank a cupful with his eyes closed. Slowly, the room began to take shape in front of him and he saw that his Arab was a tall grandfather clock wrapped in a sheet with a rope around the top. When Moggs pulled off the sheet, Alaric realized it was indeed a fine Georgian clock with carved finials.

Grimly Moggs stood beside it with his arms folded. 'You guessed, Alaric.'

'I thought – I thought for a moment . . .' Alaric quavered.

'You thought right,' said Moggs as with a flourish he opened the clock door and a mass of wires and two sticks of dynamite fell out on to the floor.

Alaric tried to throw himself under the table, but found a pile of boxes in the way, so he crouched with his hands over his ears.

'I've designed it,' said Moggs, 'so that when she opens it, this will all explode into millions of little splinters of fake furniture – a juicy conglomeration of powdered plaster and minced Morell.' Then he sighed deeply. 'The only trouble is that I can't work out the wiring. Now, I recently read where a boy in Princeton built an atom bomb and seeing as how you went to Oxford – we are in business!'

'I read classics,' Alaric said stiffly.

'Wonderful!' said Moggs. 'You'll be able to read these instructions, then. Most of them are in Arabic.' He handed a dog-eared green paper-back book to Alaric. 'It's the PLO *Guide to Guerrilla Warfare.'*

Alaric knew then that this was indeed the Titan Briareus.

'You plan to blow up Aunt Flodie?'

'What better cause is there for a freedom fighter?' said Moggs belligerently.

'I – I really couldn't!' Alaric protested. 'I mean – technically I'm opposed to violence.'

Moggs poked him in the chest. 'Then just remember this: if you don't get her, she'll get your ma! Warn your ma to handle her mail very, very carefully these days, and not to eat any chocolates she may receive. Arsenic in the peppermint creams! Augustine's done it before, she sends Flodie a box every Christmas. . . . and Honoria's famous for her letter bombs. The IRA has taken lessons from her.'

'No, no I couldn't!' Alaric staggered out to the shop, where Flodie was leaning over the bar with a glass goblet in her hand. A bemused little man was trying to focus on the glass and finding that his vision was not wide enough to encompass those orbs from horizon to horizon.

'Now this,' said Flodie professionally, 'is a perfect example of yeoman glass – look at that wrythened bowl!'

The man tried to follow the convolutions of the stem and almost twisted off his stool.

'Your wife is going to love it too. Listen to the timbre!'

The man leaned forward to listen and Flodie flicked the glass with a long silver nail. A dull and muffled pong was the response. Without a flicker of a spangled eyelash, Flodie smiled triumphantly, saying, 'You can tell by the lack of timbre that's true yeoman glass.'

Alaric staggered back into the work-room.

'Give me the book, please, Moggs. I shall endeavour to make a rough translation.'

*

As he drove out to Mockery Bend Tulliford rehearsed what he was going to say to Alice. He was quite prepared to pay her fare back to London and provide her with travelling expenses. He had the reputation of being careful with money, but this time he intended to be generous. Already she had changed the whole neighbourhood. He still remembered the blank astonishment at the Hope's End Racing Club when he had proposed Lance Weston as a member and then announced that the little ferret would be running a horse in the Invitation Mile. Syd Crockford had gobbled and swallowed, suddenly suspecting that Lance must have come into big money and Tulliford was getting his hooks into it. For Syd, money was the universal antiseptic, the absolution for all sins. He seconded Jos's proposal and determined to make a few discreet inquiries about Lance's credit rating.

The Hope's End Racing Club was indeed old New South Wales. Three generations of good blood were required for membership, or else so much money that people would generously overlook your parents. The Burtons, the Crockfords and Jos Tulliford would be joined by Australians of similar heritage from as far away as Victoria and South Australia. Now, everyone in Hope's End knew that Lance Weston was Lance Esposito, a beady-eyed little crook trying to climb so fast he was like a lizard on a hot rock. Fortunately, Tulliford stood so well with the other members that there had been no argument when he proposed Lance, only the feeling that somehow Tulliford had let down the standards of the club a long way. That feeling was still with him as he parked his convertible in Alice's driveway and walked up to the veranda. It troubled him to see the fresh paint on the walls, the new boards in the floor. To his father the decay of this house had been visible witness to the perfidy of the Tulliford will and Cavalry Barnhouse. He flinched slightly as he saw again those stony, astonished faces around the table when he put forward the name of Lance Weston as a member.

Lion came to the top of the steps, lowered his shoulders as though about to spring and snarled at him. Tulliford remembered that he had promised himself he would shoot that dog and wished he had brought a gun with him. Lion showed every tooth and Tulliford shook his fist at him in silent rage. Then he heard Alice's voice inside the house and, as she came through the door, he stepped back two paces in amazement. The house always disturbed him, but this was the transfiguration.

Alice was glowing with excitement. 'I do hope I didn't keep you waiting. There were so many eggs to collect this morning.'

Silently Tulliford took off his hat and held it as though he were in church.

At the top of the steps, Alice looked up at the sky and opened her parasol. This ensemble had been Miss Hetherington's finest achievement. The dress was in shades of lilac chiffon with a high belt embroidered in violet flowers. Gloves, shoes and purse were of a pale ostrich skin, but the hat – even Miss Hetherington had wondered if it were not a little *too* . . . until she saw it on Alice's blonde hair. A great dipping brim of lilac and a crown of crushed silk flowers, above it a parasol of purples and lavenders, rippling with frills.

When she had tried it on, Miss Hetherington had said softly and with a little tremble in her voice, 'Oh, madam, you could wear this in the Royal Enclosure at Ascot!'

Alice had never seen anything lovelier and now she was

142

going to the races with such a handsome man. She could admit that, even though she wished he had worn a morning suit and carried a grey topper instead of a suede jacket and boots, but she was prepared to make allowances for local customs.

Lavender had been Aunt Penelope's favourite colour. There was a story in the family that she was wearing a lavender sprigged muslin when the prince had insisted that she be introduced to him. Under the apricot tree, swinging gently, Aunt Penelope would sometimes hum a line over and over: 'Sleep in lavender, wake in gold.' When she asked her aunt how it had finished, there would only be a smiling silence or a ripple of chuckling laughter.

Alice told Lion to look after the house and the dog wagged his tail at her and snarled once at Tulliford. Then she smiled at Tulliford and he felt a sudden aching pain in his chest.

'Mr Tulliford, we are cousins, and I think I should like you to call me Alice.'

'Jos,' Tulliford croaked.

'I would prefer Joseph,' she said sweetly.

One minute Tulliford had felt himself to be a rational man with a reputation for common sense and shrewd business management; now he stumbled to the car like some country yokel who had fallen into a fairy ring and found himself in an enchanted country with a princess at his side.

*

Phyllis had never been to Hope's End Races before and she was relishing every minute. She lost count of the raised eyebrows as she walked past, hoping that some of those rich bitches could recognize an imported Calvin Klein original sports-de-jour. When he had not been making love to her the night before, Lance had been in a panic about his horse. It was a rangy, bony gelding and Lance swore to her that he had bought it from a reputable dealer at Flemington and that it had a long record of wins in the Northern Territory. To Phyllis it looked as though it had been ridden hard from the Territory the night before, but Lance brushed aside her questions and swore by all the saints in the calendar that this was a blood horse which would give the local nags a run for their money. Oh God, Phyllis prayed, don't let Lance try anything cheap today! Just once, let a day go past without him making a profit. But the holy medals remained silent and Our Lady of Lourdes seemed to be reaching out to the Little Flower for comfort . . . She smiled at Crystal Crockford and wondered when Alice would arrive with Jos Tulliford.

Early that morning Tulliford had phoned Syd Crockford and told him about the cows. Crystal was almost raving with worry lest Syd make a scene with Tulliford, and she had her four daughters down for the races and each one looking prettier than the next. She was certain that this mad Mrs Morell was keeping the cows out of – well, because of her being mad. Nobody in his right mind ever tried to cheat Syd Crockford, whose vindictiveness made the Chinese Tongs seem like charitable and beneficent institutions. Then Tulliford had gone on to tell Syd about the milk and the cheese, and now Crystal was afraid that Syd was planning to have Tulliford and Lance arrested at the same time. At any other time she would never have spoken to Phyllis, but today she had to talk to someone.

'I do hope there won't be any trouble about these cows, Phyllis. You know what my husband is like, he has such a strong sense of property.' And she remembered how Syd had thrown two lampshades against the wall and shattered a row of glasses on the cocktail cabinet.

Phyllis grinned and said that cattle stealing was a very serious matter.

Crystal had just returned from Los Angeles with a most expensive face-lift, her ears were aching as though someone had held her up like a beagle for a month, her eyes felt as though they were embedded in shingles and every time she smiled she couldn't feel her lips. She knew she looked ravishing. For three days she had existed on grapefruit and soy bean meal, and now her stomach was gratifyingly flat

144

under her designer jeans and her nerves were throbbing like bursting boils. All she wanted from life was to see Syd get his cows back and Tulliford marry one of her daughters. But Syd had not spoken of restitution; when he had kicked Crystal's prize Pekingese through a wire screen window, he was talking of lynching.

Nervously Crystal patted her stomach to make sure it wasn't there and looked around for her husband. Syd had a great collection of John Wayne movies and sometimes he would run four or five in succession, mouthing the lines and reaching for an imaginary six-shooter. Since dawn that morning he had been pacing up and down the living-room, muttering and firing at invisible assailants. She looked round and saw a dozen people she knew who were waving at her in an inquiring fashion – doubtless, Crystal thought, asking each other why Crystal Crockford, whose mother had been a Beale from Adelaide, was standing there talking to Phyllis Weston. Then she saw that everyone was crowding over towards the car park.

'Oh my God, please! Please don't let there be a fight at the Hope's End Races – please, anywhere but here!' And Crystal prayed with both hands on the place where her stomach had been.

She felt a nudge in the ribs.

'If you can open your eyes, Crystal, take a long look at that!'

It was like a royal progress. Alice was slowly making her way down through the crowd to the betting stand, her dress floating around her, her parasol above her head like a canopy. Every woman knew what to wear to the Picnic Races – designer sports, silk shirts, tooled leather boots with needle-thin heels – but here was Ascot proceeding towards them, summer parties by the river with swans among the reeds and punts on the stream, royal garden parties and all the splendours of Empire.

Alice could not remember when she had been so happy – such brown, curious friendly people. She knew that everyone was admiring her and felt rather as a British ambassador did when, in the full panoply of uniform and regalia, he visited a tribal chieftain in darkest Africa. She knew instinctively that these were loyal people and smiled at everyone. Then she saw Phyllis and swept down upon her like a storm of flowers.

"Phyllis, my dear, isn't this a lark!'

Phyllis could only nod. Crystal Crockford had backed away and then run to the protection of her daughters. Standing over to one side was Lance Weston and when Alice waved to him he felt his knees buckle.

'I . . . I never saw a dress like it, Alice. You look just like the fairy queen in a pantomime. I wouldn't be game to wear it to a wedding but you – you look just great!'

Alice felt this was exactly how it must have been when the Morells had open day at the Manor. Of course, Lupin Tanner had been right when she described the coloured umbrellas and canvas tents, and Alice being – what phrase had she used? – the cynosure of all eyes. Perhaps, Alice thought, it was not the past Lupin had seen, but the future. What could be more splendid than this crowd of gaping but admiring people under a brilliant blue sky? Australia, she said to herself firmly, was much, much better than Aix-en-Provence.

Crystal found her husband arguing with Tulliford and managed to pull him aside for a moment. Crockford was an irascible little man whose 'get-up-and-go' as a land developer and investor was known from Hong Kong to Hobart. He had just paid out eleven thousand dollars for Crystal's face-lift and was not impressed with the results. Besides, before he killed anyone he was determined to find out why his cows had been at Mockery Bend and how long Tulliford had known they were there, and he didn't give a damn if his daughters never got married.

Like her husband, Crystal made snap decisions and she had only needed one look at Alice Morell to see her like a bush-fire sweeping towards the house.

'She's had your cows for weeks, Syd, and she's wheedled Tulliford into keeping quiet about them. But if you're a

146

man, you'll walk right over to her now and make a citizen's arrest.'

Syd only grunted and tried to stand on his toes so that he could see where Crystal was pointing. All he could glimpse was a lilac parasol twirling against the sky. When he tried to remember where he had seen something like that before, a long-buried memory fell into his mind. Over his crib as a little child there had been a round, soft furry lilac ball which he loved to touch and hold and then, one day, his big sister came and stuffed it down the toilet. God, he hadn't thought of that for more than forty years! Crystal took Syd firmly by the arm, wondering why he was suddenly silent; ignoring the dragging pain of her ears, she set her mouth in a rabbity smile and marched him up to Alice who was still chatting amiably to Phyllis.

Crystal bridled and pushed Syd forward: 'Mrs Morell, I presume?'

Alice smiled, put out her hand and Syd Crockford took it and held it.

'My husband,' Crystal said, 'wants to discuss a matter of six of his cows with you.'

Syd looked up into the shadow of that soft lavender hat and was lost. He had made a decision. Tomorrow he would see Cavalry Barnhouse and find out the best way to divorce Crystal. If Cavalry did his stuff, then Mrs Morell would be Mrs Crockford by Christmas and he could manage to write off the cost of the divorce as a tax loss.

'Syd!' Crystal said sharply.

'I only want to know one thing,' Syd said slowly to Alice. 'Are you happy with those cows?'

Crystal felt every stitch of her face-lift beginning to throb. She tried to speak, but her jaws seemed fixed in that perpetual smile. Phyllis took her by the sleeve.

'Come on, Crystal, I'll buy you a drink.'

Two straight vodkas later, Crystal was still rigid with shock, but Phyllis was glowing with triumph as she prepared to do a little patronizing herself. Crystal Crockford whose languid blonde beauty had graced more social functions than Nola Dekyvere, and yet here she was almost crying across the bar.

'Phyllis, she's a spectacle – she's a joke – she's just outrageous. If she'd worn that at Randwick, they would have warned her off for frightening the horses. My God, does she think we're going to put her at the head of a parade or something? Does she want everyone to talk about her?'

'That's what's happening now,' Phyllis said cheerfully.

Crystal's anguish was augmented by the reports that kept coming to her from her daughters. Their father was still with Mrs Morell and Jos Tulliford had gone off to buy her ice cream, but when he got back the Burton boys had moved in.

That was too much and Crystal told the bartender to hand her the bottle. Fred and Allan Burton were the smoothest fellows in the neighbourhood and she had long ago given up hope of their picking off one of her daughters. For the last six years each had been voted the most eligible bachelor and featured in fashion magazines and social registries. Not only did they have more than their fair share of this world's goods, but they were remarkably good-looking – tall, sun-tanned, well-spoken and pleasantly aware of all they had to offer any woman. They had both studied law at Melbourne; now Fred was in Sydney and Allan in Brisbane. Both had returned to Hope's End to settle the family estate to the west of Mockery Bend. Unlike most brothers, they seldom argued with each other and had even been known to share girl friends. They both drove Porsches and they always arrived at social functions with models. Crystal saw two elegant and dismal blondes at the other end of the bar and wondered why they had not been parked with the Porsches.

'I would just love to see her birth certificate,' Crystal gritted. 'Oh God, my ears are killing me!'

Phyllis thought for a moment, then said pensively, 'I've looked at her often, Crystal, and thought as how I'd give my back teeth to look like her. But then, I get to thinking some more and I know that if I were Alice Morell I'd be a

dinkum monster. You see, I'd know that I was a knock-out
– she doesn't.'

'You're kidding!' said Crystal and hoisted another
vodka. 'I wish I'd brought some valium with me. You got
any valium with you, Phyllis?'

'If you fall flat on that new face of yours, you are going to
be in big trouble, Crystal.'

'What is going on here?' Crystal shrilled. 'What is it
about her? Every man is over there! There's your Lance.
Why don't you go over and drag him out? I thought you
working-class women had a bit of spunk. Why don't you
fight for your man?'

'I wouldn't spoil his fun,' Phyllis said.

A tableau had opened up in front of them as people
moved over to the horses. Fred Burton had just popped a
bottle of champagne and was pouring glasses all round;
Allan was obviously drinking a toast to Alice, and Syd was
frowning as he drew up a proposed settlement with Crystal.
Jos Tulliford was wiping ice cream off his suede jacket; he
had stood for so long waiting for a chance to hand it to Alice
that most of it had melted and dripped down his sleeve.
Lance was trying to slip in under Alice's elbow and whisper
something to her.

'It is crazy,' Crystal moaned. 'That is a middleaged
woman in a freaky outfit and every man here has gone
mad.'

The Burtons' two models had now drifted off and were
standing with the four Crockford girls. Even at this distance
they could hear Alice's laughter rippling towards them and
every flourish of her parasol seemed like a victory flag
waved over their heads.

'Phyllis, how old is she?' Crystal moaned.

'About forty-two, forty-three maybe.'

'And she has a son – who isn't exactly legitimate, and
she's a Morell, which means she's mad as a snake, and . . .
forty-three!'

'There's more juice in a ripe peach than a green apple,
Crystal.'

149

'But there are five men over there with her – and two of them are our husbands. Lance, I can understand. We all know Lance, but Syd doesn't go for women – he's only wrapped up in money and John Wayne.'

'It sure is a sight,' Phyllis said, smoothing out the creases in her pants.

'Why – how is she doing it – what is happening here?' Crystal screamed.

'I don't know exactly, but there was a book we all had to study in primary school, Crystal. We had to learn one sentence off by heart. Yes: "Men, it has been well said, think in herds; it will be seen that they go mad in herds, while they only recover their senses slowly, and one by one." I never forgot that, it seemed the truest thing they ever taught me in school.'

'That's a load of crap!' Crystal slammed her glass on the counter and it shattered into a dozen fragments. 'I'll tell you what this is. You ever seen a bitch in heat run through a town on a hot afternoon, with every dog after her? That's all that is!'

'Please, Crystal,' Phyllis said coldly, 'you are speaking about Alice Morell, who happens to be my best friend. And for married women like us, she's better than an insurance policy.'

Alice was radiant with happiness. If only Alaric could have been here to meet these charming Burton brothers and dear little Mr Crockford, who was so intelligent she didn't have to explain the laws of trespass and rights of free warren to him, he had just accepted her right to his cows. Tulliford had managed to move in beside her and asked if she wanted to see the horses before they raced.

Lance was at her shoulder, trying to whisper something.

'Dynamo – my horse. Put all you've got on her, Mrs Morell!'

Alice smiled, but she remembered the name. Fred and Allan were telling her about the term they had spent at Oxford after graduating from Melbourne. They had, of course, heard all about Alaric's fame as a classicist there and Allan was certain he had had dinner with him in college on a number of occasions.

The horses were being assembled with their jockeys and Alice furled her parasol and walked around them. Tulliford could see that she did indeed know horses. Dynamo, Lance's gelding was prancing nervously by the gate, his jockey – a stolid little oriental dwarf – already in the saddle. Alice stopped and nodded in approval before a black mare with four white socks and a sparkling white blaze down her nose.

'That,' said Alice, 'must be from Hyperion. You can always tell that line.'

'You should see my horse,' Syd said. 'I paid twelve thousand dollars for him and I only race him socially.'

'Is this your mare, Joseph?'

Tulliford nodded, then asked her how she knew it was from the old Hyperion bloodline.

'One white foot, keep him not a day;
Two white feet, send him soon away;
Three white feet, sell him to a friend.
Four white feet, keep him to the end.'

'Would you like me to put something on Jos's mare for you, Alice?' Allan was beaming down at her.

'I'll add something to it,' Fred said, cursing his brother silently for being so fast on the uptake.

'No,' said Alice thoughtfully. 'If I had any money, I'd back Lance's Dynamo.'

Four men looked at her in amazement, then stared at the brown gelding with its rough head and flat ears.

'If you want to back Lance's moke, then Syd Crockford will stand by your judgment, Alice!' Whereupon Syd Crockford, that man of instant decisions, rushed off to the betting stand followed by the Burton brothers and Lance.

'You're wasting their money,' Tulliford said. 'My mare's unbeaten.'

'I don't think she'll win today, Joseph,' and Alice smiled

151

as the Burtons, Crockford and Lance rushed back to hand her a selection of tickets. True to form, Crockford had waited to see what everyone else was putting on for her, then doubled the amount. He knew that to make money, you had to spend money. In this case he was going to outbid the competition for Alice Morell.

Later, as they drove back to Mockery Bend, Alice was trying to fold her winnings into neat piles and cram them into her tiny purse.

'You should have brought a sack with you, Alice,' Tulliford said bitterly.

'I'll count it when I get home. I really think I must have a thousand dollars here.'

'Will you tell me one thing? How did you know Lance had doped that walking mound of dog's meat? Did he tell you?'

'Good heavens, no!' Alice sounded genuinely shocked. 'I intend to speak to him most severely about it, but as soon as I saw the carotid artery in its neck pulsating so irregularly and the way its eyes were popping, I knew he'd tampered with the poor brute. Your mare was the finest horse there, Joseph, but nothing could have beaten Dynamo this afternoon.'

'I propose him,' Tulliford ground his teeth. 'I have him made a member of the Hope's End Racing Club and the first thing he does is run a doped horse.' He did not add that the only reason he was now living in a fog of embarrassment was because of Alice Morell. When Dynamo had come in from the stretch coated in foam from nostrils to tail, everyone had known the horse had been fixed. But there was no swabbing at the picnic races, no investigations, because it was assumed that every man who brought his horse there was a thoroughbred gentleman.

He pulled in to the steps of Mockery Bend and Lion rushed out to greet his goddess. Something about the dog reminded Tulliford of Syd Crockford and that smooth-talking Fred Burton. Neither of those boys had been real men since they went off to private boarding schools and university.

'I really shall have a word to Lance about that horse, Joseph. I had a great-uncle who used to dope all his horses before he sold them. He could make a twelve-year-old gelding look like a two-year-old. We were so ashamed of him in the family –'

'Alice,' Tulliford had made up his mind, 'would you like me to bring over that mare so that you can ride it – before you leave here? I gather you do know something about horses.'

'Joseph, how very kind of you!'

'It's nothing.' He walked her to the door and was at the wheel of his car in six strides. Alice watched him drive off and found herself marvelling at the length of his legs and the way she had felt when his thigh brushed against hers in the car. Once, Aunt Penelope had watched the hunt ride back and said softly:

'Horse and man, the staying power is in the legs.'

She wished Tulliford had invited her to the dance that evening, but she supposed that one must conform with local customs. Fred Burton had explained to her that it just wasn't done to take the same girl to the races *and* the dance unless you were formally engaged to her. He had suggested that he drive out with his brother and pick her up about eight o'clock.

She changed, fed the cows and the chickens, gave Lion his dinner and then opened the wardrobe in her bedroom. The kerosene lamps were lit and a sudden surge of excitement swept over her as she looked at the long rack of dresses. If only Alaric could be with her! She missed her son, but her faith in him was unshakable. Soon he would return with the estate settled and there would be all that money to invest in the farm, and a rose garden.

She laid a pale blue crêpe covered with crystal beads on the bed and decided to wear the pastel mink with it.

*

153

Moggs attached a wire and jumped back as Alaric screamed,

'The red to the yellow! No! The white to the yellow. Red to yellow could have blown us up.'

'Have no fear,' Moggs said. 'There is an unseen hand directing us!'

'I'll do what I can, but I'm not going to be here . . . when it happens. I know I'm an accomplice, and that what I'm doing is weak and cowardly . . .' Alaric shuddered as a thousand Sunday sermons concerned with honour, truth, fair play and doing the right thing crowded his mind. He stood up and turned to face the Titan.

'I can't do it!'

'Think of your mother,' Moggs said.

'I've done all I can. It's not as though I can read blasted Arabic! I've done my best – my worst, I should say.'

'Then it's ready for her!' Moggs did his shuffling, sliding dance around the clock. 'I bring her in here tomorrow, tell her this old clock was just delivered. She'll want to look it over and get me to make her ten more exactly like it. And while she's opening the door I'll . . .'

Alaric jumped. 'Please, don't touch it now!'

'We'll be across the road in the pub hoisting a jug, Alaric.' Moggs hugged him and he felt his ribs crack. 'Waiting for the fire brigade to arrive. And then a free man!'

'I still can't see why you don't leave her now? To be free, all you have to do is . . .' Alaric paused feeling that somewhere he had missed a nuance of meaning in Moggs' smokey accents.

'I shall be a free man – a widower!'

'A widower? But you *can't* be that – unless you're married.'

'I told you I was bound in servitude to her, didn't I? That means marriage where I come from, mate.'

Alaric was hugging himself with jubilation – married, Flodie had no claim to the estate: she was a Moggs, not a Morell!

154

'A night of shame, mate! I'd carried the banner that afternoon at Maroubra and she waved to me from the crowd. I can't explain to you properly what happened after that, except that she had a bottle of cherry brandy and it was hot and we were in the dunes and Flodie said she liked my hands – I couldn't tell you where my hands were when she said that. Clever hands, she said. Oh my Gawd, I was punished! She took me home and I woke up in an ormolu bed and she said I'd promised to marry her.' His voice became frenzied and he jumped around the table showering sawdust at every step. 'Chair-legs into dining-room suites – clever hands – a brass moulding into a bedstead, a marble chip into a coffee table, a –'

'Moggs! You don't have to kill her! You can get a divorce!'

'No, I can't! I have religious scruples.'

Alaric tried to push Moggs away from the clock, but they fell on each other and Alaric tripped. Reaching for a hold, he pulled open the clock door. They both flung themselves face down as a spaghetti of wires slowly trickled out, followed by the dynamite which fell with a dull plop on the floor.

Moggs looked up in disgust. 'And that is the result of an Oxford education.'

'If you want a tradition of terrorism, go to Cambridge,' Alaric retorted.

*

Confronted, Flodie tried to deny it, her bosoms heaving like buoys in a stormy sea, but Alaric pointed out that he had seen the marriage certificate in Moggs's Bible.

'Oh! You will pay for this, you little reptile!' Flodie hissed.

'Aunt Floddie, you are no longer a contender for the estate,' Alaric said firmly.

Flodie moaned.

'There are only three left now: Aunt Augustine, Aunt Honoria and my mother.'

'Ask her if she's had any exciting mail recently. You have no idea what Augustine is like and you've never met Honoria. Augustine put a trap-door spider in my knickers when I was nine. Honoria pushed me out of a dinghy in Middle Harbout and threw a pail of cat's meat after me to attract sharks. Oh, you poor deluded little dusthead, your mother will never beat my sisters. She's weak and stupid and English and they'll eat her alive if she doesn't have enough sense to get married.'

'My mother – married?' Alaric laughed at the absurdity of the suggestion.

'On the contrary, she sounds just like Betty. She'll throw in the towel and scream to us for mercy.' And then Flodie began screaming in earnest as she too remembered that night in the sand dunes and a wedding so quiet that a row of pigeons on a nearby roof were the only interested spectators.

As Alaric left the shop with his valise he felt like Hercules who had been enslaved by the Lydian queen, Omphale, and set to work spinning and singing love songs when he should have been off in search of the golden apples of the Hesperides. So it was Hercules who caught a cab out to Cremorne where Aunt Augustine was Mother Superior of an Order of Judgment nuns. With Aunt Flodie married, now he had only two women to convince that they should share the estate. He began to laugh in the taxi at the idea of his mother getting married like Aunt Betty – or anyone else for that matter. The time for those frivolities was long past so far as his mother was concerned.

*

Crockford almost collided with Tulliford as they turned into the driveway at Mockery Bend. They both had to pull abruptly to the side as the Burtons drove past with Alice on the front seat next to Fred. Allan was hanging over from the back so far that he could almost have been said to have a seat in front too. All three were laughing so loudly that they did not even notice Tulliford's convertible in amongst the wild fennel and Crockford's Mercedes at an angle against the fence.

Crockford got out and stamped with rage. He would have been there half an hour earlier had he not been forced to listen to Cavalry expound the new family law in New South Wales and women's property rights. The first thing he had done when he came home from the races was lock himself in his study and call Cavalry long-distance. The Burtons might have taken a jump on him, but Crockford knew he could put $5 on the table for every one of theirs, and if Alice Morell were smart enough to run off his cows and Tulliford's poultry and get free labour on her property from Lance Weston, she sure as hell wouldn't sell herself cheap to a Burton. The fact that Alice had taken his cows and got away with it, made Crockford salivate for her like a hungry dog. She was a bloody marvel!

Tulliford saw the lights of the Burtons' Porsche vanish over the rise and wondered why Alice had not waited for him. He realized he had neglected to speak to her about the dance, but assumed that Phyllis or one of the other women would have told her about it, and he had been quite prepared to take her. Why was he hearing what his wife Chrissie said to him half a lifetime ago? 'I could live with a thief or a liar, I wouldn't draw the line at a lecher or a drunk, but you are a bore and every minute in your company is like a rehearsal for eternity!' And that after a month, and then her name in all the papers with Alonso de Madariaga, king of the Mexican meat industry, and one of his oldest friends asking him if he had failed to get it up on the wedding night. He had not thought about Chrissie for years and yet now . . . he felt as disappointed as a child who is promised a treat and then denied it without reason.

'You should take better care of your cousin, Jos,' Crockford snarled at him. 'She shouldn't be in that car with those Burton kids.'

Every time Crockford thought of the Burton brothers they became younger, and now he could see them with scraped knees and toffee-apples.

'You know what a kid is like at the wheel of a fast car. I made a special trip out here to speak to her about those cows, only to find she's been rushed off by those two delinquents.'

He could see them now, heavy-eyed and unshaven, shooting up in a dark doorway before lurching out in pursuit of pillage and rape. As he thought about rape, he began to pound on the door of Tulliford's car.

'I intend to take every care of my cousin, Syd,' Tulliford replied coldly. 'She will be returning to England very soon and then maybe this area can settle down and be the way it was.' And as he swung the wheel and turned towards the track, he added, 'And keep your fists off my car, or I'll use mine on your face!'

When she returns to England, Crockford thought, it will be on a honeymoon as Mrs Sydney J. Crockford the Third. Both men drove to the wool-shed so lost in their dreams that they almost collided again as they parked.

Crockford's wool-shed was hung with lights and lanterns, the floor sanded and polished for the dance. The Hope's End Racing Club liked to think it maintained its dinkum Aussie traditions by using the wool-shed, but this also meant that the dance was held on Crockford's property and no one had a greater sense of personal property and who should be invited to use it than Sydney Crockford. As people said, Crockford never spent a dollar unless he got two back, and over the years he had made an invitation to this dance as prized as a free pass to the Black and White Ball.

In her bedroom Crystal was trying to blot her mascara with Phyllis's help, but she couldn't feel her eyelids. As Crystal moaned, Phyllis felt thrills of rapture running up from her toes: she was here in Crystal Crockford's pink and beige bedroom, sitting in front of a dressing-table that was covered with photos of governors and politicians, knights and minor aristocrats. If only she could go to the phone and casually tell her daughter in Canberra that she was helping Crystal to dress – Crystal Beale, you know?

'Let me tell you about Sydney Crockford when I met him, Phyllis. He had nothing except money – Sydney J. Crockford the Third! His grandfather ran the biggest two-up game in the western districts, and his father was into S.P. bookmaking before he went into politics and really found out where the money was. But my father was governor of South Australia, I am a Beale. Tonight I am going to wear the dress that I wore when I was wearing myself out on Sydney J. Crockford's behalf in London at the Embassy Ball last April when . . .' and she almost slid off her stool.

'I'd go easy on the valium if I were you, Crystal,' Phyllis said as she propped Crystal upright.

'It's a Hardy Amies model – the pink taffeta. Oh, Phyllis, I wish we'd been friends years ago!' Crystal said, and began to cry, again smudging her mascara.

Alice's entrance was an even greater sensation than at the races. All the women had shaken out ball-gowns and were stiff with satin and pleated silk. When Crystal arrived she was wearing long white gloves which she had dragged over her elbows like mail armour. Three valiums and a fifth of vodka later, she felt ready to confront Alice on the dance floor, but as soon as she saw her she was defeated. Phyllis kept telling her to calm down, not to worry, that Syd was all right and had never had a notion more romantic than a stock merger in his head, but Crystal could only shake her head in disbelief and wonder why she could not feel her tears if indeed she were crying. Her whole face was numbly frozen, all she could do was hope she was smiling.

Lance was standing directly behind Phyllis and pinching her bottom when Alice arrived with a Burton on either arm. She shimmered across the floor in blue and silver and as she passed, the crystal beading of her dress sounded a

159

thousand small chimes. Phyllis felt her backside would drop off if Lance pinched any harder, but she flexed for more and winked at him over her shoulder. Lance's little beady eyes were like a ferret's demented with lust after it has cleaned out a rabbit-hole.

The band began and Phyllis saw Alice smile at her escorts and walk towards her.

'Phyllis, would you mind very much if I had the first dance of the evening with your husband?'

Alice did not know the local customs, but she did remember that on servants' night the lady of the manor always had the first dance with the butler. Aunt Penelope had always said it was more important to have a handy butler in the house than a good cook.

'It would be my pleasure, Alice,' Phyllis replied and pushed Lance forward. He almost fell at Alice's feet, but she guided him on to the floor and – with a few discreet nudges and one deft kick – kept him off her dress and silver sandals.

Tulliford thought it was one of the most humiliating experiences of his life: his cousin dancing with that little creep, Weston, whom he had proposed for the Club and who had undoubtedly made a bundle by running a doped horse. And what could people assume from that except that he was in on it? Everything stemmed from Alice Morell – she had arrived in the area like a noxious weed and now she was choking the life out of the whole country. He decided to have a few words with Fred Burton, who was leaning against the door in a white tuxedo and staring at Alice. Crockford had already taken Allan aside and was glaring up at him, his bald freckled head dark with rage.

Alice did her best to talk to Lance, but it was as though he had suddenly been struck dumb. He still could not believe it. He – Lance Weston – dancing with the most gorgeous woman in Australia in the most exclusive wool-shed in New South Wales. And all the silver-tails were standing around envying him: Crockford and those tailor's dummies, the Burtons, and especially Mr Righteous-

160

Public-Spirited-Tulliford, our next Senator. Well, now it was Tulliford on the short end of the stick, Tulliford who had missed the boat and was up the river without a paddle Triumph was confusing Lance a little, but Phyllis could feel his jubilation and rejoiced with him as she danced sedately with a lean stockbroker from Newcastle.

Three dances later, Crockford had Alice on the floor and within thirty seconds had proposed to her.

Alice wanted to laugh, but she had been taught never to mock a man in his cups. Dear little Mr Crockford – he had been so understanding about the cows.

'Alice, I'm putting it to you straight. Crystal and I have come to the parting of the ways and I want to marry *you*.'

'Dear Mr Crockford, it's such an honour . . . that I shall have to give it great thought.'

She knew that when he was sober he would have forgotten all about it, and that if he did remember then he would be everlastingly grateful to her for pretending the incident had never occurred. She wondered when Joseph Tulliford would ask her to dance, but that was the only disappointment of the evening. He had stood there watching her and glowering like the villain in a pantomime. When she smiled at him, he deliberately looked away and frowned at a limp potted palm. Finally, she walked over to him at supper and asked why he seemed so upset. It was then that he learned of the perfidy and lowdown cunning of the Burtons and decided that the time was long overdue for someone to take the starch out of their fancy frills. The sight of them in ruffled shirts was making him feel ill, and one of them was even wearing white shoes like a ballet dancer. Their very appearance was an affront to decency. When Alice Morell was safely back in England with her son, where they both belonged, he would straighten out the neighbourhood and the Burtons with it.

*

In Sydney, Cavalry Barnhouse was making some fast calculations. It now seemed that there were only two heirs left to

161

the estate. He was quite certain that Crockford would marry Alice Morell; he had never known anything to deter that little bald-headed bullet once it was set on target. So, Flodie was married – that had surprised him – leaving only Augustine and Honoria. But if either one died, then he would have to relinquish control of the Tulliford estate. He crumpled the sheet of yellow paper and threw it across the room. Fafnir the dragon was stirring on his gold horde, jets of steam curling from his great nostrils, and all around people trembled. Then Cavalry laughed and three typists in the outer office fainted.

Chapter Eight

Alaric had never seen walls so high. They loomed over his head like a fortress or a penitentiary. And the only entrance seemed to be a tiny porthole in a heavy oak gate. There was a bell chain. He pulled it and waited, listening as the sound echoed off into silence.

Twice he spoke to an unseen face on the other side of the gate, twice pleaded that he had urgent business with his Aunt Augustine, and twice the door of the little portal was slammed on his fingers. He went back to his hotel and tried phoning, but no matter what he said there was the same cold response as though the words were being measured from a medicine spoon: 'Mother Augustine is in retreat and can see no one.'

Alaric fumed – it was cowardly for anyone to retreat for as long as his aunt. He wished he could recover the spirit of Hercules, but he felt more like a blind Tiresias. He decided to try to force his way into the convent. Having taken a course in mountain climbing in the Pennines when he was a student, he did not think a convent wall would provide too much of an obstacle.

As he was trying to get a toehold, he looked up and saw that the top of the wall was set with an artistic arrangement of broken bottles. He was hanging there for a moment, at a loss whether to climb higher or jump down, when he felt his left foot supported and held and looked down into the grinning face of a policeman who was obligingly providing him with a hand hoist. The policeman laughed and shook his head as Alaric scrambled down.

'Believe me, mate, you won't find a damn thing over those walls!'

Alaric coughed and tried to explain his purpose, but the policeman continued, 'Don't believe the stories you've heard about nuns – I was taught by them and they're a mean, narrow-minded bunch of great women!'

Alaric was blushing and knew it.

The policeman was middle-aged, with a paunch hanging over his belt and tight crinkled ears. When his hand fell on Alaric's shoulder he felt his knees sag.

'Son, I want you to listen to me real good now. I can see you're a Pom – and I know they start you late over there – but what you want to understand is that your feelings are natural.'

'I would hope so,' Alaric said faintly.

'You're not gay, are you?' the policeman asked roughly.

'Good heavens, no!'

'That's what I thought. Because if I thought you were a fucking fairy, I would kick you from here to the nearest lock-up. No, I can see you're a normal backward kid, so I have some advice for you. Go down to North Bondi and head for the rocks – it's topless there. Go right round the rocks and it's the full job.'

'Indeed?' Alaric said, wondering if this was indeed a policeman or a tout for the Sirens who lured men with their sweet song and then ate them.

'But, if you have a few bob, I would advise you to try the Marie Rose Motel off McLeay Street. A very refined place. My boy, a night there would set you up as a man and you wouldn't be trying to climb any more convent walls.'

163

'Thank you, officer,' Alaric said as the policeman walked off, muscles and fat rippling under his blue shirt.

Alaric was baffled. Nobody would answer his phone calls save in curt monosyllables. He had not even spoken to his aunt, and always in his mind were Flodie's threats and warnings. He knew his mother was partial to chocolates – and what about letter bombs? By now he had seen enough of his aunts to appreciate that they were homicidal maniacs, and he knew his mother to be as helpless, trusting and guileless as a cocker spaniel puppy. The walls frowned down at him, the gate remained closed, and he stamped up and down to the opposite pavement wondering what magic words opened it.

Alaric was just about to return to the warmth of his hotel (an insidious cold wind had taken up residence at the convent gates) when a taxi pulled in and a small, pretty girl got out slowly and put a large suitcase on the kerb. She smoothed her plaid skirt, adjusted the comb in her long fair hair and reluctantly paid the cab driver his fare. Then she walked up to the gate, paused and sighed, walked away, stopped again, looked up at the walls and sighed once more.

In five seconds Alaric was beside her.

'Excuse me.' He tried to pick up her suitcase, but she snatched it from him and seemed about to scream.

'Oh please, don't be afraid, I'm Mother Augustine's nephew.'

As introductions go, Alaric felt that it was rather like saying he was Dracula's brother, but the girl was looking thoughtfully at him. She had never heard of muggers looking or sounding like this. His blond hair curled over his ears and his eyes reminded her of a favourite movie star whose name slipped her mind.

'I really don't think it's good for either of us to be standing here in the cold, Miss . . .', Alaric hesitated, but she did not.

'Can't we find somewhere warmer than this?' she asked, 'Somewhere we can talk – and get to know each other?'

164

When Tulliford rode over to Mockery Bend the next day with Blaze on a leading rein, he thought at first that the racing club was conducting a meeting on his cousin's front veranda. The Burton boys were sitting on the steps drinking tea with an elegance which disgusted him, Crockford was expatiating on the care of dairy cows and wondering when he could get a chance to ask Alice if she had made up her mind about his proposal. He knew women did not think as fast as men and was quite prepared to give her a little time.

Alice seemed delighted to see Tulliford and insisted on taking Blaze round to the stable, but Crockford and the Burtons appeared to have received an unseen signal and just drifted off. Tulliford was building up to a cold rage and they all knew about the Tulliford temper. What enraged him more than anything else was Lion. One of the Burtons had tied a ribbon round his neck, and there was the best working dog in New South Wales swanking about with a blue satin bow behind his ear. It was revolting!

'Have you heard from your son, Alice?' he asked.

'Yes, and it's such wonderful news. He's trying to make an appointment to see Augustine – she's the nun – and once she has agreed to share the estate, that only leaves Honoria and he'll have accomplished everything. Oh Joseph, he's such a brilliant boy, so energetic and resourceful. No wonder those Burton lads made a point of getting to know him at Oxford.'

'From what I hear tell of the way they spent their time at Oxford, I doubt if they were meeting your boy, Alice.'

'Rubbish! I showed them his picture just now and they recognized him immediately.'

Tulliford felt that he should acquaint his cousin with a few facts of bush life.

'Alice, those boys are trying to get off with you.'

She was puzzled for a moment, then laughed. 'Of course they are. Boys of that age always flirt with older women.'

165

'You're encouraging them?'

'Yes, a little. It's great fun, you know, but it does seem to upset Mr Crockford. He proposed to me last night,' she added absently, stroking Blaze's nose.

'He *what*?' Tulliford felt the whole country around him was exploding in madness.

'Such a funny little man!'

'Crockford has never had a reputation with women. He's only interested in making money!'

'Ah, perhaps that's why he keeps telling me how much money he has. Money is such a boring subject, isn't it?' And here Alice sighed.

There had been a fixed point and somehow Tulliford intended to find his way back to it.

'I'm going to arrange for you to leave here, Alice.'

Suddenly she rounded on him, her voice cracking with anger.

'How dare you try to force me out! I have a right to this property, and my son is going to ensure that it becomes mine! You may think you're being kind to me, Joseph, but your cruelty is enough to break my heart. This is going to be my farm. Already I have a herd of cows and some of the best chickens in the area. I am making a living – and when the estate is settled, this will be the finest property in New South Wales. I shall have roses and there will be swans on the stream and peacocks in the front garden. I can already see what this place will be when Alaric comes back!'

Tulliford had wanted to respond when she spoke of his chickens and Crockford's cows, but there was a terrifying intensity about her dream which silenced him.

Within the moment she was downcast and appealing: 'Do forgive me for speaking so heatedly. If my Aunt Matilda could have heard me, she would never have forgiven me for raising my voice.'

Tulliford had lost his fixed point once more and doubted whether he would ever be able to find it again.

'You don't fit in here, Alice. I don't think you're right for this place.'

166

He remembered what his father had once said about 'morels' – that they were a kind of mushroom. But whereas the mushrooms of meadows and woods rose up with the morning sun and died at noon, the morels endured for ever in the ground, poisoning the earth.

'Why do you dislike me so much?' Her hand was on his arm and he felt an aching pain across his chest.

'Because . . . I *don't* dislike you, Alice. I just know that what you're doing here is not feasible, and that you make people do strange things. And half the time I don't know what you're saying, and I can't believe I'm hearing myself when I answer you.' It was a long speech for a Tulliford and that, too, he felt was a sign of the effect she was having on him.

Lance drove up then, with his hopeless passion and a large tray of bedding geraniums. Tulliford left them planting by the front steps and decided that Alice needed live-in help at Mockery Bend before she returned to England. He considered her chances of inheriting the estate to be as wild and improbable as fountains of water in the Nullabor. He nodded to the postman as he drove past the gate and noticed that everything was being delivered to the front steps these days.

The postman winked and shouted, 'They're sending her chocolates by mail now!' and held up a large gift-wrapped box.

*

Alaric could not think of any warmer place than his hotel room, and there was no warmer spot in the room than the bed. He found out her name after they had made love.

'I thought I had a vocation,' Bernice said.

'Oh, but you have,' Alaric breathed and they fell into another Lydian clutch.

'You could have been a classical scholar – I've never known anyone pick it all up so quickly,' said Alaric, and this time she showed him that a Thessalonian thrust could be improved upon.

167

'Why? Why did you ever want to be a nun?'

'I'm not sure,' Bernice said as she shook her hair out of her eyes. 'I guess I was never sure whether I wanted to be a nun or a key punch operator.'

They talked and Bernice finally understood why it was imperative that Alaric should see his aunt.

'Yeah, I kind of felt that way about my mother,' Bernice said. 'You get so damned sorry for them when they're old, and do you know what it costs to put them away in a half-way decent home these days?'

It came to Alaric as an inspiration, as though the god Hermes had fired his mind with a strange vision. Afterwards he realized it might have come about when they were measuring each other by tongue lengths in bed and arrived at the sticky conclusion that they were exactly the same height.

'You couldn't!' Bernice squeaked. 'We – we're different!'

'But the clothes . . .' said Alaric.

'Oh, Jesus Christ!' screamed Bernice and rolled over and over in bed.

'I think,' said Alaric, 'that *you* should think very seriously indeed about this vocation of yours. I mean, I have heard that once in they nail you to the floorboards, so to speak.'

'I could be a key punch operator,' Bernice hesitated.

'I think you should go and stay with my Aunt Betty in Killara and see what family life is like. You said you were an only child, Bernice.'

'Well, maybe . . .'

'I'll pay for your ticket and when I've settled this estate business with my aunt, we'll try a slightly more exotic form of the Lydian clutch.'

Bernice's eyes were narrowed and she was panting slightly. 'Show me now, and it's a deal!'

*

Alaric found it difficult to walk in heels at first, but he was

168

quite used to wearing skirts from all his experience in school and college plays. His fair hair and pale complexion had made him the obvious choice for every part from Desdemona to Titania, while as Cassandra he had been a sensation. He knocked at the little portal, then pulled at the bell chain. He was so intent on listening to the bell that he did not notice the portal open. The gate seemed to swing on oiled and silent hinges and Alaric fell back with a stifled scream – but it was only a tall, white-robed nun who took him by the elbow and yanked him inside. Ahead, he saw a Gothic mansion set behind dark cypress and yew with spiked turrets and narrow, recessed windows. The nun jerked him along as he stumbled in his heels on the gravel path.

'You are late, Sister Bernice. Mother Augustine has no time for the tardy, and there is only repentance for the reluctant of spirit.'

When he finally stood before Mother Augustine of the Order of Divine Judgment, Alaric felt that he was looking into the eyes of the Sphinx without the saving ingenuity of Oedipus. There was no brightness in her eyes, their sombre darkness seemed to draw all light from the room and extinguish it. As he looked up, he felt as though he were being drawn irresistibly into a pit of steel ashes where many souls had died in unutterable torment. The whole room seemed to be filled with the echoing shadows of their cries.

He had dressed hurriedly in the long brown robe of a novice and had gratefully put on a pair of rope sandals. Mother Augustine looked down and began reading his records. She looked up and smiled thinly.

'I am gratified to see that we are not going to have any difficulties with hair, sister.'

Nervously, Alaric tried to push a short curl back under his wimple.

'I'm very sorry, Mother. I did mean to have a haircut –'

'It is the approved length, sister. The last novice we had here complained and I had to shave her myself. Hair is a vanity.'

She sat back and contemplated Alaric with the faintest gleam of approval in her ashen eyes.

'Now, Sister, you may have heard that our rule here is strict?'

Alaric murmured, *'Is ordo vitio careto, caeteris specimen esto* – let this order be free from vice and an example to others.'

Mother Augustine half-rose from her chair with a gasp of pleasure. 'Latin! You have the sacred tongue! But I did not see this anywhere in your records, Sister Bernice.'

Alaric bowed his head lower and tried to recall what it felt like when he was a first-former being dressed down by a senior prefect for spitting in the holy water font.

'Humility – the first sign of grace,' and Mother Augustine smiled and sighed. 'No doubt you've heard of my trials and tribulations with the bishop – a worldly man. As for the cardinal, the less we speak of him the better. He wants to investigate my rule here. And can we find hope in the Holy Father – alas! The sad permissiveness, the spirit of satanic anarchy that now prevails within the Church appalls me. But Satan will never govern within these walls – *is ordo vitio careto* – yes, and when providence ordains, which will not be long now, I shall take all my sisters to a place of purity.'

She paused abruptly and pushed a box of peppermint creams across her desk to Alaric.

'Would you care for a peppermint cream, Sister? They are of my own making – the manufacture of chocolates is a small source of revenue for the Order.'

Alaric looked down at the glossy little chocolates and shivered. 'I – thank you – I feel . . . chocolates are an indulgence.'

Mother Augustine slowly closed the box. 'Excellent, Sister. Conquer the appetite and you have won a victory in Satan's kingdom. We had a sister here last year who developed a passion for chocolates,' she sighed heavily. 'In greed she lived, from greed she died.'

Alaric murmured faintly, *'Requiescat in pace.'*

Augustine wagged an admonishing finger, 'Ah, but she won't, sister. She is burning now in intolerable torment. We can take comfort in that thought. There will be less temptation when I take my Order from this place to Mockery Bend.'

Alaric could not help but look up suddenly.

'You may well be surprised, my child. But I intend to make a place called Mockery Bend the site of a new Order. And when I have thirty million, let any bishop or cardinal try to give me orders!'

She slammed the palm of her hand on the desk and the whole room seemed to shake.

'I,' she said slowly, 'have received my instructions from God. To found a new Order far from the city and the ways of men. *Valet anchora virtus . . .*'

Alaric finished the quotation for her; '*Fides servanda est.*'

Mother Augustine leaned back in her chair and felt strangely moved by this young novice. She could not recall ever having been drawn to a sister so strongly. But she knew it was the Latin – the bond of the sacred tongue between them. With training, she would put Sister Bernice at her right hand, and one day she might tell her of the blessed events which led her to become Mother Superior at the early age of thirty-seven. By act of God, when only a novice, she had been set to work in a hospice for the dying, and where others quailed she grew in strength and grace. It was extraordinary how many of the aged whom she nursed with such tenderness insisted on changing their wills and leaving their entire fortunes to her. She smiled reflectively, and Alaric felt that the Sphinx was flexing its claws and licking its chops.

'Do you know that I taught myself Latin as a small child in order to read the Holy Fathers?'

Alaric tottered off to his cell and dreamed all night that he was tied to his bed, with Aunt Augustine pushing one chocolate cream after another into his screaming mouth.

*

Alice was trying to comfort a shaken Crockford when Tulliford drove up in his station wagon. In the back he had a miserable, terrified pair of Greek migrants. Unlike Lance, who specialized in illegal Asians, Tulliford had applied for migrant labour and one day received a letter telling him to meet two Greek farmworkers – m. and f. (married) – at the airport. He had collected them and for a month they had buried themselves in a room at his property, barely eating, and covering their heads whenever he tried to speak to them. He finally decided to see if Alice could find out what was wrong with them, and if she was able to do so, she could have them. He also liked the thought of her having some protection in the house, with the Burtons making constant calls.

The Greeks remained in the car while Tulliford tried to work out what had happened to Crockford. At the best of times he looked as though he had been hammered together from rough lumps of wood by a jobbing carpenter; now he was lying back in a chair, rigid and with a glassy stare. Alice was just applying a cold towel to his forehead and she looked up at Tulliford with such pleasure that Jos felt a sudden desire to kiss her, but he restrained himself.

'Oh Joseph, I'm so glad you're here! Something so frightful has just happened to poor Mr Crockford!'

Crockford moaned and kicked his short legs feebly.

'The dear man was getting out of his car when a crow fell out of the sky and hit him.'

Tulliford leaned over and saw that there were some odd scratches on Crockford's bald head.

'A crow,' Tulliford said heavily, wondering why everything seemed to shift off balance whenever he met Alice.

Crockford sat up, bristling, 'You heard what she said, Jos! A bloody great dead crow landed on my head. It almost knocked me out cold!'

Tulliford shook his head and tried to remember when Syd Crockford had ever made a joke or even showed the faintest glint of humour. He walked to the edge of the

172

veranda and asked if anyone had set out baits for crows. All around the house there were dead crows and Lion was just investigating one. He smelled it, then backed away, whining.

'Yes, you can see them,' Alice said. 'It's extraordinary.'

'Anybody setting poison?' Tulliford asked.

'No,' said Alice. 'I'd just fed my chickens and I brought a box of chocolates out here on the veranda. I knew there'd be people dropping in this afternoon, and I thought we could all have chocolates with our tea. Well, the next thing the cows were out and Lion and I had to go and bring them back, and when we looked at the chocolate box – it was empty.'

'Crows. They'll eat anything,' Tulliford said.

'But it couldn't have been the chocolates. Look, there's the box – it came from Sydney, so I'm sure Alaric sent them to me. He knows I have a sweet tooth.'

Tulliford decided that if he thought about it, his reason would be seriously affected. Crockford was still moaning about his head when Jos asked Alice if she could make use of a couple of Greek farmworkers.

Alice looked down at the station wagon and saw the pair holding on to each other and praying.

Instantly, she ran down to them and flung open the door of the wagon. Tulliford decided this was an appropriate time to have a short word with Crockford.

'Syd, what's this I'm hearing about your proposing marriage to my cousin? Seems to me you have a wife already.'

'It's a lie.' Syd sat up and wiped his face with the towel.

'I heard you'd been doing some fast talking to Cavalry Barnhouse.'

'That's the truth. I've just been rearranging some of my assets.'

Crockford was no fool and he had been genuinely alarmed when Barnhouse told him of divorce settlements that required property to be split right down the middle, fair and square. He had therefore ordered Crystal a new mink, promised her a vacation in California, and while she was recovering from her face-lift with valium and vodka, had requested she sign a few odds and ends. He hoped that by the end of the month he would satisfactorily have re-arranged his estate in such a way that Crystal would be dividing one small corner with him. He knew how to lie low while negotiating take-overs, and when it was expedient to go private, and he did not mention to anyone save Barn-house that he was going to make Alice his wife.

He was just about to make a few general comments on rumours and gossip in a place like Hope's End, when Alice came up to the house speaking Greek to two voluble and excited Cretans. She ushered them inside and emerged a little later, laughing.

'Oh Joseph, those two poor souls have been terrified of you! They thought they were being sent to an internment camp. What *did* you say to them?'

'I didn't say anything.'

'Well, but how could you expect them to understand English if you couldn't speak Greek?'

The logic of this escaped Tulliford, but he noted bitterly that Crockford was nodding his head and beaming approval at Alice.

She explained that she had been sent to a finishing school in Corfu run by a certain Reverend Felix Rabbits and his wife. It was cheaper than Switzerland, and it did mean that Aunt Matilda could say her niece was being finished in Europe.

Ten minutes later the woman came out with a tray of tea, while her husband was out collecting the dead crows and piling them in a mound to be burned. It seemed to Alice that there was a dead crow for every chocolate in that box she had left on the veranda.

*

Alaric did not find the routine of the convent difficult after Eton. Bells rang for compulsory prayers and the nuns were expected to spend a great deal of their time in silent meditation. Shaving was a problem, but Alaric was very fair and had a downy beard that only required attention every three or four days. When that was necessary, he crawled into a closet and attacked himself with a dry razor by the small flame of a cigarette lighter. The difficulty was with some of the other novices, two of whom seemed drawn to him and kept trying to sit next to him at mealtimes. Once he caught Mother Augustine's approving eye when he deliberately changed places to avoid sitting next to Sister Paula.

He did not know how to speak to his aunt about the estate without revealing his identity. There were moments when the ashen pits of her eyes seemed to glow; then he thought of her chocolates and how a succession of unexpected deaths in the Order had allowed her to become Mother Superior when most nuns had barely finished a novitiate. If she was the Sphinx, then he must fathom her riddle as Oedipus had done.

Washing seemed a perfunctory affair, done in a bowl in one's cell, and Alaric had occasionally found himself reminded of the warm, pungent animal odour of an English public school in winter. Then, briefly at breakfast, Mother Augustine announced that all sisters would be required to assemble in the shower room immediately after vespers, and to bring their own towels.

Alaric was petrified and began to shiver as they made their way down a dark, slippery corridor to a concrete cellar with one shower stall lit by a bare electric globe.

Sister Paula had wriggled next to him and whispered, 'Oh, sweet Jesus, there's no hot water!'

There was only one tap for the shower and the temperature of the cellar was that of a meat freezer. After intoning a prayer, Mother Augustine disrobed and stood under the shower, soaping herself vigorously. She did not flinch as the icy water bounced off her firm flesh and, while murmuring the litany of the saints, Alaric could not help observing out of the corner of his eye that Mother Augustine had the form of a ripe Juno.

The older nuns followed, cringing and bleating as they soaped and rinsed, then stood blue and spastic with cold against the colder wall.

Mother Augustine seemed impervious to the elements. Contemptuously, she raked the novices with an ashy stare, saying, 'The flesh is the enemy – the flesh tempts – the flesh corrupts. Therefore, we must punish and subdue the flesh. We must learn to enjoy the rigour of icy water on our vile bodies. Next to flagellation, there is nothing better for the spirit than cold showers in winter. It is our duty to demonstrate the triumph of spirit over flesh. Sister Paula, to the shower!'

Alaric glanced wildly around him, but there was no hiding place. Each nun in turn had to stand under that shower in the unwinking glare of the single globe.

Sister Paula dropped her robe and stepped shaking under the spray. As the water struck, she screamed and began to shake and jerk with the agony of cold, her breasts swinging to escape the water, nipples like small iced grapes.

Mother Augustine's voice rose to a scream of fury,

'Do not display yourself, Sister Paula! You are exulting in your body! You are deliberately cavorting in a passion of lust! Lower your eyes, Sisters, from this spectacle of infirmity. Here is our sister glorying in the profanity of her jerking limbs dancing to the command of Satan. Lust! The demon of lust is devouring her!'

Sister Paula fell out of the shower and was bundled into her robe by one of the older nuns. Mother Augustine stood over her like a pillar of cold righteousness, the exterminator of all forms of carnal knowledge. Hysterical and trying to wipe soap from her eyes, Sister Paula was begging forgiveness, imploring understanding for her weakness.

Mother Augustine smiled grimly and ordered a penance of thirty days without blankets on her bed. She was impatient of restrictions placed on her authority by priests and generally took confessions herself. As Sister Paula crouched sobbing against the wall, she turned to Alaric.

Alaric took a deep breath and tried to remember shower

176

nights at Eton – how you occasionally had to protect yourself from playful attacks by older boys, and what the arts of towel fighting were. With one swift movement, he dropped the robe and wrapped the towel around his waist; then he stepped into the shower with the cry of 'Deus id vult!' 'It is the will of God!' – the mighty shout of the Crusaders as they besieged Jerusalem.

Standing with his back turned to them, his words still ringing round the cellar, he turned on the shower. Alaric did not flinch but soaped himself vigorously, thankful that the cold had shrunk everything to less than normal size. Then, with a swooping glide which would have done credit to Sally Rand, he retrieved the towel, covered himself and slipped the robe over his head. He had seen old ladies getting in and out of bathing costumes on the beach and knew the technique.

Mother Augustine was exultant! Here was her disciple! Her chosen one! She turned to the nuns, who were now so deaf with cold that it was with difficulty they heard even her clarion tones.

'I have never said this before of any Sister, but of our beloved Sister Bernice, I feel a new glory has entered our Order. Humility, modesty, an absence of all vanity – and she despises her fleshly body.'

The nuns tottered off to their cells, but Mother Augustine motioned to Alaric to stay. She could not explain what she had felt when she watched Sister Bernice under the shower except that . . . she had been stirred.

'Sister Bernice, you may come and pray with me in my cell tonight.'

'I am not worthy,' Alaric whispered.

'No, but you may prove to be so,' Mother Augustine said firmly and gently. 'You will read to me from blessed St Boethius.'

Mother Augustine lay stretched on her bed like a medieval saint, with her hands folded in prayer upon her chest. Alaric knelt beside the bed and, despite the cold, was almost beginning to enjoy the sonorous periods of Boethius as he spoke of the virtues of abstinence and the joys of continence.

Mother Augustine opened one eye and looked at him. 'We shall continue our spiritual exercises through the night, Sister.'

She may have sensed a declining fall in Alaric's voice, because she motioned for him to approach the bed.

'You may share my bed in sisterly devotion. Continue reading.'

Alaric climbed awkwardly into the bed and lay next to his aunt. Her body glowed with a furnace heat and he found that he was getting comfortably warm. As he read, Mother Augustine murmured responses in excellent Latin. Alaric admired her accent as he turned the page and read on.

'The light is upon my eyes and not upon the page, Sister. Adjust it accordingly.'

A small reading lamp was against the wall and as Alaric continued reading (it was a particularly interesting passage with a fine example of the ablative absolute) he reached across his aunt to adjust it. Suddenly she stiffened and Alaric thought he had startled her with a sudden glare from the reading light. He tried to move it closer to the wall and she stiffened, her eyes like vast glowing cinder pits.

'Your hands! They are both above the covers!'

Alaric acknowledged that they were and then realized that a part of him had responded to the warmth of his aunt's body.

He flung himself over to the edge of the bed and tried to think of cold showers, syphilis and sharp kicks in the groin at football. But nothing could restrain the arrow of Eros once it had found a target.

'I felt you touch me, but I *saw* your hands,' Mother Augustine said in muted frenzy.

'I – I couldn't help it! I'm trying, but I can't control it! Sometimes it happens at the most awkward moments – when one's dancing or at the pictures, often when one's asleep.'

Mother Augustine sat bolt upright in bed and glared at

178

Alaric. Then she held out her arm and pointed to his private part. 'Satan! Get thee behind me!'

Alaric blanched. 'Mother Augustine, I couldn't. Not with a woman!'

'You – you're not a sister,' she hissed.

Alaric bowed his head. 'I'm your nephew, Alaric.'

'Worse than Satan,' Mother Augustine shrilled.

She looked wildly around the cell and seemed about to scream so Alaric flung himself on top of her, clamping a hand across her mouth.

'If you scream, Aunt Augustine, I shall tell the whole convent that you deliberately smuggled me in here to satisfy your lust.'

'Lust!' Augustine went deathly pale and began to struggle. She was a powerful woman and even though Alaric tried to imagine he was in a football scrum, still she managed to pin him to the bed. Her face was close to his and he felt her hot breath.

'Do you think you can frighten me with a threat like that? I survived my sisters. That should be proof enough that I was under divine protection. I have my faith –'

'And your reputation, which will be in shreds. Who do you think the bishop will believe? I can get an excellent reference from my college chaplain. I have a confirmation certificate. I was a choir-boy until I was twelve. I –'

'The bishop!' Augustine groaned and heaved the full weight of her body down upon him. Alaric fought, managed to slide out and, by hooking his leg round her thigh, land on top once more.

Gasping, he said, 'This could be a secret for ever. I could leave the convent tomorrow . . .'

Augustine seemed to breathe her assent to this suggestion.

'Provided,' Alaric said slowly, 'provided that you sign a legal waiver to Mockery Bend. It's here in the Boethius – between the *Iamne igitur uides quid* and *Firmis medium uiribus occupate.*'

'Give up my inheritance?' Augustine moaned.

179

'To my mother.'

'How do you know she's alive? Doesn't she eat chocolates?'

'Listen to me carefully, Aunt Augustine. If you don't sign this waiver, I shall start screaming for help, and when all the Sisters arrive I shall tell them that you wanted me to commit vile and unnatural acts.'

'I'll defy you!'

Alaric's face was very close to Augustine's now, their lips almost touching.

'I shall make a special point of telling the bishop how you wanted me to . . . to get . . . behind you!'

Augustine sighed and asked for a pen. Alaric was about to climb out of bed when she grabbed him by the ankle and they began to wrestle again.

All through the convent the screams and cries echoed, while the nuns prayed that the spiritual exercises would not be too exhausting for their beloved Mother and young Sister Bernice. They listened for the whip and the whining rhythm of flagellation and rejoiced when they heard a mounting scale of moans rise to a crescendo of two piercing screams – screams which were repeated again and again through the night.

Alaric could barely walk as he tottered to the gate of the convent. He would have liked to forget the whole night, but he felt as though he had had long and passionate intercourse with the hydra. One moment he was being strangled, the next he was being tickled into a delirium of ecstasy. At the gate he wondered if he had energy enough to pull back the bolt. As he mustered his last remaining strength, there was a violent pounding on the other side, accompanied by muffled shouts. The wooden planking shuddered and he realized that someone was trying to beat it down, or open.

He reached up and loosed the bolt. The door swung wide and Bernice almost fell in.

'You are in my way,' she said coldly and picked up her bag.

180

Alaric was still dazed. 'I thought you were at my Aunt Betty's?'

Bernice's words came out in a torrent: 'Oh, I found my vocation all right! I *want* to be a nun! I never want to see a kid again as long as I live!'

She started up the path, then stopped.

'And let me tell you what's wrong with being a key punch operator. Key punch operators get married!'

She ran up to the convent shouting at the top of her voice, 'Mother Augustine! Mother Augustine! I'm here! I want to come in! Please! Please let me in!'

Chapter Nine

Cavalry Barnhouse brooded over the news like one of the larger granite eagles in the lobby. Damn that snowy-haired, sissy-looking kid! He had watched him winkle out of the office with his bum waving an invitation to the world and felt sure that Gerda would beat him into the ground with a nudge of a niblick. But Gerda was dead, and Flodie was married. How could he not have known that? There were no secrets of the Morells to which he was not privy, no plots by sister against sister that he had not watched and sometimes discreetly encouraged. Barnhouse had studied the Morells ever since he read the Tulliford will at his father's elbow, and he thought he knew every crease and wrinkle of their lives. But one dead, one married and now Augustine had signed a waiver. And the kid had gone straight to a local solicitor and had it notarised. My God! It was like walking across your own lawn in the calm of the early morning and being attacked by a ferocious dandelion!

The will was as precious to Barnhouse as habeas corpus – an expression of justice, a confirmation of all his faith in law to make money at the expense of and despite clients. And now, there were only two heirs. Honoria . . . yes, he could rely on her. He leaned back in his chair and stared up at the fresco on his ceiling of Moses receiving the tablets of the law from God. He had managed to stall Crockford with his crazy notion of marrying Alice Morell. What was going on up there at Mockery Bend? Barnhouse had taken him through the new family law clause by clause, he had told his staff to move slowly on the transfer of assets, but Crockford was like a man who has just sprinkled cocaine on his corn-flakes.

The thought of there being no Morells left to inherit the estate filled Barnhouse with horror, as though that young blond, pruney-voiced kid was dragging him remorselessly into a Götterdammerung. The gold would be torn from him, the fortune snatched from his control! He would personally have to see to it that Alice Morell remained single and that Honoria fixed the nosey kid once and for all.

Alaric met Moggs at a small pub in Paddington, where they shared a beer and a large quantity of curried prawns. The shaggy Titan had been making inquiries about Honoria and it seemed that she travelled around a good deal, but she was now in her favoured spot – a small flat in Kettle Street, Redfern. Alaric pulled out a Gregory's and located the street without difficulty, as Moggs shook his head and a small dusting of sawdust fell into his beer.

'The beast was cackling about it, Alaric. She said Honoria was the smartest of them all, with an honours degree in philosophy from Sydney University.'

Alaric did not feel that Moggs would appreciate his views on colonial institutions of higher learning, so he simply asked, 'Has Aunt Flodie been talking to her?'

'I couldn't say. But she was laughing fit to bust on the phone to someone.' He paused. 'And you watch out for yourself too, mate!'

Honoria in Redfern, only a few hours' drive away from his mother! He could see his mother scrubbing the floor in one of those frightful smocks that Phyllis had given her, pushing a bucket of suds across the floor, oblivious to a crouching figure behind her with an axe in her gnarled hands.

'First, I think I shall call on Barnhouse and tell him what progress I've made, then I'll see Honoria and get her to sign an agreement.'

Moggs grinned over his mug. 'All I can say is, I reckon you're a bloody marvel, Al! You just seem to *make* things happen. Well, next time you hear from me, it'll be an invitation to the funeral.'

Alaric blanched.

'No, don't worry,' Moggs said as he sifted some more sawdust on to his plate. 'It'll be nothing electrical. I know where my talent lies.' His voice dropped to a husky whisper. 'I am in the process of constructing a special ceiling over the workshop. When she's next in there poking around, I pull a rope, and . . . bingo!! Four tons of scrap metal land on top of her!'

Alaric neither approved nor criticized the Titan's plan. He knew that most of the Titans, including poor Briareus of the hundred hands, had come to pretty sticky ends.

Late that afternoon, he was in Cavalry Barnhouse's office being handed a straight whiskey from a Florentine cocktail cabinet of the sixteenth century. Barnhouse was radiating a geniality that would have made every lawyer in Sydney rush for the fine print and footnotes.

'I am amazed at what you have done, my boy. Have you seriously never thought of reading law? I think I could find a place for you here in the firm. Of course, I would naturally have to consult with my partners, but –'

Alaric smiled faintly. 'Law is the last refuge of the failed scholar,' he said, quoting one of his favourite tutors at Merton. 'I simply must get this estate settled before I can get back to some serious work on Theognis.'

Perseus did not return without the Golden Fleece, Hercules brought back the golden apples of the Hesperides to Eurystheus, and he was going to save his mother from Mockery Bend and the Morells from poverty. He raised his glass and drank a quiet libation to the gods, then asked

Barnhouse about Honoria.

The solicitor was watching Alaric and regretting the abolition of the old statutes that permitted torture as a process of law.

'Honoria Morell – some would describe her as an eccentric old lady – certainly a character. Basically a charming and learned woman. You may find you have a great deal in common with her.'

'Really?' said Alaric. 'But wasn't she educated here in Sydney?'

Barnhouse's hands tightened like claws on the edge of the desk. 'Nevertheless, I think you may find her your intellectual equal, Alaric.'

Alaric was still aching from his hydra-like night with Mother Augustine and said, 'Mr Barnhouse, I have found it necessary to exercise the greatest caution when dealing with all of my aunts.'

Barnhouse had not found a weakness in Alaric yet, but he was known to be relentless when examining clients. Now his voice became dulcet, his manner one of fatherly concern.

'I am a little troubled about your feelings towards your mother. Some might say that you were suffering from an Oedipus complex.'

Alaric raised his eyebrows, finished his drink and stood up.

'Mr Barnhouse, it was Freud who conceived the idea of an Oedipus complex at the theatre as the result of an imperfect classical education. A more thorough reading of Sophocles would have taught him that the moral of the play is not to argue with old men for right of way on a narrow road, and never to ignore oracles or the gods may curse you by making you marry your mother. I have no desire to marry my mother, nor has anyone else, but as her son I have a responsibility for her welfare. Therefore, I intend to see that she is provided for.'

With $30 million, Barnhouse thought – and I bet you were the kind of kid who was pinching pennies from your

184

mother's purse when you were three. With difficulty he assembled the blocks of his face into a smile.

'I wish you the best of luck with your Aunt Honoria.'

As Alaric was ushered out, Barnhouse gave two instructions to his secretary: 'Get me a direct line to Hots Morell – and bring me the Arab file.'

*

Phyllis could not really explain the way she felt: like the uneasiness before a bout of influenza, but not a physical weakness, more of a nervous anticipation which was closer to excitement than sickness. It was as though she could sense a shivering premonition of change.

Lance shrugged and pointed to the sky. 'Some more rain coming, love.' His voice dropped and he spoke almost to himself. 'Ever since she came, it's been like a miracle, dams full, grass up to your knees.'

'No, it's more like an earthquake. I remember a couple of tremors we had when I was a kid. It was terribly still and hot, you could hear yourself breathing out, when suddenly the cat came screaming in from the yard with its fur on end and every dog in the neighbourhood started howling. The next instant all the glasses in the pub began to shake. It was over in a second, but it was queer while it lasted, Lance – very queer.'

'Never been an earthquake round here, Phyllie.'

Alaric had phoned them last night and told them that there was only one aunt left between his mother and the Tulliford estate. My God, Phyllis thought, $30 million! They had discussed the money on their way out to Alice's.

For once Crockford was not on the veranda and his absence was explained by Fred Burton. He was lying on the floor playing with Lion when they arrived, while Allan showed Alice how to plait a cowhide whip. Alice was laughing and refusing to look, saying that she never used a whip when riding or on the cattle. As they made themselves comfortable, they gathered that Crockford was bringing over another four cows to build up Alice's small herd. He

185

had gone over the milk and cheese figures with her and finally convinced her that six cows were not showing sufficient profit, whereas with ten she would be financially sound.

Lance sat watching Alice in quiet rapture, still not quite able to believe that he was sitting with the Burtons, that he had made a killing on the Hope's End Mile and no one had threatened to lynch him. It was just like the Marists said at school – you had to be in a state of grace, and he knew where that grace came from now. Phyllis wondered why Alice did not wear white more often; it made her look so young.

Fred gave Lion another friendly wrestle and sat down next to Phyllis.

'My brother and I are having a real family fight, Phyllis.'

'You two fighting? I can't believe it, Fred. I always heard the two of you shared everything.'

'Not this time,' Fred said, his handsome face puckered like that of a spoilt child.

'Not bloody likely,' Allan replied, and underneath his wide grin Phyllis could sense the same tension she had felt in the car when they were driving.

'I reckon I am on the inside track because this intelligent animal,' and Fred tweaked Lion's ear, 'this fine specimen of doghood clearly prefers me to my brother.'

As though to confound this statement, Lion immediately went over and put his paws up on Allan's lap.

'See,' said Fred, 'he's telling Allan that right now!'

'You be the judge, Phyllis. You're a publican's wife, so you must be a good judge of men. Which one of us should Alice marry?'

'Oh, I've decided that already,' Alice laughed before Phyllis could speak. 'I'm going to marry both of you, and both at the same time, with Lion to give me away.'

It all ended in a joke, with Lance insisting that neither of them were fit to clean Alice's shoes, but Phyllis could not shake off that feeling. Men think in herds and go mad in herds – but which one would recover his sanity first? Cer-

186

tainly not Lance; he had gone down to the front gate to help Crockford truck in four cows. And not the Burton boys; they had ridden off whooping and yelling, trying to shoulder each other off the track as though they were Snowy River cowboys. That only left Tulliford . . .

'You seen Jos lately, Alice?'

'Phyllis, what's wrong with him? He says he wants me to leave here, but you can see how it's all working out. I'm going to have ten cows. Jos had a miserable childhood because of the will, but neither of us is responsible for what happened so long ago. He knows how successful I am here, and he's given me so much help, yet . . . he keeps telling me to go.'

'He's in love with you, Alice, just like the rest. He's another hopeless passion.'

'No,' Alice's voice was quiet. 'It isn't hopeless. I've always dreamed of the past and it was Henry Morell there. But now I keep thinking about Joseph, and sometimes I imagine it was not Henry with me in Provençe but . . . ' Her voice faltered.

'You better talk to Alaric before you do anything rash, Alice. Mind you, I don't think Jos is the marrying kind, not after that little episode when he was a kid, but you have a remarkable effect on men.'

Alice smiled and shook her head. 'Dear me, Phyllis, you remind me of Lupin Tanner and her stories. I never argued with her because she did enjoy them so much, but we can't live in daydreams, we must accept facts. And the fact is that I feel sure Honoria will share the property with me.' Then she paused. 'And I am equally sure that Joseph Tulliford will spend the rest of his life trying to drive me away from here because of his grandfather . . . '

She faltered and started collecting the cups and plates into neat piles. Maria came bustling out and took the tray from her, scolding her.

'I used to do everything for Bessie. Now Maria and George take care of everything. I go out riding on Blaze – but Joseph hasn't been here since he brought me the horse.'

'Alice – if you had the choice, what would you do? Take the estate, or marry Joseph Tulliford?'

Alice looked at her in astonishment. 'Phyllis, what a curious question! What choice could there possibly be?'

That afternoon Tulliford stopped his car to watch the Burton boys ride past with Alice on Blaze. She was dressed in an English riding habit of black cloth that seemed of the same shining texture as Blaze's silky coat. She waved as she rode past, but Tulliford could not lift his hands from the wheel. He felt the same grinding pain across his chest and tried to shake the image of her from his mind. He was a rational man, but there seemed no way of escaping the lunacy she was spreading across the country. There was talk of Crockford divorcing his wife, the Burton brothers proposing to her and Lance Weston faithful to Phyllis. The natural order at Hope's End had been set at odds and yet, when he was with her, he felt the same strange dreaming shake his concentration and send his thoughts into perilous and delectable countries . . .

*

The taxi driver refused to take Alaric to Kettle Street, saying the neighbourhood was too rough after dark, that last time he had been there he had had a rock thrown through his back window. Only after Alaric pressed $5 into his hand as an advance tip had he been persuaded to screech to a stop outside a ramshackle block of flats, then he swung round and drove off with a smell of burning rubber joining the other rank odours of the cul-de-sac.

Alaric wondered at his Aunt Honoria choosing to live in such an area. As he stepped across the gutter, over a broken-nosed derelict, he remembered Flodie's marzipan house in Paddington and wondered why Honoria would want to live in the seediest part of Redfern. Then his heart leapt up as he beheld a pile of rotting garbage by the front steps. If she was as poor as this, she would jump at the chance of sharing the estate. Why had he been so foolish as not to see her first?

He bounded up the slimy, rank stairs with certain knowledge adding wings to his Gucci loafers. It had been an old crippled woman who begged Jason for help to cross the stream when first he set out in search of the Golden Fleece. And that old woman had been the goddess Juno in disguise, who guided and befriended him ever after. Yet even Jason, Alaric thought, would have quailed at the sight of his Aunt Honoria.

At first sight she looked like a bag lady, but there was a jaunty opulence about her rags which defied the dirt and overpowering smell of cats. Her wasp-black eyes were surrounded with peeling layers of multi-coloured mascara which gave her face the appearance of a raddled but intelligent insect. She seemed overjoyed to see Alaric and pushed him into a room where a gigantic, mangy, brindled cat sprawled across a mound of clutter that might once have been a sofa.

Alaric tried to remember how offended Jason probably was when he met the disguised Juno and smiled.

As Honoria threw back her head and laughed, her hat and a tattered red wig fell off to reveal a small head covered with a dirty mould of furze.

'Little Alaric – little Alaric from Eton and Oxford – and now he's come all this way to see his dear old Auntie!'

'Delighted to make your acquaintance, Aunt Honoria.'

'Hots. The name is Hots. Never answer to anything else. Sit down, lovie,' and she pushed the cat along the mound of old papers, rags and cardboard cartons.

Before Alaric could speak, she was hugging her knees and rocking back and forth with laughter.

'Here to arrange a settlement, eh? Forget it! But I must say,' and she put her head on one side, 'you're a real Morell. You know what morels are, don't you? Black nightshades that grow best on old coffins and broken tombs. Fancy, a pretty little boy like you bumping off Gerda!'

Alaric tried to interrupt with a full measure of justified indignation, but Hots had reached down into the mess and

189

pulled out a bottle of gin. She took a swig and offered the bottle to Alaric, who shuddered and refused.

The black eyes narrowed to glittering pinpoints as she swallowed, then pulled out a small packet of white powder and sniffed greedily. Burping and sneezing, she seemed to grow in size and vitality, and Alaric began to think less of Juno and disguise than of the witch in *Hansel and Gretel* who fed on the flesh of roasted children.

'Gerda was tough, brutal and strong. Flodie had her own way with razor blades and Augustine – my God, *she* knew more about poisons than Lucrezia Borgia. And they were all after me because I was the eldest. Now I've beaten them all – thanks to you, lovie!'

She leaned over and pinched Alaric's knee. 'I bet you've got pretty legs.'

Alaric tried to look over her head and directly at a broken mirror on the opposite wall.

'There is my mother, Hots.'

'So there is. I wonder she hasn't been blown up or poisoned by now.'

'I do not know how anybody could be so unreasonable! There is an enormous estate and all you have to do is agree to share it.'

'Share! Who says I should share anything? Let me tell you something, lovie. I am the philosopher of the family. My sisters – bright enough – but *I* had intellect. All my life I've proved that crime pays and sin wins – and vice will always be victorious. I've always done the exact opposite of what people say is good and proper and I've got a small fortune tucked away. Not thirty million, mind you, but a neat bundle. Drugs, guns . . . you name it, and I've got the goods or the contacts.'

She took another swig and another sniff from the crumpled envelope and even the cat seemed affected by the cloying sweetness of the aroma floating over its head.

'But, Hots,' Alaric was genuinely puzzled, 'if you did inherit Mockery Bend, what would you do with it?'

'Spread my gospel to the world – give every kid a gun, make dope as free as bubble-gum, and then I'd sit back here with Felix and die laughing while the children killed their parents and the world ran mad. You can think of me as Pandora, lovie. Just let me have that money and I'll open up such a box of grief that this planet will explode!'

Alaric was dumbfounded. Hots rocked back and forth, laughing, then looked at the cat which was scratching itself. She grabbed it and dropped it in Alaric's lap where it dug in, its claws ripping through his trousers and into the flesh of his thighs.

'While I get some tea, you can flea the cat. I don't mind fleas myself, but I can't stand to watch him scratch.'

Alaric hesitated and Hots grinned. 'If you want to talk settlements and negotiations, you're going to learn a lot of new things, lovie. Like learning how to flea a cat.'

Alaric bent over the cat, which began to purr and knead his legs with its claws, but he was determined that he would not leave until Hots had signed an agreement. There would be no homecoming without the Golden Fleece, no matter what ordeals he had to suffer and how many humiliations he had to endure.

Alice was in the kitchen sorting laundry with Maria when Phyllis hurtled through the door. Everything was beginning to erupt in Hope's End. Last night Crockford had pushed another document under Crystal's bobbed nose and asked her to sign it. Instead of letting him guide her hand across the dotted line, she had taken the pen and lunged at him with it. It had taken major surgery to remove the pen from his chest and now Crockford was recuperating in a hospital room in Melbourne with Crystal screaming abuse at him from the hall outside.

As Phyllis fell breathless into a chair, Maria greeted her amiably in Greek and went off with a pile of folded sheets. Phyllis had driven too fast for her own nervous well-being – her fingers still felt stiff from clutching the wheel. But at least she had got here before anyone else and so was the first with the news.

'Have you come out to tell me about poor Mr Crockford,

Phyllis? He is all right, isn't he? The postman told me this morning.'

Phyllis sighed with relief. So Alice hadn't heard the big one!

'Let me get you something to drink, dear.' Alice poured a lemonade and Phyllis threw it down her throat.

'I'm told it was an accident and that he is going to recover. Imagine falling on a ballpoint pen!'

'Then you haven't heard?' asked Phyllis.

'I just said –'

'About the fight at the Pub.'

'One day I may get a telephone here, but there is some equipment I need to buy for the dairy first.' Alice poured herself some lemonade and sat down with her friend. It was very odd how difficult it seemed to remember Morell Manor these days; even Aunt Penelope's voice had dwindled to a whisper that came to her just before she was falling asleep. And Henry had taken to wearing high boots and carrying a slouched hat.

'The fight, Alice!'

Alice apologized for wandering and prepared to concentrate, but really it was more interesting to think of the old orchard she had found by the stream than to listen to an account of some bar-room brawl.

'Fred and Allan . . . that's how it began.'

Alice sighed and said she hoped the boys had not been drinking.

'They were drinking all right and arguing over you. Then they decided that the only fair thing to do was toss a coin. Fred won and they shook hands and hoisted a few more drinks for old times' sake. I must say that Allan is not a poor loser, I always said he was a nice kid.'

Alice was beginning to frown. 'Phyllis, do you mean they were mentioning my name in a public bar?'

'Your name, for crying out loud, Alice! You were all they were talking about. You *were* the fight. Well, that didn't start until Lance came in and Fred had just called for drinks all round. Everyone was drinking to Mrs Frederick

192

Burton the third. Now, you can imagine how Lance felt, so he threw a punch at Fred and then raced off to get Tulliford.'

'Tulliford!' Alice stood up and almost shouted the name.

'Fortunately, Tulliford was at the gas station, otherwise Fred and Allan might have caught Lance and killed him.'

'This is monstrous!'

'Love, this is Hope's End, and I knew something was brewing and those men were going to fight. The fight lasted more than an hour. Tulliford called them both out and they fist-fought up and down that street from one end to the other. Lance was offering to help Jos, but he pushed him off, so Lance started taking bets on the side and cleaned up a bundle. I mean, Fred was always supposed to be good with his fists and those boys have fought together before. Oh sweet Jesus, I wish I'd been there, but I'm certainly glad I got out here before Lance arrived with the news.'

Alice walked over to the window and stared down at the orchard. To be fought over as though she were a prize cow in a herd of bulls!

Phyllis was at her elbow, touching her gently.

'Love, you're all right, aren't you? I mean – men will fight for what they want. Nothing's going to change that.'

'Oh, but it will change if there's nothing to fight for.'

'I just thought you'd like to know that Jos won,' .Phyllis concluded lamely.

Alice's gaze was steady as she looked across from the orchard to the meadow land on the other side of the stream where her property ended.

'Nobody has won anything. I'm not a prize in a raffle, Phyllis. I'm not a Christmas hamper at the church bazaar. When Alaric gets back, the estate will be settled and I shall farm here – alone if I have to. Alaric may not want to be a farmer, but nobody here – no one from the past – will make a single decision for me.'

She stood very erect, as though offering formal challenge to the past and the future, while Phyllis stared at her in amazement. There seemed to be a sudden stillness through

193

the house, then suddenly it was as though they both heard a soft rippling laugh and the rustle of a swing in the air.

'You never find diamonds standing up.'

Only Alice heard Aunt Penelope, but immediately she sat down and shakily poured herself another glass of lemonade.

At exactly the same time that Tulliford and the Burton boys were fighting for Alice down the main street at Hope's End, Hots was leading Alaric through her domain to a used-car lot. He knew now that only his aunt could live safely in such a neighbourhood. She swaggered along, tripping over a trailing shawl, stopping every few yards to sniff or swig from the bottle she carried in a grocery bag, and then people would step aside for her. One man tried to stop her, but Hots laughed in his face and said something which sent him running down a side street. Some avoided her face, a few nodded and smiled, some touched their hats as though in salute.

Alaric had been with her for two days, pleading and arguing. Then, late that morning, she had climbed out of the cavern of old rags where she slept and announced that she was sick of him hanging round the house and it was high time he learned a trade. He had no idea where they were going. Every street seemed littered with garbage and strewn with waste paper.

In the parking lot, the cars looked as though they had huddled together for safety. Hots walked around them spitting, then she stopped in front of a black Buick.

'This'll do. I like black cars! We can pretend that it's a hearse and we've got your mother in the back,' she cackled and opened an old lizard-skin bag. Muttering, she fumbled in its depths, finally pulling out a large ring hung with innumerable keys. Swiftly, she proceeded to try one after another in the door lock.

'This . . . this is your car, isn't it?' inquired Alaric nervously.

The door opened and Hots slipped off the key, handing it to Alaric with a leering smile. 'You can drive. The airport –

194

you'll see the signs.'

A stolen car and he was at the wheel, with a fiendish old woman beside him gulping gin and sniffing cocaine. No hero ever had to endure an ordeal like this.

'I travel a lot,' said Hots reflectively. 'I'm always on the lookout for business.'

'Please, Hots, please can we talk about the estate? As it is, neither you nor my mother can benefit. But she wants to share – she always has.'

'You poor little dope. What did they teach you at Oxford?' Hots chuckled. 'Your mother will never live to inherit Mockery Bend. First thing I'm going to do is have her run out of the country as an undesirable alien, and you'll go with her unless you decide to stay with your old Auntie Hots. Now, before she's shoved out I'm going to make you sorry you ever had a mother.'

Alaric tried to concentrate on the road and the traffic. Once a police car moved alongside and he felt an overwhelming urge to wave and scream for help, but the car moved swiftly on ahead and he saw that Hots was waving and blowing kisses to the two cops. He had no idea why she wanted to leave the city, nor where they were going.

When they reached the airport, Hots ambled through the crowds in front of the ticket counters with Alaric trailing miserably behind her. The red wig and the bedraggled hat were hanging askew over one ear and a tuft of grey furze had emerged. There seemed no purpose to her shifting, aimless meandering. Then abruptly she stopped near a long queue of people checking in baggage. Softly, moving with extraordinary speed, she passed behind a dark-jowled man and snatched his bag. In the next instant she passed it to Alaric and told him to run.

Alaric stood there holding the suitcase, transfixed with horror as the man reached down for his bag, then looked wildly around. He saw Alaric and shouted. Hots was screaming at him and Alaric fled with whistles sounding around him and a blare of voices.

Hots stood back approvingly. 'I knew he had good legs.

You're going to make a fortune out of those legs, Hots old dear!'

Alaric barely knew how he had arrived back in Redfern. Outside the airport he was caught up in a mob of American tourists and bundled aboard the bus with them. From the back window he saw police cars arriving at the main entrance and a blur of uniforms. He made his way back to Hots' neighbourhood more by instinct than guided by road signs.

The bag was heavy and he wondered if he should drop it in the nearest pile of garbage. Then he decided to place it in front of Hots and call the police. Yes, he felt sure she would be back at the apartment, and there he would threaten to reveal everything to the police unless she signed a waiver. After Aunt Augustine, he was beginning to feel quite an expert at blackmail

Just as he was about to enter the crumbling entrance to Hots' building he felt a searing blow at the back of his neck. When he spun round, he saw two men with murder in their faces. One pushed him back against the wall and the other grabbed the case.

'We run for Hots. Nobody muscles in –'

He fought back, trying desperately to defend himself against their knives, kicking and punching. Then a car turned the corner and the two muggers pushed Alaric into the doorway and raced down the side alley with the suit-case.

Bleeding and bruised, he half-crawled, half-climbed the stairs to the door. She was in there and he could hear her cursing Felix. He leaned against the door and it creaked open.

'The case! You got the case?' She rushed past him to see if it were in the hall.

He tried to explain what had happened and her fury rose to a screech of incoherent rage. She gasped, groping for words, then flung herself into a chair and reached for the gin bottle. Only when she had swallowed a good half-pint did she have breath enough to speak.

196

'That bag contained ten kilos of pure cocaine. I had the tip-off about it. And now, because you were too pansy to defend yourself and too stupid to head for the car, a pair of cheap little muggers have a million dollars' worth of dope.'

Alaric sat on a pile of old clothes, feeling blood seeping down his sleeve. Felix came over and tried to crawl into his lap.

'You, with all your fancy notions about the estate! Let me tell you, lovie, your mother is going to be deported. But before she's thrown out she'll be facing a long, stiff gaol sentence – and you can imagine what they'll do to someone like her in prison, can't you?'

Alaric tried to speak, but he did not seem able to lift his head or focus. It was only now that he could see the two men who had mugged him. One had gap-teeth and a gold earring, the other was blotched and bald-headed. He felt sure he could describe them to the police if only they would stop swimming around him now, their faces blurring and bloating.

'I've got a few things prepared for your mother that will make her toes curl. It's very important to have good friends in this cruel world,' she said sententiously.

At last he managed to raise his head. She was sitting there with her hand around the bottle, grinning at him like one of the harpies that fed on human flesh and fouled what they could not eat.

He knew he must kill her. Either he destroyed her or she would murder him and his mother. As though afflicted with some paralysis, he fell on his knees, then pulled himself upright. He would throttle her, choke the poisonous life out of her.

The room swayed and dipped but still she sat there, her gaping grin mocking him. He dragged himself forward and collapsed at her feet. Then slowly, he pulled himself up by the table and as he did, Hots gently slid sideways, her hand still gripping the bottle. He touched her, but there was no breath and her eyes were glazing.

In the kitchen he managed to fill a dish with water and

197

tried splashing her with it. But she was quite dead. He sat back on his heels and felt the great hero's brief pang of regret when the last dragon lay dead.

After pouring some more water over his own head, he took stock of his injuries. The knife slash in his arm was no longer bleeding and a gash across his hand now seemed no more than a deep scratch. First he would call the police, then he would return to Mockery Bend with the Golden Fleece. It was all over now. He had secured the estate for his mother, and he knew she was a generous woman who would be happy to let him continue his studies. He shook his head, for even the nature of those studies seemed to have sifted from his mind like dust.

By the phone he noticed a crumpled pile of envelopes skewered on a bent nail – they all bore the discreet imprint of Cavalry Barnhouse's firm. It only needed a few seconds for him to read and understand who was arranging to have his mother deported, and there was mention of other things besides.

He reached for the phone and looked out of the window, then moaned with terror. A long grey Mercedes was in the street outside, and in it were three Arabs. Felix wound himself around his ankle, purring.

*

Tulliford did not know why he was driving out to Mockery Bend or what he would say when he got there. A puffy swelling had closed his right eye and his chest felt as though someone had just run a mob of cattle across it.

He was half-way up the drive when Maria ran out of the house to him, crying and shaking her fists in the air. He tried to understand her, but she was wailing in Greek and all he could think was that it was typical of Alice to keep a servant who couldn't speak a word of English. She cried and pointed over to the orchard, then threw her apron over her head and sat down in the middle of the driveway, howling.

Lion came up and fixed Tulliford with his yellow eyes,

198

paused for an instant and ran off at a loping stride towards the orchard. There Tulliford found Alice lying under a tree, staring sightlessly up through the branches. And he knew why she had gone beyond tears to a mute grief beyond all feelings. His anger had vanished, leaving only an agony of remorse and bitterness. Bending down, he touched her gently, but she did not seem aware of his presence.

'Alice, I'm very sorry. I – I didn't know you loved him. I didn't mean to hurt him so bad, but he's young and he'll be OK.'

Alice turned her head slightly and looked at him as though he were a stranger.

'I kept thinking he was too young for you. I should have known that love doesn't take much account of age or sense . . .'

Alice seemed puzzled and put her hand to her head. Then as though she had suddenly remembered, she began sobbing and tried to roll over and bury her face in the grass.

'Please Alice – if you'll just say something to me!' His voice was pleading, but her sobs became wilder.

He tried to stroke her hair, then he put his arms around her shoulders and lifted her to him. She struggled to free herself, but he held her, turned her face up to his and kissed her. Now he would have to say it, even if it meant having a pain across his chest for the rest of his life.

'Alice, I swear I did not intend to hurt Fred Burton so badly. I know you love him, and I . . . I'm prepared to apologize to him and bring him out here to you.'

Gasping for air, Alice managed to find breath enough to speak.

'Joseph Tulliford, you are the most stupid man I've ever known!'

Tulliford thought for a moment, but he still continued to hold her, feeling her breasts against his chest.

'Do you think,' she said, 'that I'm crying for Fred Burton or any other man? Look at those!' She pulled two letters out of her skirt pocket.

'One of them says that I'm an undesirable alien suspected of trafficking in drugs and that I must be in Sydney to answer charges tomorrow. The other is from the Department of Taxation, and they say that I've been making money here illegally and breaking so many laws I lost count of them – and that I must give them everything and pay a fine too!'

At that moment Tulliford left the world he had known for ever and entered the strange, dreaming country he had so often glimpsed since Alice came to Mockery Bend.

'They won't do a damn thing to you, Alice. I'm going to marry you. And just let those bastards try to push Mrs Jos Tulliford around!'

Alice protested that he did not love her, that she irritated him and he had not even met her son. Tulliford could only hold her more tightly and kiss her when he couldn't think of an answer, which occurred very frequently. They argued and Alice found herself kissing him when he wouldn't listen to her, helping him take off her dress and sobbing with joy as she ripped off his shirt.

Alaric, who was a conoisseur in this and many other matters, would probably have considered their lovemaking crude and uninspired, but neither had been given a classical education, so they came and spent with passion on the grass. Tulliford was beginning to find himself at home in that strange countryside, and he knew that he would never be able to find his way back to what he had been and known. Abruptly, he sat up.

'My God, Alice, I've taken advantage of you!'

Alice looked at him sleepily. 'Oh Joseph, I'm sure I couldn't possibly be pregnant yet.'

'Alice, this was . . .' but he could not describe even to himself what had happened. 'We are going to be married tonight. I can get a tame minister in Hope's End to do the right thing by us.'

'I really should discuss it with Alaric, Jos.'

'Alice,' Tulliford was genuinely shocked, 'don't you realize what we've just done?'

She kissed him on his bruised face and laughed. 'I could never forget how wonderful it was. But it's odd, I can't really imagine then – everything's *now*.'

Tulliford had his pants on and was looking around as nervously as though he had just made love in Martin Place at lunchtime.

'I really should talk it over with Alaric,' Alice said.

'Alice, this is not something you can tell a grown-up son. My God, Jos Tulliford making love in the open like – like . . .' but he too was finding it difficult to remember what he had been.

Alaric phoned the pub at Hope's End and got Phyllis who gave him a number to ring at St Mary's. Lance answered in a falsetto voice which changed immediately when he realized who it was.

'You can't be too careful in this business, mate. Now, I want you to barricade the door and I'll be there within the hour with friends. You're lucky you caught me here on a delivery.'

It was fortunate indeed that Lance had just driven down six Moluccans from Queensland. They were tough, mean little men and he rather liked the idea of knocking some of the spunk out of them before he shipped them on to a vegetable grower in Victoria.

He lined them up and addressed them in slow and careful English: 'I do not wish to discourage you as new Australians, but we have a problem.'

The men muttered and one, Lance noticed with satisfaction, reached for his belt.

'But nothing we cannot overcome if we are prepared to do a little fighting.'

The Moluccans brightened up considerably.

'There are three rich Indonesian gentlemen who are planning to pick you up along the road and take you back to prison.'

'We die first,' a wiry, scarred little man said.

'I propose,' Lance beamed at them, 'that we should attack first. I shall see that you each have a machete and I will back you up with a shotgun. I trust,' he said severely, 'that I do not have to use it.'

The sheikh had been planning his revenge for some weeks now, and he was not going to sit in his car any longer waiting for Alaric to emerge . . .

Lance found the whole episode very disappointing. It was less of a fight than Hope's End had seen that morning. Six machetes and a shotgun were more than the sheikh and his guards could stomach, even though they kept trying to explain that all they wanted was Alaric's right hand.

They were roughed up under Lance's supervision and then kicked down into the street where some of the local residents were assembling like jackals for the pickings. The Mercedes was stripped and burned as the Arabs fled in considerable disarray. They were picked up by the police at the end of the street and immediately arrested on a number of charges ranging from creating a public disturbance to carrying an offensive weapon.

Alaric refused to get into the station wagon without Felix, even though Lance pointed to the sign that forbade the carrying of pets except in cages. Some of the Moluccans complained that they were allergic to cat fur, but Alaric would not relinquish the red-brindled Felix. Dimly he wondered if the Golden Fleece had felt like this in Jason's arms – warm and alive and covered with fleas.

Phyllis wanted to drive out to Mockery Bend that night, but Alaric was falling across the table with fatigue.

'We'll take him out first thing in the morning,' Lance said.

'Poor kid – he looks so beat up,' Phyllis said gently after she had strapped his arm and found some flea powder and cold lamb for the cat.

Lance was rocking to and fro on his feet with excitement.

'How's about,' he said, 'If I go there tonight and tell Alice that she is now worth $30 million?'

'No.' Alaric looked up suddenly and his voice was firm. 'I

shall tell her myself. She'll never have to worry about money again, and I can –' but he was no longer certain what he wanted to do. Lance and Phyllis carried him to bed and she tucked him in like a child.

Lance looked down at him and shook his head in admiration.

'You know, I thought he was gay. But he's a great kid, Philly. Think of it, four aunts – two he knocks out of the running, and two he kills. He's a bloody hero!'

Epilogue

This is the way Jason, Hercules and all the heroes felt, when they came home victorious. Alaric was happy to let Lance and Phyllis nudge each other and laugh in the front seat while he leaned back with Felix. Of all the Morells from the beginning of time, he had done the most for his family. Thirty million dollars! The amount kept sounding in his head like a crash of cymbals.

'Will you take a look at who's pulling in!' Phyllis's voice was shrill with indignation.

'I thought he might be here!' Lance's two front teeth were jutting out and he looked as though he had just seen a plump and crippled rabbit in his path.

Cavalry Barnhouse was about to step from his car when they parked behind him.

Alaric could scarcely recognize the house. He had left it a patched shambles; now it was spruce with paint and ten cows were just being taken down to the stream to pasture.

'My boy!' Cavalry Barnhouse came over with an out-stretched hand which Alaric ignored. 'I wanted to be here to tell your mother the great and wonderful news that she is now heir to the Tulliford estate!'

'I bet!' thought Lance, and spat so close to Barnhouse's black kid loafers that he shifted nervously.

'Your mother is going to need guidance in the management of this estate, Alaric, and you no doubt will want to become a member of my firm,' Barnhouse beamed, but Alaric remained stonily silent.

Phyllis laughed, strolled over to the garden, picked a geranium and tucked it behind her ear. Then she grinned at Barnhouse and said, 'You know, Cavalry, you'd make a dingo's poop smell sweet.'

At that moment Alice came out to the steps. She was wearing a long peignoir of lace and satin which Miss Hetherington had packed herself, sighing with regret that royal eyes would never see it. Her hair was a mass of tangled curls and her eyes were soft and sleepy. She saw Alaric and screamed.

'Oh, my darling boy! Oh, Alaric!' She cried and wept and clung to him.

Alaric was prepared for an outburst of joy, but wished that his mother were less demonstrative in public.

'Mother,' he paused, trying to remember the speech he had prepared, something simple and dignified. Instead, he shouted, 'She's dead! Aunt Honoria's dead and you've got the lot!'

Alice was suddenly still.

'Mother, I didn't hurt her! I didn't kill her! She died from drink and God knows what. But you are now the heir. This is why we left England!'

Barnhouse was determined to take charge, even though he sensed a certain hostility around him and felt the gold was no longer his to gloat over and guard.

'I can appreciate your shock, Miss Morell. But as the last unmarried Morell you are now heir in the state of New South Wales and . . .'

At this point Tulliford came slowly out on to the veranda, his sheepish but contented expression indicating that he had spent a happy but fairly sleepless night at Mockery Bend.

'Oh my God,' thought Phyllis, 'don't, *please* don't let it be legal!'

Alaric stared at his mother, but he could not read the expression in her eyes. It was as though she had become a stranger to him.

Very quietly she said, 'This is my husband. I am Mrs Joseph Tulliford.'

Phyllis tore the flower out of her hair and stamped on it, crying, 'Alice, you fool! One night and it's cost you thirty million bucks! Mother of God! That must be the most expensive lay in history!'

Barnhouse seemed to be crumbling, he could only falter, 'Married, legally?'

205

'By the Reverend Heston, last evening,' said Alice.

Alaric felt chaos closing in upon him. So this is what happened to the hero when he came home with the spoils of victory.

'Couldn't you – couldn't you have waited at least until I got home?' he asked, grief and anger breaking his voice.

Tulliford saw what had happened and sat down on the steps, his head in his hands. He was almost crying.

'Alice! Oh my God, I've robbed you! If I'd only shown a little strength of mind down there in the orchard. If I hadn't let go – what can I do to make it up to you? What can I say?'

'You can say nothing, Mr Tulliford,' said Alaric bitterly. 'Had it not been for you, my mother would now be a rich woman. If only she had let me look after her, she'd have thirty million dollars. But this is how it was when Jason brought back the Golden Fleece and set it down at the feet of Pelias, expecting a little praise and a lot of gratitude. What did he get? Pelias ignored it and said he would have preferred a polyester doubleknit. And when Hercules handed the golden apples to Eurystheus, he was told he should have brought back a bag of grapefruit – and when Theseus slew the Minotaur, the King of Crete told him it was "be kind to bulls week". Oh yes, and let us not forget Aeneas, who carried his old father to safety and placed him gently on the future site of Rome – and then the rotten old twit said he'd sooner be back in Troy. The only thing I've got out of all this is a bloody cat!'

Felix purred and climbed up on to Alaric's shoulder.

'I have been humilated and beaten, I have gone through one miserable and disgusting ordeal after another – for nothing – for nothing at all . . .' He leaned against the car and wept, and Phyllis felt like crying with him.

Lance moved up to Barnhouse, spat again and said in a whisper,

'Who gets it, Cavalry? Who gets the big bucks now?'

Barnhouse coughed and tried to look away.

Lance repeated, 'There's got to be an heir, Cavalry, you rat!'

206

'The estate,' Cavalry said brokenly, 'in the event of the demise or marriage of all existing unmarried Morells, reverts to the eldest male of the Tulliford line. So Jos gets the lot!'

Tulliford stood up and shouted, 'I won't take it! I won't touch one cent of that money. It's my wife's – it belongs to Alice.'

Alice slipped her arm through his, hugged him and smiled, 'Jos, this is the way it should be.'

'Damn!' Alaric said.

'I can't take it, Alice. I shall have it all made over to you.' Tulliford stood in front of Alaric, saying over and over that he wanted no part of the Tulliford estate, that he wished to heaven he could live yesterday afternoon again and then nothing would have happened down there in the orchard.

Alice turned to Barnhouse and said in a small, firm voice, 'Mr Barnhouse, you can see how dreadfully upsetting all this is for my husband. My instructions to you are that the papers be drawn up by tomorrow morning. Then we will sign everything here.'

Barnhouse tried to reply, but could only nod in agreement. He stared down at those wide grey eyes and felt suddenly that the jury was in and the verdict against him. It seemed that all his law books were blowing away from him like shreds of paper, and three generations of Barnhouse stewardship of the largest estate in Australia were being snatched from his hands. He had been defeated by the terrible power of goodness.

'The estate will be in my name – as my husband wishes,' said Alice.

And then Barnhouse felt that the Australian constitution could not withstand her smile, and even habeas corpus was in danger. But he mumbled that he would have everything ready for her, everything she wanted.

Alice reached up and kissed Tulliford, then stroked the cat.

'What a very nice cat, Alaric. Lion needs a little friend. How very thoughtful of Aunt Honoria to leave you her pet.

You must promise to take care of it.'

Phyllis took a deep breath and leaned against Lance for support.

'She's got the lot,' she said.

Tulliford put his hands on Alice's shoulders as though taking a solemn oath. 'Alice, whatever you want, you're going to have. Whatever you say, it's yours right now.'

'I think,' said Alice thoughtfully, 'what I would like most of all now is a swing under the apple tree in the orchard.'

And then they all heard the laughter.